Robinson Crusoe 2244

A Novel

E. J. Robinson

ROBINSON CRUSOE 2244
Copyright © 2014 *Erik J. Robinson*
http://erikjamesrobinson.com

Edited by Jessica Holland
Cover Design by Jordan Grimmer
Formatting by Polgarus Studio

For my parents,
Who gave me a love of words.

And for my wife and sons,
Who give me the love to use them.

PART ONE

"... and now I saw, tho' too late, the Folly of beginning a Work before we count the Cost."

-Daniel Defoe

Chapter One
Walls

"I love Tessa Saah!"

The scream exploded from the boy's lungs, but as his voice had yet to crack, it came out sounding more like the shriek of a dying animal or a woman in peril.

They were sure to wake the Red Guard now.

"Merciful Crown!" Slink hissed as his head dotted back around the Keep's bend. "For the love of the Eight, Robinson, shut up before you wake the entire Township, you fool!"

Robinson laughed. He didn't care. He *was* a fool—a fool for love and he wanted everyone to know it.

Slink had an immediate urge to throttle his friend, but this wasn't the time or place. For one thing, they were in the process of committing a crime that could get them both banished to the outer Regens. For another, they were currently perched six stories high in the sky, pressed flat against the wall of the Tower Keep, on a ledge barely wider than a man's foot, in the chill, howling wind.

What in the name of the Eight was he doing up here?

It wasn't the fact that Robinson was the son of Tiers and he was the son of a Wall guard. The unspoken rule that *his kind* needed to defer to *theirs* was flat-out stupid and went against everything the One People were supposed to stand for.

And it certainly wasn't because Robinson was too athletic for him. If anything, Robinson was undersized and a bit chubby for his age (although Slink would never say it aloud—his friend was sensitive about such things). Yes, Slink might look like a giant when standing beside him, but that was only due to his most recent growth spurt (and his father's genetics). He still retained the uncanny dexterity—honed by years of sneaking around the hidden paths of the city—that had helped him earn his nickname.

No, he and Robinson had been friends since their first days of school, which had come as a surprise to most because A) fraternization between Nobes and Mucks was frowned upon, and B) Slink's family was cheated out of a second child when Robinson's mother gave birth to twins. They should have been bitter enemies. They became best friends instead.

Even now, Slink knew Robinson wasn't simply acting out. Sure, he'd made an arse out of himself plenty of times before by playing the fool and engaging in acts so unconscionably illegal or immoral that they should have both walked the Road long ago. He didn't even believe Tessa was the real reason for his outburst—though he had no doubt the sentiment of his declaration was true. No, the reason Robinson was shouting at the top of his lungs was much simpler: he had never seen the Township from on high before.

Robinson Crusoe was born in the year 2228, and at sixteen years old, he had lived his entire life in New London, sequestered behind the Wall that surrounded the four square kilometer sanctuary his ancestors had carved out centuries before. The impermeable, unyielding Wall—a dozen times the height of a man, built of stone and dirt and blood—served to keep all threats out while also keeping the citizens in.

In the courtyard of the Crown below them, Red Guard would be patrolling at the crack of dawn. Beyond the six spires surrounding the Tower Keep were the Flats, where the underclass lived in cramped quarters overrun with rain. To the right, the Clutch, where the merchants peddled their wares.

At the Township's heart sat the communal fields, divided by only a narrow, winding road—the Red Road—that led to the Western Gate and also up to the Shelf, where the Tiers and their families looked down upon all else from a golden perch, but one that still sat in the shadow of the Wall. There, Robinson could see his father's estate, tucked into the north-easternmost corner, its grounds larger than any other, but not for the size of their home, which was surprisingly modest, but because of the flyer livery, which dominated half their land.

Even the Pate above—that massive slab of rock split only by the Tongue, the river that fed all—was inspiring from here.

But what truly stayed Robinson's heart was what lay beyond the Wall. To the west was the Great Atlantica. To the east, Isle Prime, the continent of Europa, and the last refuge of mankind following the Great Rendering. Here, for the first time, he realized the enormity of the world and how small his place was in it.

"Come on, Robinson," Slink grumbled. "The sun is almost up. Do you want to do this or not?"

"Of course."

"Then look there. The second window is the one you want. That's where I'm told *it* is being held. Take your look and get back as quick as you can."

"You're not coming?"

"I have no desire to see that thing. I have enough nightmares as it is."

Robinson clapped him on the shoulder. "I appreciate this, my friend. You can't imagine the amount of bragging I'm going to do in school today."

"Of course I can," Slink said. "I am your *best friend* after all."

The words barely left his lips before his giant hands locked onto Robinson, swung him over the abyss, and deposited him on the other side of the ledge. It was such an effortless, graceful act that Robinson never had time to be scared.

Rounding the bend, Robinson was met by the sun as it emerged through the clouds. As he neared the first window, he fell to his knees to creep underneath it. Only when he heard a peal of drunken laughter did he realize what a stupid idea this was. He could get into so much trouble. Then again, it was the kind of brash, arrogant act that would ensure his reputation for a lifetime. He pressed on.

It wasn't until he was passing under the window's ledge that the sneeze struck him. He covered his mouth, but it was too late to pull it back. He hunkered down for what seemed an eternity, before eventually relaxing. He had gone unnoticed.

It was precisely that moment when the windows above him blew open and a gauntleted hand clamped onto his coat.

"And who do we have here?" a deep voice said.

Chapter Two
Secrets

A turn later, Robinson's Red Guard captor delivered him by carriage to his father's estate. As they passed through the front gates, his ears barely registered the rocks kicked up by the carriage wheels or the sound of the leather reins going taut as they lurched to a stop.

Vareen, the family's aged housemistress, answered the door. She had become the closest thing to a mother the children had since their own died six months earlier. Even from the carriage, Robinson could see her face fill with disappointment.

Once inside, Vareen directed him past the kitchen where the staff prepared breakfast. They continued on into the sitting room.

"Your father has company in the study. Wait here until he can get to you. And mind your tongue."

Company wasn't a common occurrence at the Crusoe estate, so when Robinson heard several deep voices from under the partitioned doors, he crossed the room and gently set his ear to them.

"We must be careful. The man has spies everywhere."

"Forget his spies! Time is running out. We need to act now!"

"You always want to rush in headfirst, with no thought to the consequences."

"The consequences have always been the same if we fail. But if we succeed …"

"Once we start down this road, there will be no turning back."

"Only a coward would want to."

Voices erupted in unison, but Robinson recognized none of them. His hands suddenly felt damp. The situation inside grew tenser by the moment. The tenor of anger gave way to mistrust and even fear.

And then all at once, the arguments ceased. A new voice spoke, calm and sure. Robinson recognized it as belonging to the Tier of Transportation, a man who was also his father.

"Sers. We all have much to lose by acting. But failing to act presents an even worse fate. The Campaign moves forward. Each and every one of you must ask yourself, here and now, will I support it or stand against it?"

The room went quiet. Robinson didn't know what this Campaign was, but even the mere mention of it set his heart thrumming in his chest. He didn't know why. He wanted so badly to see what was happening on the other side of those doors. Finally, when he couldn't take it any longer, he bent down to the keyhole for a glimpse inside.

And just as his weight shifted, the floorboard under his feet groaned. It was a subtle sound, but it sent a jolt of terror straight through him. He quickly stood up, about to back away when the doors were thrust open and his father met him eye to eye.

"Father," he stuttered. "Uh …Vareen asked me to tell you that breakfast is ready."

Leodore Crusoe was dressed in grey slacks and a grey doublet with a bootlace tie. His black hair was slicked back to tight curls that billowed over his collar. His beard had been trimmed that very morning, but it was his eyes, so thin and foreign, that froze Robinson in his tracks.

Even more disconcerting were the dozen or so guests spread about the room. They were Tiers and not of minor houses or faux titles. These were men of power from all over the Isle—men who rarely gathered together outside the council and never in secret.

What are they doing here?

"Fellow sers," Leodore finally said, "My eldest, Robinson."

"Your Tierships," Robinson said while bowing with an open hand facing them, thumb curved in. It was an old tradition, the One and Four. The open hand symbolized that he held no weapon. The inverted thumb meant he was positioning himself between them and harm, which signaled that he was a friend.

Several returned the gesture, though none bothered to bow. Robinson recognized several of the men. Fonel Keric, Tier of Water Resources. Byron Frostmore, the flamboyant Tier of Horticulture. The elderly Vonus Cork, Tier of Agriculture, scowled from the corner. But it was Roland Fallow, Tier of the Exterior, whose presence surprised Robinson most. It was well known Ser Fallow and his father didn't get along.

"Perhaps it is time to wrap this up," Leodore said.

The men muttered quick assents.

Leodore turned back to his son. "See that Tannis and Tallis are dressed and ready for breakfast. I'll be along shortly."

Robinson nodded and bid a quick goodbye before leaving the room.

Once in the kitchen, the twins questioned Robinson fervently about what he had seen, but he gave little away other than to say, "Of course they welcomed me. Now that I'm to be an apprentice, they value my opinion about certain things."

The twins looked at him with awe. But his pleasure quickly ended when the final carriage left the grounds and his father returned and slapped him across the face.

"That is the last time your antics embarrass me."

Vareen and the twins gasped. Leodore had never struck any of his children before. Tears sprang to Robinson's eyes.

"Ser," Vareen pleaded. "It was a harmless prank."

"Harmless? Scaling the Tower two days before the Day of Naming when every Tier from around the Isle is in New London? Damnit, boy! You couldn't have picked a worse time if you'd tried! Should that Red Guard report back who was in attendance here, the Iron Fists will be breaking down the door before the staff can hide the silverware!"

"I assure you, Ser," Vareen said calmly, "that man did not so much as glimpse who or what was inside the parlor. And did he not accept your token?"

"The word is *bribe*," my father said. "And just because he accepted it doesn't mean he won't write a report later."

Ser Crusoe's eyes fell back on his son. "When I think of the tutors we wasted on your education. And the dance masters and the elocution lessons, and for what? So my son could be the laughing stock of the entire Isle? Thank the Crown your mother cannot see you now!"

Before he turned and fled, Robinson saw a glint of something lustrous clutched in his father's hand. It was attached to a long, thin chain. Only later when he calmed down did he realize it was his mother's locket.

He had not seen it since she had died.

A half turn later, Vareen appeared at the Livery door and saw Robinson sitting at a small desk tinkering with leftover components. She never understood where the desire or imagination to create came from, but it had always been present in the Crusoe line.

"What are you building?" she finally asked.

"It's a tracking unit. You can carry it aboard a ship or on your person and if you're ever in trouble, you push this and it will emit a pulse that will help others find you."

Vareen knew what he was thinking. Had his mother been in possession of this device, she would have still been alive today.

"It's brilliant, Robinson. Everything you create is. You're just like her in that—"

His hands stopped churning. "What does it matter? Thanks to the Eighth Law, it will never even see the light of day."

"The Eight are here to protect us."

He stifled a laugh before looking up. "Does he hate me, Vareen?"

"No, Child!" she said, stepping close. "Your father loves you very much. He is just … These are difficult times. There is a change in the air, something I have not felt in a very long time. It's like the coming of a storm. Your father feels it too. It's why he met with the Tiers today. Leodorc has always had a deep love for the One People, as did your mother. Both felt it incumbent upon them to preserve what our ancestors built."

"But we have a good life here. Why would he risk that by consorting with men like Tier Fallow?"

"Because not all views look out from the Shelf. Most have no windows at all. Isn't that terrible, considering how big the world is?"

Robinson nodded, but he wasn't sure. New London was the only world he'd ever known.

Vareen lifted his chin. "You're too young to worry about such things. In two days' time, I will dress you in your finest and load you into your carriage for the Crown. And there, you will hear your name spoken in front of the entire One People. And I will watch you on the Feed as I did your father, and I will cry because you will no longer be the boy I have held and loved and watched grow. You will be a man—an apprentice to your father. And maybe then we can set about finding you a wife."

She saw him smile oddly. "Or have you found one already?"

"There is no one," he said, frustrated by his transparency.

She clucked. "You have always been a terrible liar. At least with me. Now come. We must clean you up. You're already late for school."

He looked at the clock on the wall. "I have plenty of time. The carriage trip only takes a quarter turn."

"Your father took the carriage a while ago. You'll need to go in on foot."

Panic immediately swelled in Robinson's chest. He quickly ran for the door. Vareen yelled at him. He needed a bath, but before she knew it, he was halfway down the road. He'd already enraged one of the two men he feared most in this world.

He was about to face the other.

Chapter Three
Crimes and Punishment

The Academnia had been one of the first buildings built after the Wall had gone up, so no one could have foreseen the area around it going so quickly to seed. But the irrigation to the communal fields had been improperly engineered and the result was constant flooding to the streets surrounding the school.

Over time, the underclass had built a beehive of stacked domiciles and shanties to live in, but they were often flooded, earning those citizens who lived there the slur, "Muckbacks." Robinson had never used the word himself. After all, his best friend was one of those citizens, but few children of Tiers gave them the same courtesy, as evidenced by the scrawl over the bathrooms that read, "Nobes only, no Mucks allowed."

When Robinson arrived at his classroom, he found the door locked. It wasn't a surprise. Taskmaster Satu was as strict about punctuality as he was about everything else. Through the window, he saw the class rigid and attentive as always. His only relief came when he spotted Slink inside. He had successfully managed to escape the tower, though Robinson was sure he bore some guilt over leaving his friend behind.

Robinson took a deep breath and knocked. The door opened slowly.

Taskmaster Satu wore his usual burgundy robe, fringed with gold leaf brocade around the neck that designated him as Taskmaster Overseer of New London. His hair and beard were both long and grey, but it was his penetrating eyes that had weakened the knees of generations of students and sent many from the rural Regens scrambling back to the safety of their homes.

"Citizen Crusoe," he enunciated with relish. "You are late. You know the penalty for tardiness in my class. You will return tomorrow with a five-thousand-word essay enumerating the myriad ways in which you have hindered my teachings over the years. This, you shall read for the amusement of your fellow students and myself. Good day."

He slammed the door in Robinson's face.

Robinson knocked again.

When the door opened this time, Taskmaster Satu's nostrils were flaring. In his hand was a long, slender riding crop made of yew that extended from a worn handle, down a narrow shaft, to a leather tongue keeper that was cracked with age and overuse. It was an implement Robinson was very familiar with.

"My apologies, Taskmaster, but there is no school tomorrow. Today's our final day."

His teacher feigned surprised. "Is it now? How foolish of me to assume that I, your teacher, might have some say in the fulfillment of your academic obligations. By all means, come in! Come in, so you might inform all my charges of their fate as well."

As he entered, Slink rolled his eyes and most every other student frowned with irritation. Only Jaras Saah, seated in the back, wore a perverse smile.

Robinson was about to head for his seat when the crop barred his path.

"*Before* you take your seat, there is some business we must attend to, yes?"

He knew what was coming. "Yes, Taskmaster."

"You have willfully interrupted my class. I will have an explanation."

Robinson knew he'd have no problem fabricating an excuse, but Taskmaster Satu would then have the right to vet that excuse, which, given this was the last day of school and how such an act could further cement his reputation, was not beyond him. If a student was caught in a lie, he could be brought up on charges in front of the Tier of Civil Obedience, which was a grave thing. He could easily tell some smaller lie, something Slink could corroborate, but if the Red Guard did indeed file a report, then Slink too would be disciplined, and his punishment would be far worse. Robinson had only one option.

"I have no excuse, Taskmaster. My tardiness is no one's fault but my own. I apologize to you, my fellow classmates, and all the citizens of the One People."

His disappointment was evident. He'd clearly been itching for a confrontation. "Your sentence is two lashes. To be exercised"—he brought the crop down with a snap that made most in the room jump— "immediately."

Robinson swallowed and began rolling up his sleeves.

"Unless, you think it unnecessary."

"Taskmaster?"

"As you say, citizen, this is the final day of your education, which would imply there is nothing more I can teach you. If that is indeed the case, then your tardiness is inconsequential. You have learned all that you need to move into the world and rightly take your place as your father's apprentice. Is that how you see it?"

Robinson knew he was being baited, but he had no intention of giving him what he wanted. "I doubt there will ever be a day that you couldn't teach me *something*, Taskmaster."

"Well said. Very *diplomatic*. But I'm not speaking in riddles. There is no subterfuge on my part. You have always been one of my brightest students. Or am I mistaken?"

The students shuffled, eager to see where this was going. Robinson felt a flare of anger. He'd already had a tough morning and didn't deserve to be singled out like this for being a quarter of a turn late, so he ignored Slink's subtle shake of his head.

"No," he said finally, "you're not."

"Excellent! So, theoretically, I could pose to you any question and you should be able to answer it."

"Theoretically. If the question was based on the curriculum taught to us here, under this roof."

"Or on things I am sure you have knowledge of?" he asked.

"A difficult concept to verify since no one knows my mind but myself."

"An excellent point! Let's find out. Shall we say six questions?"

He still wasn't certain he wanted to do this, but the idea of beating Taskmaster Satu at his own game was too much to turn down.

"Six is fair. But what happens if I answer one incorrectly?"

"Then, as the ancients used to say, *the punishment should fit the crime.*"

"I'll be kept an extra quarter turn after class?"

The class tittered nervously. Taskmaster Satu grinned.

"No. You will receive a lash for every question posed."

Six lashes! By the Spires, Robinson had never taken more than three and had never heard of anyone taking more than four. As tempting as it was, he had doubts he could bear the pain of six lashes, much less the unending humiliation that would accompany it.

"I think I'll take my two lashes and move on, Ser. After all, I was late and that punishment *more* than fits the crime."

"Pity," his teacher said. "Though I'm not surprised. Over the years, I've made similar offers to a handful of students and all but one declined."

"Then he is a better man than me."

"Of that, there is little doubt. Even less since he was a *she.*"

"Forgive my assumption. I'm sure *she* was a remarkable student."

"A remarkable citizen," he corrected. "She too refused the challenge at first, but if memory serves, she came up with an interesting counterproposal."

"Which was?"

"That her fellow students be allowed to pose the questions. Ironic that you did not think to do the same."

"I admit it's clever, but how is it ironic?"

"Because the woman in question was your mother."

The blood instantly ran from Robinson's face as a buzz moved through the room. Taskmaster Satu's eyes never wavered.

"And to answer your next question, yes. She replied correctly to all six queries. As I said, she was a remarkable citizen, an exemplary student, the best I've ever taught, which is why you, her son, are such a disappointment. But to quote the ancients once more, 'Virtue is not hereditary.'"

"Thomas Paine," Robinson said, immediately. "I'll consider that the first question, *Taskmaster*. Pick your students."

Chapter Four
Entrapment

"You heard the rules, citizens. Common knowledge of things Ser Crusoe should know. Let's start you off with an easy one, shall we? Citizen Grey."

Slink's head bolted up in surprise. "Taskmaster?"

"Any question will do," he said.

Slink looked confused and then asked one of the most basic things he knew. "What are the names of the five continents?"

Taskmaster Satu made a "tsking" sound and rolled his eyes.

"Europa, A'tacia, Afranzique, New Zaustria, and NuGee."

"NuGee is a colloquialism and not a particularly inventive one," Taskmaster Satu said with a sigh. "Can you give me the fifth continent's proper name or shall I declare this contest over before it's even begun?"

"New Glacia, Ser," Robinson said, and out of spite, he added, "Once called Antarctica."

Many in the class looked confused. Taskmaster Satu nodded but leaned close to him. "Careful, boy. Some names are forbidden for a reason."

He next called the very pedantic Aris Green, who deliberated carefully.

"Name the capital cities of the eight Regens and their primary export."

Another easy one.

"Regen 1, North Hub, textiles. Regen 2, the Sunderlands or 'Twin

Rivers,' fresh water fish. Regen 3, Lake Stone Grize, lumber. Regen 4, South Hub, livestock. Regen 5, Dragoon, minerals and metals. Regen 6, Shir'ton, grains. Regen 7, Vento, agriculture. And Regen 8, New London, attractive people." The class giggled even as Taskmaster Satu frowned. "And leadership, of course."

Taskmaster Satu nodded toward Bevin Vig, who stood with a flip of her curly hair. "Name the three divisions of Academnia and the five subcategories of each."

Robinson yawned. "Of the General Approved Disciplines, there is Mathematics, Human Science, Language, Civil Obedience, and Labor. Of the Advanced Disciplines, there is Medicine, Physics, Selective Defense Training, Lineage and Childbearing, and Communications. Of the Forbidden Disciplines, there is History, Engineering, Literature and the Arts, Chemical Biology, and Ideo-Religious Studies."

Flora Sunchild, a daft girl from Regen 1, raised her hand eagerly.

"What are the Eight Laws of the One People?"

Robinson looked to his teacher as if to say, "This is the best you have to offer?"

"In the winter of the Great Rendering and the fall of man, We, the One People, do pledge this oath: that never again, by cause or deed, shall we affect harm or injury to man or beast, earth or sky, ocean or—" he recited.

"Citizen Crusoe," Taskmaster Satu interrupted. "Your talent for memorization, while no doubt *impressive* to your fellow students, bores me. For brevity's sake, summarize please."

"Of course. The First Law stands on equality. Each of us is a uniform piece of the larger whole. No man, be he farmer or Regent, is above the other in the eyes of us all."

Robinson almost gagged saying it.

"The Second Law condemns all written works, since knowledge and history is authored by the corruptible. This is why Taskmasters like yourself do not teach from books but from memory, and why our papers are burned at the end of each year. From mouth to ear, thus knowledge is passed, from parent to child, from first to last."

"You segue to the Third Law well," Taskmaster Satu said.

"Thank you. The Third Law tells us that every skill and trade must be passed from parent to child to ensure both purity and dedication of the craft."

"And do you like flying, Ser Crusoe?" Taskmaster Satu asked innocently.

Robinson smirked. "As I am yet an apprentice, Taskmaster, it is illegal for me to participate in my father's trade, but when I find out, you'll be the first to know."

"How considerate of you."

He continued, "The Fourth Law centers on the Wall or what happens on this side of it. As populous dissemination once led to global strife, we stay sequestered within the realm of our Eight Regens and Isle Prime. In this, we maintain our peace, health, and security from now until the end."

"The end of what?"

"Whatever end we face."

"But the Eight ensure the One People will live forever. Or do you not believe in the Law?"

"I meant until our individual ends, Taskmaster. We all die. Is it not an *expirable* offense to suggest otherwise?"

Taskmaster Satu nodded in appreciation. "Continue."

"The Fifth Law is the condemnation of violence. It ensures that any hand raised by one Citizen against another shall pay the ultimate price."

Robinson looked to Jaras Saah as he said it and watched him sneer.

"Continue."

"The Sixth Law regulates the use of music and dance, as endorsed by the Council of Tiers. At no time, however, may music incorporate vocalizations or may dance adopt a provocative tone given their inherently corruptible natures."

"Your own song and dance is coming to an end and we are all thankful for it."

"The Seventh Law outlaws the practice of ideology and religion, since they are the reasons most often blamed for the Great Rendering and the fall of man."

"As if man's nature should share no culpability," Taskmaster said, seemingly to himself. "And the last. The Eighth Law?"

"The Eighth Law denounces technology and all of its pervasive forms."

"For invention is the lowest form of magic. It is easier to take a thousand lives with a button than a single one with a blade. Wouldn't you agree?"

"I wouldn't know," Robinson said honestly.

"Hmm. I had heard somewhere that you enjoy to tinker."

"Only when the Feed in my room is acting up, Taskmaster."

Robinson's point was obvious. How can we claim to honor the Eight when things like electricity, flyers, and the Feed were being used more and more?

"Citizen Crusoe has answered five questions successfully, albeit it softballs, every one."

"Softballs?" someone asked.

Taskmaster Satu waved her off. "Does anyone have a question that might challenge this truant fellow?"

Several hands went up, but none of them gave Robinson any worry. It was only when Jaras Saah's hand went up that a nagging doubt pricked at him.

"Citizen Saah."

Jaras stood. He was the tallest boy in the class, behind Slink, but despite his proper attire and handsome looks, his veins pumped only cruel blood.

"How many beds are there in the gaoler's cell of the Tower Keep?"

And in that instant, Robinson's heart ceased to beat.

Chapter Five
A White Dress

He'd been ambushed.

Jaras knew Robinson had been caught scaling the Tower Keep that morning and had shared the news with Taskmaster Satu. If he admitted to the act, he would be forced to go before the Tier of Civil Obedience, Tessa and Jaras's father. If he lied and was exposed, his punishment would be much worse. He gave the only answer he could.

"I'm afraid I can't answer the question," he muttered.

"Do you mean to say you *don't know* how many beds are in the Tower Keep?"

"I just can't answer the question."

"That is unfortunate," Taskmaster Satu said before calling Robinson to the front of the room.

He tried not to let his knees shake as he peeled back his shirt cuffs again and exposed forearms that were white and toneless.

"Citizen Crusoe, the punishment for your transgressions is six lashes. Do you have anything to say?"

Robinson swallowed but shook his head. In the back, Jaras grinned.

Taskmaster Satu raised the whip high and brought it down hard against Robinson's naked flesh. The sound was enough to make most students wince.

Crack!

With the second whip, two angry red welts ballooned on Robinson's arms and sweat tickled his scalp.

Crack!

The pain was so intense that even the simple act of curling his fingers sent needles shooting throughout his body. A tear coursed down his cheek.

Crack!

When the fourth strike buckled his knees, many students looked away. The fifth drew sobs. Robinson would not look away. Eventually, he locked eyes with Slink. A single nod was enough to buoy his spirits. He could cry no more.

"Are we done?" Robinson asked after the final lash, his voice oddly steady.

Taskmaster Satu nodded minutely.

For the rest of the class, Robinson sat in silence. When the final bell rang, the pall immediately dispersed and chatter erupted as students spilled from the room.

"Citizen Crusoe," Taskmaster Satu called, "a moment please."

Jaras Saah paused, but eventually filed out too. Slink was the last to go.

"Do you know what your problem is, Crusoe?" His voice was weary. "Your problem is that you spend every waking moment trying to be clever. Ignorance is a terrible misfortune, but cleverness without wisdom is a far greater evil."

"Is that a quote?"

"Consider it a gift. To remember our time together."

"I have a feeling you, Ser, will reflect more fondly upon these days than me."

"I wouldn't be so sure. Youth is the carrot before the stick. In my classroom, you have tasted both. There may come a time out there when you realize I've taught you more than you know."

"At least out there I'll be free to make my own choices."

He chuckled. "A man has free choice to the extent that he is rational."

"Thomas Aquinas."

This time he blinked. "Your mother gave you a fine education. And a dangerous one. But here is one from Ser Aquinas that you might not know: 'Three things are necessary for the salvation of man: to know what he ought to believe; to know what he ought to desire; and to know what he ought to do.' You know none of these. And until you do, I'm afraid you will always be a danger to yourself and those around you."

Robinson shook his head. He was tired of lessons and brutality. "It doesn't really matter, does it? In two days, I will stand before the Regent on the Day of Naming and hear my name read aloud. And then I'll be on my way to becoming a Tier myself."

"And that will make you, what? Exempt from trouble?"

Robinson shrugged. "If not trouble, at least the lash."

For the first time, Robinson saw not contempt in his teacher's eyes, but pity. "Oh, dear boy. If only that were true."

Outside, Tessa was waiting. She was dressed in white with sleeves of lace. Her golden hair spilled over her shoulders in curls as she ran to him.

"Robinson!" she cried, gently taking his hands. "Is it true? *Six lashes?*"

"I guess good news really does travel fast."

"Don't be flippant! The man is a menace! Really, something must be done."

"Like what?" he asked. "He spoke of my mother and I got upset. I played right into their hands."

"'Their?' Who—?" And then she saw it on his face. "Not Jaras." She cursed. "I swear, my brother's cruelty knows no bounds."

"We can't really blame him, can we? After all, I have stolen his sister's hand."

She offered a faint smile. "You've stolen much more than that."

Then she looked down at his arms and her smile disappeared. "He can't be allowed to get away with this."

"He can and he will. He has never liked me. I don't know why. The point is moot anyway. School is over. I'll never have to face him again."

Her anger dissipated and she kissed his forearms gently. The bruising was garish, but she didn't care. Among all the male children of Tiers, there were more handsome, more politically inclined. But she had chosen him. They kissed.

"Kissing a *Muckback*, Tessa?"

They spun to see Jaras and his friends approaching. "And in public no less. Have you no shame?"

"I don't like that word, Jaras. And he is a son of Tiers, just like you and me."

"He's nothing like you and me. He makes friends of Muckbacks, sneaks around the city like one, and now he's soiling you with his very presence."

Robinson took her by the hand. "We should go."

"Go? But the fun is just beginning." Jaras's hand shot out and latched onto his forearm. Robinson couldn't help but squeal with pain. Tessa tried to peel her brother's grip away, but he was too strong. He was laughing when a voice behind them sounded.

"Problem?"

Everyone turned to see Slink approaching. When he stepped right up to Jaras's face, the smaller teen leaned back, but he didn't retreat. "We're sons of Tiers, *Muckback*. One strike against us and you'll be walking the Road before a turn is up."

Tessa pushed her way in between them. "And one strike against either of them and I'll tell father. And then we'll see who'll be walking the Road."

"You wouldn't dare."

"Try me."

Jaras was considering his next move when a Taskmaster happened by. He smiled and waited until he was gone.

"I'm so sick of you, Crusoe. Sick of your face. Sick of your family. Sick of your name. Stay away from my sister or else."

"Or else what?" Robinson asked.

"Or else the real fun will begin."

His fellow sycophants laughed and followed Jaras as he turned and strode away.

"I'm sorry," Tessa said. "I don't know what gets into him. He's never like this at home."

"Are you all right?" Slink asked.

Robinson looked at Tessa, who cozied up next to him. "Never better."

Slink grinned. "Well, there's nothing less attractive than an oversized third wheel, so—"

But before he finished, the Second Spire's bell tolled. Tessa's brow furrowed, as she was first to grasp the sequencing of tolls.

"We need to find a Feed," she said.

"Why?" Robinson asked, turning to Slink. "Is that a Wall alarm?"

"No," he answered gravely. "It's a toll of Expiry. Someone is about to be executed."

Chapter Six
The Red Road

The inner-quad was so packed with students that it was impossible for the trio to get a glimpse of a Feed monitor. The message was clear however. Someone had been found guilty of treasonous acts and a sentence of Expiry was to be exercised immediately in the Crown Square.

The queue for carriages leaving the school was long, so Slink led the others on a serpentine jot that spilled out at the eastern end of the Clutch, near the Crown itself.

A sizeable crowd had already amassed with Tiers taking position outside the stores while ordinary citizens filled the streets. Renarch Uth, who had designed Tessa's spring wardrobe, frowned when he saw Slink but knew better than to speak up while his friends were present. His apprentice even ushered over water, unbidden.

It wasn't long before the Second Spire bell tolled and a contingent of Red Guard took positions in front of the crowd. Over the open Crown Gates, the Feed display flickered to life. All eight Regens would be watching.

Public sentencing was a bizarre affair. It was one of the few occasions when the Tiers and the underclass took in anything side-by-side. But everyone was there, infusing the air with a perverse sense of excitement.

The scene brought to mind a memory of when Robinson was a small child sitting on his father's shoulders, jeering with the crowd as a condemned matron accused of theft was marched down the Red Road before him. He remembered his mother pulling him to the ground and scolding him. He hadn't understood the harsh look in her eyes that day. Now that he was older, he realized it had been disgust.

The massive swath of bodies kicked up dust as citizens craned their heads. Robinson scanned the faces across the street until he spotted his father huddled in a darkened alcove, talking furtively with Tier Fallow and Tier Cork.

"Tessa, have you heard something about a campaign?"

Her nose crinkled oddly. "No. What is it?"

He shrugged and then deflected. "Something one of the Nobes at school mentioned, but I only caught the word in passing."

"You don't remember who?" she asked offhandedly.

He shook his head, though it troubled him to lie. Not that it mattered. When the bells tolled for the third time, she grabbed his arm and said, "Here they come."

Through the Crown Gates, a battalion of Iron Fists emerged. The Iron Fists were the Regent's elite guard, kept for his personal security and for battling renders. They wore bulkier uniforms with iron plating covering their shoulders and torsos. The iron gauntlets they wore gave them their moniker. It was said one strike with an Iron Fist could crush a man's skull with ease.

Once they were in position, the Crown officials followed, led by Tier Vardan Saah, Tessa's father. Her chest swelled with pride as he strode forward in his crisp, navy uniform with a narrow line of red running down one side. His clipped, dark hair sat comfortably above a high collar. He wore no facial hair but had deep-set eyes that always drew people's attention. Accompanying him was Brapo Liesel, a towering figure rumored to be the city's executioner and the personal tracker of any who fled over the Wall.

At last, the Regent appeared, adorned in navy and gold, his halo of silver hair shining like a crown. To the people, he raised a single hand of One and Four. The crowd immediately returned the gesture. The Feed cut to a microphone raised toward him. His eyes, filled with both sorrow and resolution, perused the crowd until the din had settled.

"Let the condemned stand forth before us."

From the gates, two Iron Fists led the hooded perpetrator in chains. The crowd jeered so loudly that he actually tripped and had to be dragged the rest of the way. The Regent held up his hand, silencing the crowd once more. Then he nodded to Tier Saah, who made his way to the dais.

"Before you stands a man," Tier Saah spoke, his voice smooth like cream, "faceless. Unknown. Born of flesh and blood—like all of us—and imbued with the power of choice and free will. But unlike you and I, who serve the One, this man serves himself. Would you see this man for who he is? For *what* he has become?"

The crowd answered in unison as bodies pressed forward. Bloodlust was thick in the air. Even Robinson found himself gripping the railing as Tier Saah called for the prisoner's hood to be removed.

The crowd gasped. The condemned man's head hung low, his ruffled hair covering his face. As the prisoner's name sped through the mob, the furor escalated until it was deafening. Finally, he looked up. Robinson inhaled.

"Who is it?" Tessa asked.

Robinson shook with disbelief. "Byron Frostmore. They're executing a Tier."

Tessa and Slink were equally stunned. A Tier hadn't been executed since well before the teens were born.

"What could he have done?" Tessa asked.

Robinson shrugged but didn't dare look at her for fear she'd see the doubt building in his heart. The man was being tried for treason. And yet that very morning, he'd taken a secret meeting with his father and the others. Were they also involved? Would that explain his father's angry outburst? If so, they were all in jeopardy.

Exile and Expiry.

These were the two punishments any citizen faced. To be Exiled was to be banished beyond the Wall, left to the horrors of renders and the wild things of the world. Death was certain, but the means were unknown.

Expiry wasn't nearly as vague.

A rush of people swarmed forward and tore Tier Frostmore from the stage. His clothes were ripped from his body and he was dragged into the street. The mob spit and threw things as he passed. Already the heavy chains bit into his legs, drawing blood that stained the road red, which was how it had earned its name. Through it all, the entire spectacle was broadcast with remarkable clarity on the Feed overhead.

Tessa turned, tears in her eyes. They both knew the journey that awaited Tier Frostmore. It was a long, hard slog through the Clutch and Communal Fields, and all the way to the Western Gate. Only there would the crowd be held back as the Iron Fists dragged him to the cliffs that overlooked the sea. Would he leap of his own accord? Or would he tarry out of fear or pride and force the gauntlets to end it for him?

"I have to go see my father," Tessa said unexpectedly.

To their right, the Regent and his guard left the stage, but Tier Saah remained. Robinson could see by his demeanor that the scene affected him too. He'd always heard disturbing things about the Tier of Obedience, but now he was unsure what to believe. In the space of half a day, so many things had happened.

Robinson reached for Tessa's hand. "Go on. Put this from your mind. Tomorrow we become apprentices. Tomorrow we'll be Named. After that, nothing can keep us apart."

"I can't wait," she said before quickly kissing him on the mouth and dashing away. He watched her until her golden locks disappeared among the crowd.

"You knew him," Slink said suddenly. Robinson didn't have to ask who *him* was.

"Not really. But he was one of us. The idea that this could happen so quickly ..."

"I'll walk you to the Shelf."

"You can't look after me forever, Slink. One of these days, I'm going to have to learn to take care of myself."

Slink chuckled. "There's a terrifying thought. Stick to the streets. Most of the mob is gone or sated, but you don't want to test them when their blood is up."

Slink clouted his friend on the shoulder and left.

After he was gone, Robinson looked back to the stage and felt that cold chill crawling up his spine. Vareen was right. A change was coming. Slink seemed to have felt it too. Had he known the enormity of what was in front of him, he might have done things differently. But fate had other ideas in store.

Robinson took one last gulp of his water and then turned to go. For some unknown reason, he paused to look back over his shoulder. Most of the Tiers had cleared out of the Clutch but one had remained. It was his father, and he was watching him.

Chapter Seven
Tears in the Rain

Robinson was relieved to learn that Vareen had not let the children watch the broadcast, but they hadn't missed the news of their older brother's punishment.

"Six lashes!" Tannis exclaimed. "That has to be a record!"

"You're famous!" Tallis said and everyone laughed. They asked how much it hurt, but Robinson fibbed and told them "not much." Afterward, they played Over the Wall, Under the Wall, their favorite game.

Word finally turned to the ball set for the following night and Tallis beamed.

"Vareen is putting the final touches on my dress tonight," she said excitedly.

"And my suit was done yesterday, but we're not allowed to see them yet," Tannis added.

Vareen stood nearby, helping clear the plates from the table. "It wouldn't be fair to present your outfit separately. You'll just have to wait until the 'morrow."

A patter of rain splashed the window and the staff quickly brought in the clothes from the cords outside. An hour or so into the game, one of the twins looked up and saw Leodore watching from the doorway.

"Father!" they both cried and hugged him around the waist. He smiled, and for a moment, he looked like the man Robinson knew from before his mother had died.

"Children, I'd like a few moments with your brother. Please."

When they were gone, Leodore sat in a chair opposite his son. "I'm sorry I struck you today," he said softly. "No excuse is worthy."

"It was foolish of me, Father. I deserved—"

"No," he said sternly. "No child should ever fear their own parent. There are too many threats in this world—too many greater dangers—for them to fear coming home. And this will always be your home, Robinson. No matter how old you grow or which direction life takes you, you will always have a place under this roof. You and Tannis and Tallis. I hope you know that."

Robinson did. And then he sought a question to fill the silence between them. "Why did Tier Frostmore walk the Road?"

Leodore sighed. "I wish I could tell you, but it's for the best that I don't."

"I'm not a child. You can trust me."

"I know that, but you're not exactly a man yet, are you? Men don't scale towers before the crack of dawn on a lark. Why did you do it, by the way? I forgot to ask."

"I heard they were keeping a render there. It's been years since anyone glimpsed one outside the Wall. Many believe they no longer exist."

Leodore snorted. "Oh, they exist. Maybe their numbers have waned here in the south where the walls can't be breached, but in other Regens, and on other continents, they are very real and very dangerous. Now, I have a question of my own. What's the story with you and Tier Saah's daughter?"

Robinson's heart picked up pace, but he didn't dare look away. "Tessa? We're classmates. And friends."

"You looked very *friendly* today."

Robinson could only shrug. Then his father asked the question he'd been dreading. "Do you love her?"

He could not lie, so he simply nodded again. Leodore leaned into his chair, looking infinitely weary. His fingers dipped absently into the small pocket of his vest. Robinson saw a glint of silver there.

"There are things I should have told you about her father long ago. Things I had hoped to say once you finished school and joined me in the trade. I see now I've waited too long."

"Father, I would never jeopardize—"

Leodore held up a hand to silence him. "I cannot forbid you from attending the ball. Your absence would draw too much attention. And attention right now is the last thing either of us needs." He looked at the bruises on his son's arms as he said it. "But I can and will insist you stop seeing this girl immediately."

"But, Father! We're in love!"

"Of your sincerity I have no doubts. And maybe the girl loves you too. Who knows? All that matters is that you are my son and I know what's best for you. I forbid you from having contact with her. And if you defy me on this, I will have no choice but to see you apprenticed to another Tier. Someone in the far Regens to the north where you'll be safe. From others … and from yourself. Do I make myself clear?"

Robinson was too stunned to answer.

"I'll take your silence as assent. Please don't test me on this. What I do—what I have always done—is for the sake of this family. Your mother would have done the same."

"No, she wouldn't have!" Robinson said. "She would never agree to this!"

"Your mother knew the value of sacrifice better than any other, Robinson. I only hope you are spared that pain."

Even as his father walked away, Robinson knew he would defy him. He and Tessa belonged together. Regardless of the rift between their fathers, he knew in his heart they would risk the Wall, the Road, and everything short of dying to stay by each other's side.

As dusk arrived, the rain slowed to a drizzle. Robinson sat on the porch, watching the clouds turn pink to the east. A screen door squeaked. Vareen sat down beside him.

"He doesn't know what real love is," Robinson said. "Or maybe he did once and has forgotten."

"Is that what you believe? That after six months, your mother's memory has passed from his mind? You're not that big a fool, boy."

Robinson hung his head. "What history is there between father and Tier Saah? I know they're both on the council. And rumor has it one of them will succeed the Regent when he retires. But it goes deeper than that, doesn't it?"

Vareen nodded. "When your father was your age, your grandfather made a pact to marry him to the daughter of the Tier of Rivers."

"Wait. You mean, Tier Saah's wife?"

"She was Janal Florencia then. Some say she was the most beautiful girl to ever walk the Isle. He used to visit her at the House of Healers where she apprenticed. But it was during those trips that he noticed a second girl who was beautiful in a different way. Strong willed but compassionate. And she had a gift for medicine that went far beyond those who had come before."

"Mother."

Vareen nodded again. "Alan Crusoe was not a man to be defied, especially by his own blood. He threatened to Exile your father and disown him. Even beat him senseless. But none of these could change his heart. When the Naming Day Ball arrived, Annabess and your father stood before the entire Crown and abdicated their apprenticeships for each other."

Robinson was stunned.

"No one had ever turned their back on the Tiers before. They were prepared to live the lives of ordinary citizens or accept exile themselves. Your grandfather knew it was no bluff. It cost him most of his political clout, but in the end, Leodore remained a Crusoe and your mother along with him."

Robinson couldn't believe it. Abdicating an apprenticeship? He'd never heard of such a thing.

"I don't tell you this story to give you *ideas*," Vareen said. "Those were different times. But they do illustrate one undeniable truth: the greatest love anyone can hope for is the one for which you are willing to sacrifice everything. Make sure this girl is worthy of that before you do."

Later that evening, Robinson lay awake in bed, listening to the rain and trying to process all he'd been through and all he'd heard that day. He wondered if he'd have the strength to do as his father had and stand in front of the entire One People and choose exile because of love. If nothing else could make him a man in his father's eyes, that would. But deep down, he knew the truth. He was a boy. And that was a man's act.

Just as he began edging off to sleep, Robinson heard a knock at his window. He slid tentatively out of bed and crossed to it. Tessa was outside.

She was crying.

Chapter Eight
Forbidden Things

"My father has forbidden me from seeing you," she sobbed as soon as Robinson opened the kitchen door. He quickly hustled her into the parlor where they could whisper without worrying over waking the staff.

"Mine gave the same order," he said.

"What can we do? We're not enemies. I don't even understand what they have against each other."

She was soaked through, so he bid her to wait as he went to retrieve some towels. When he came back, she had wandered into his father's study. He was nervous. They were never allowed in here. But his father had gone out earlier and still hadn't returned.

Tessa was staring at a sketch of Robinson's mother, shivering. He wrapped a towel around her.

"You never told me what happened to her."

"Surely you heard? There was a medical emergency in Regen 4. She took a flyer and it crashed on the way there."

"But why didn't she just use an authorized pilot to fly her?"

"None were available."

She set down the photo and turned to embrace him. "I want us to start a life together. A family. But I feel as if something is about to happen."

"I feel it too."

"Earlier you asked me about the word campaign. Well, I snuck into my father's office at home. I'm not proud of it. The truth is I didn't expect to find anything. But there was a document on his desk with that word."

"A document?"

"A *confession*. Tier Frostmore's. He admitted to being part of the campaign, the gist of which I took to mean a revolt."

"Against who?"

"Who do you think? The One People."

Robinson felt a sickening hollowness in his stomach. "Did Tier Frostmore mention any collaborations or implicate anyone else?" he asked nervously.

"No. He had something on his person. A tincture of some kind. He drank it when the guards weren't looking. That's why he was acting so delirious yesterday. Robinson, do you suspect your father could be involved?"

The question rocked him. "I can't say. Is it any more improbable than yours?"

"No, but I hope in my deepest heart it's neither."

He agreed. They held each other and talked until their worries were tempered. The rain had lessened but not abated. She noticed something on the desk.

"What's this?"

Tessa picked up a slightly curved instrument made out of wood and pulled two halves apart, revealing a shining blade within.

"Be careful with that. It's very old."

"Is it sharp?"

"I don't know and I don't want to find out."

"This is contraband."

"I know. *Very old* contraband. My father says it's been in our family for centuries. It was a gift from a foreign merchant to one of my ancestors when the Crusoes owned ships instead of flyers. It even has our family crest engraved there. See?"

"It's beautiful," she said before setting it down. "What are we going to do?"

Robinson thought long and hard. "As I see it, we have two options."

And as he spelled them out for her, Tessa's eyes grew wider and wider.

Shortly after she'd gone, Robinson returned to bed but still found sleep elusive. He had never doubted his father but was troubled by his many secrets. He needed to defuse his suspicions and one thing kept coming to mind—the object his father held most dear.

Robinson hadn't been in his parents' room since his mother died, and sneaking inside felt like a terrible violation. But when he saw his father's suit hanging on the bureau, he couldn't help but check the vest pocket. He found his mother's locket.

It too was very old, made long before the Great Rendering. None could confuse it as contraband, however. It was handcrafted with an elegant flower center-set. Robinson smiled. Holding it felt like holding a piece of her.

But as he moved to return it, he felt something shift subtly inside. He looked closer and noticed a locking mechanism. He didn't know what he would find, but his hands trembled when he depressed a small button. The locket split in half. Inside were two things: a small piece of paper and a circular disc. He knew the disc carried information. It was illegal for all but the Feed operators to possess. He unfolded the paper only to see it had a single number written across it:

3853772

He had no idea what it meant, but he knew it was important.

The following evening, the family were dressed in their best clothes and rushed through the rain to load into the carriage.

"I want you to be on your best behavior, children," Vareen said as she continued to primp the twins. "This is a big day for your brother. Today, he becomes a man."

Robinson blushed.

"Are you going to watch it on the Feed?" Tallis asked.

"I wouldn't miss it for all the five continents!" Vareen said.

As Robinson was about to enter, Vareen pulled him into a hug and whispered into his ear, "I'm very proud of you. And your mother is too."

He smiled but entered quickly, hoping she couldn't see his tears in the rain.

The muddy roads and spate of carriages made the ride longer than normal. It felt muggy inside the carriage despite the thunderstorm.

"Roderick Illus said the ancients used to be able to predict the weather years in advance," Tannis said unexpectedly. Tallis asked if that was true.

"No one knows the weather before it knows itself, dear. Though I daresay calculating it a few days early was more than likely feasible."

"How?" Tannis asked.

"The ancients once deployed sentinels to watch the skies from above."

"Sentinels?" Tallis asked.

"Satellites, I believe they were called. Machines. One of the many wonders that elude us. And if we're lucky, always will."

"Why?" Tallis asked.

"Because any machine that is built for one purpose but can be used for another is dangerous. I shouldn't've mentioned it. Even speaking of such things violates the Eight."

"Father," Tannis said. "Vareen said she wouldn't miss the ball for all the five continents."

Leodore grinned. "Do you doubt her?"

"Of course not, but Roderick also said there are seven continents, not five."

Leodore's mouth grew tight. "Someone needs to speak with Tier Illus about his son's prattling."

"So it's not true?"

Leodore sighed. "Yes, it's true. Our world has seven continents, not five. But two of those continents are forbidden to us. They are where the Great Rendering began and were lost to horrors I dare not speak about here. Their evil drove man to the brink of extinction. Those who survived agreed long ago never to risk return."

Father checked his pocket watch and shook his head. They had barely passed the communal fields and still had the span of the Clutch to navigate. "Let us speak of something lighter. Robinson, your friend Mayfus must be excited to attend his first ball."

Mayfus was Slink's given name. The Naming Day Ball was the only time the Underclass got to attend an event inside the Crown.

"Excited would be an understatement," Robinson replied. "Slink's been calling in all his father's favors in hopes of earning an apprenticeship with the Tier of Media."

Leodore shook his head. "Your friend has no chance of working on the Feed."

"Why not? I've seen the underclass get apprenticed."

"Sure, in the northern Regens, and from Tiers foolish enough to believe they can make a statement. But not here in the capital, and not by Balthazar Abett."

"What if you made an introduction on his behalf? If Tier Abett met Slink, I'm sure he would find him qualified and very deserving."

"*Deserving* has nothing to do with it. Mayfus is the son of a Wall Guard. It is his place to stand the post *with* his father and when he passes, *in his stead*. Just as it is your place to one day supersede me. These are our customs. These are our traditions."

"That doesn't make them right."

Leodore looked at his son anew and was surprised to see the boy didn't avert his eyes. He was riding to the Naming Day Ball in his crisp suit, looking more and more like a man. *Too soon*, he thought. *I still have so much more to teach him.*

Chapter Nine
The Naming Day Ball

The Naming Day Ball was in full swing when Tier Crusoe and family entered the Great Room, but many heads still turned to mark their entrance. Leodore received respectful bows and One and Fours by every Tier he passed, but Robinson saw a few whisper or sneer after they'd moved on. Still, his father had an aura about him that created a kind of buffer as he walked, like a deep-hulled river craft that others avoided for fear of getting caught in its wake.

The decorations in the massive ballroom were lavish with crimson banners that hung from balconies and giant chandeliers laden with candles glimmering brilliantly from above.

Feed cameras moved effortlessly through the room. The attendees coveted the attention, sporting artificial derision while showing off their finest garments.

Servers came and went from the kitchen, carrying plates of mouth-watering dishes as delectable odors filled the room. Others carried crystal decanters of wine and spirits. That night, not a single glass would run dry.

At the foot of the grand staircase, Tier Saah and his family held court amongst a number of Tiers. As the Crusoe family passed, the two patriarchs exchanged nods, but it was Tessa's eyes Robinson held until her brother stepped between them, glowering.

Eventually, the twins were sent to the South Hall to join others their age, while others drew Leodore to the far end of the room. Robinson was left alone.

"Well, look who decided to show up," a familiar voice spoke.

Robinson turned to find Slink standing with his father, the Bull, Captain of the Wall Guard. He was a daunting figure, barrel-chested and thick-armed, with ruddy skin and a dense, golden mustache flecked with red. His uniform was perfectly starched, with silver buttons that were only outshone by the pride in his eyes.

"Slink! I mean … Mayfus. There you are." He nodded to his father. "Ser Grey."

"It's 'Bull' tonight, son. And from now on, I suppose. How are ya? Nervous?"

"A bit."

"Shoulda seen this one. Preening in front of the mirror like a wee mare—"

"Dad," Slink growled.

"All right then. I'll leave you two to it." He shuffled awkwardly off.

"I swear he's more of an embarrassment than the pimples that ambushed me this morning."

"He's just excited," Robinson said.

"I don't know what for. I might be getting Named, but tomorrow I'll be standing the Wall right behind him. Have you seen it yet?"

"*It?*" Robinson asked.

"The render. It's in the East Room. Thought there'd be more to it, really."

"Show me."

"Nuh-uh. I need to practice my words. I only have one chance to stand before the Crown. I don't want to screw it up."

Robinson pressed through the clogged dance floor and made his way to the East Room, only to find it overrun with people trying to get a look inside. A few exiting looked pale and repulsed, but many others appeared excited.

When Robinson finally made his way to the front, he found a cage perched on a small platform. Inside was a creature, humanoid in shape, but with three legs rather than two. One arm was stunted, flopping like a child's, but its other was grossly distended with ropy muscle and a fist larger than a cantaloupe that bore talon-like claws. Its flesh was wet, intermingled with blood and pus that ran from ulcerated pocks tattooing its rigid back and chest. Despite these horrors, the creature looked sickly and sallow. Several children from Tier families stabbed it with blunt sticks, laughing as it howled.

"Well, boy? Is it everything you imagined?" a familiar voice asked from behind him.

Robinson turned. "Actually, Taskmaster, it looks rather pathetic."

Taskmaster Satu sneered, his eyes red from too much drink. Robinson had never known him to drink. "Does it now? I wonder if you'd feel pity for it if there weren't bars between you. Or if you two met on the other side of the Wall?"

Robinson shrugged bravely. "Give me a weapon and I like my chances."

This time the teacher laughed. "You wouldn't last a day outside and we both know it." He watched the boy deflate. "Your mother held a similar compassion for these abominations. She tried to see their humanity through the disease. Look what it got her."

"My mother died in a flyer accident. What do you mean?"

Taskmaster Satu seemed to want to say more. Then he looked around. "Nothing."

"You've always hated me. I never understood why."

Pity bled across the teacher's face. "I don't hate you, boy," he said softly. "Only what you're destined to become."

"And what is that?" Robinson asked.

Taskmaster Satu nodded toward the surly crowd. "One of them."

By the time the Spire Bells began to toll the start of the ceremony, the rain outside had grown into a heavy downpour. Thunder could be heard over the music and once, the lights in the Great Room fluttered.

Robinson joined his group of schoolmates to the left of the grand staircase just as the Regent and his Retinue arrived. Tier Saah took up position next to him, his head held high, his mouth a grim line.

Robinson's chest felt tight. He knew what he was about to do would rock the Townships, if not the very Isle. It might also destroy his father. But if he loved him, he would understand. He looked to Tessa. When her eyes met his he smiled, but she looked more nervous than he did at what was to come.

"Citizens of the One People," the Regent began, his voice melodious as it played over the Feed. "Tonight we celebrate the Day of Naming. It is a sacred tradition that began over two centuries ago, given to us in the form of the Third Law by our founders to ensure our continued way of life. Here, tonight, your children—*our children*—will take the final step in joining us in full citizenry by hearing their names read aloud and accepting apprenticeship in their parents' trade."

He nodded and a group of Taskmasters stood up behind him. One familiar face was conspicuously absent.

"In adherence to the Third Law, I give you this year's Named."

With the reading of each name, one of Robinson's classmates crossed to the dais and was offered apprenticeship under one of his or her parents' names. Each accepted to the applause of the crowd and to the occasional sob of family members. Seleen Cottsfold, Powe Lawrell, Tius Absroy. Each proudly accepted their calling. And then Jaras Saah's name was called. Robinson's blood boiled as he walked smugly forward.

"Jaras, as first son of your parents, you are named to the apprenticeship of your father, Vardan Saah, Tier of Civil Obedience. Do you accept this calling?"

"Yes, my Regent," answered Jaras. And as if fate designed to punctuate the moment, a streak of lightning and the roar of thunder set the lights fluttering again.

"Then may your addition be a boon to the One People until the end of your days."

Tier Saah beamed as his son returned. Robinson's gut continued to twist until Slink's name filled the hall.

"Mayfus Grey, your father is Captain of the Wall Guard, is he not?"

Mayfus looked confused. This was irregular. "Y-yes, my Regent."

"A fine position for an apprentice. The Wall is always in need of good men. But as a student under my tutelage, you have proven yourself capable of more. Because of your accomplishments and your father's exemplary service to the One People, you have been nominated for apprenticeship with Balthazar Abett, Tier of Media. Do you accept this calling?"

Slink was stunned. Robinson's head snapped to the back of the room where he found his father's eyes. He knew in an instant this was his doing, not for Slink or to make a political statement, but out of love for his son. He felt joy for a moment, but it was tempered by the pain he knew would follow.

"O-of course, Ser!" Slink said as he found his voice. "It would be an honor!"

A hum ran through the crowd. As Slink turned toward his father, the Bull's eyes brimmed, likely for the first time in his life. And then Robinson's name was called.

"Robinson Crusoe."

His chest tightened as he walked toward the stage. It was as if every sight and sound fell away, except for the beating of his heart. He glanced at Tier Saah, but his gaze remained fixed elsewhere.

"Robinson Crusoe, as first son of your parents, you are named into the apprenticeship of your father, Leodore Crusoe, Tier of Transportation. Do you accept this calling?"

His voice was suddenly lost. He tried to steady himself, aware that any awkward movement or errant glance might diminish the appearance of his conviction. Every set of eyes in the room was on him. Every viewer across the Eight Regens was watching the Feed. He was ready to sacrifice everything for Tessa.

And then the lights went out.

Several screams permeated the room, but Tier Saah called for order. The lights returned a moment later. Robinson looked up to find the Regent's eyes blank.

"Ser?" he queried.

And the Regent toppled to the floor, a knife in his back.

Citizens screamed. Guards rushed forward. Tier Saah rushed to the Regent's aid. But Robinson's eyes were wholly fixed on the handle of the blade and the crest that bore his family's name. His head instantly turned to Tessa, whose eyes held immense pity but no love.

Then his father's voice rang out.

"Robinson, run!"

Chapter Ten
Flight!

The Great Room erupted into chaos. But it was not the Red Guard or Iron Fists that dragged Robinson from the floor; it was Jaras and his friends. They hustled him through a side door just off the kitchen that led to a darkened alcove where they threw him down and pummeled him with kicks and punches.

"You should have seen your face," Jaras said, sputum flying from his mouth. "That moment when you knew you'd been played for a fool. Did you really believe my sister would fancy a little nothing like you?"

"The twins—" Robinson started but was rocked by another punch that brought an explosion of coppery warmth to his mouth.

"Gone! Gone! Like Daddy, they're all gone! Just you now but not for long!"

Robinson tried to get up but was shoved down again.

"You want to run? You want a chance? All you have to do is beg."

He said nothing and was punched in the gut again.

"Come on, rabbit. Beg. You know how it's done."

Robinson shook his head and was pummeled again.

"Just give us a whimper, yeah? A little snivel and it'll all be over. It's who you are."

As hard as he tried, Robinson couldn't contain the quiver in his lip. Finally, he said, "Please."

Jaras sneered again. "Since you asked so nicely …"

Jaras grit his teeth as he reared back for the final blow. Robinson closed his eyes. But before the blow came, a rush of air blew into the room as a shadow slammed into his attackers. One by one, they cried out as the sickening notes of violence built up to a crescendo.

Robinson's vision blurred, but when it returned, he found himself moving through a series of tunnels that snaked through rock, scaling up and down with the smallest of lanterns to light their way. A meaty hand was wrapped under his arm, willing his legs to move.

They finally emerged under the eaves of the Seventh Spire. Slink peeled back a shroud of ivy that led to the Tongue.

"The Tiers all fled for the Shelf. The people are rioting and the Red Guard will learn of your escape soon. If we don't get you across the river now—"

Robinson tried to thank him, but his tongue was severely swollen and his mouth had gone numb.

"Save it, Nobe. We've got a lot of ground to cover."

Slink waited and then pulled him out of the tunnel and rushed them across the street. He was just about to turn into the Clutch when a contingent of Red Guard appeared two blocks away. He froze. And then a carriage skidded to a halt in front of him. The door blew open and Taskmaster Satu flung an arm out.

"In here, boy!"

Slink debated a second before helping Robinson inside. Taskmaster Satu told Slink to get home as quickly as possible before slamming the door and ordering the driver to go.

"My father …" Robinson mumbled.

"Fled with the children, but they will be coming for him. He has papers at home. Your mother's things. With any luck, we can beat the Iron Fists there and meet him."

"She lied to me," he sobbed, tears falling freely. "She said she loved me."

Taskmaster Satu was overwhelmed with pity. "We suspected they might be using her to glean information from you."

"*We?*"

"My allegiance has always been with your parents and the One People. But we needed a way to prove my loyalty to Tier Saah. My loathing for you was part of that."

Robinson felt like a fool. Outside the carriage, he witnessed the looting of merchant businesses. A gang of thugs had taken up anything resembling a weapon to meet the Red Guard in the street.

"Is this what Tier Saah wants? The end of the One People? Is that what the campaign is about?"

"Oh, no. Tier Saah has set his sights on something much bigger and grander."

The carriage was suddenly rocked from outside. The driver tried spurring his horse through the mob, but a horde of men overtook it and soon it toppled over. Robinson crawled out from underneath the wreckage and set off for the estate on foot.

Taskmaster Satu, bloodied but alive, stumbled out after him, calling his name.

A quarter turn later, Robinson was halfway up the Shelf when he smelled the smoke. He knew immediately where it was coming from. The panic brewing inside him reached a fever pitch when he rounded the bend and saw flames billowing out of his family estate.

He turned the corner at the rear of the house and saw Vareen lying outside the door. Her throat had been slit, her scarlet lifeblood pooling around her. Robinson was not surprised, however, to see a knife in her hand. It was tipped with blood. Lying next to her was the family driver, his skull bludgeoned and gaping.

Robinson rushed into the kitchen, immediately inhaling a lungful of smoke. He grabbed a wet rag to cover his face and stumbled toward the children's rooms. They were empty. Then he heard a noise coming from the parlor.

Halfway through the main hallway, Robinson jumped over a burning beam that had split the roof wide open. A torrent of rain spilled in but failed to quench the fire.

When Robinson entered the parlor, he saw Brapo Liesel behind his father, a garrote wrapped tightly around his father's neck. Brapo was bruised and bloodied, but it was clear this fight was almost over. The teen charged the assassin with a scream and leaped onto his back, gouging at his eyes. He let loose a heavy backhand that sent Robinson sailing. His yellow teeth glowed ominously in the flames.

"I get extra for you!" he said, scooping up a dagger.

Robinson froze with fear. But as the brute stepped forward, Leodore unexpectedly kicked out, knocking his attacker off balance. Robinson's instinct took over and he charged, burying a shoulder into the goliath's chest and sending him cartwheeling over his father's desk. Brapo's body clipped an oil lamp and he landed on top of it with a crash. The liquid soaked into his clothes an instant before it took to flame. Brapo became a whirling conflagration, a dervish of brute flesh and unrequited sin.

Over the roar of the fire and their attacker's screams, Robinson pulled his father outside just as a winded Taskmaster Satu arrived.

"Is he alive?" Taskmaster Satu asked.

Robinson checked his pulse. When his father stirred, Robinson asked about the twins.

"Sent … away …" Leodore gasped before thrusting something into his hands. "Now you … must go … too."

Robinson refused to leave, so Leodore turned to his teacher. "To the flyers … now!"

Robinson screamed as Taskmaster Satu grabbed him, but he was too weak to fend the old man off. Robinson screamed his father's name, but the roar of the flames swallowed his words. As the smoke blotted out the night, the last thing he saw was his father raise his hand in a One and Three, symbolizing they would always be together.

Taskmaster Satu dragged Robinson across the field toward the livery. In the distance, they saw lanterns approaching. The Red Guard was closing in.

Robinson stumbled into the livery as his teacher opened the front gates.

He ran for the nearest flyer.

"You know how to fly one of these things?"

Robinson nodded numbly. He had watched his father teach many pilots the skill. "Good," Satu said. "Fly as far away as you can. Find a place to hide. Preferably some place cold. The renders don't like the cold. Can you remember that?"

Robinson nodded again.

"When the time is right, your father will come for you. Do not give up hope."

It seemed like an impossible promise, but in a night of horrors, hope was all he had to grasp. He wanted to say more, but his teacher waved, and then picked up a mallet and set to sabotaging the other flyers.

Robinson activated his flyer controls as he'd seen his father do many times. He wasn't even sure if he was doing it correctly until the thrusters thrummed to life. The ship rose and slowly powered through the livery gate.

Outside, the Red Guard had overtaken the estate. Robinson waited until the gravity drive was fully charged before giving the engine power and pulling back on the yoke. It soared up and out over the Pate. As he banked toward the ocean, he stopped to take one last look at the Isle and the inferno that marked the end of his life. He knew at that very moment, he would never see this place again.

As the craft sped over the surf, Robinson scanned the array of foreign knobs and dials and wondered how on earth he was going to survive.

Then two words appeared on the screen before him: ENGAGE AUTOPILOT?

With no other choice, he selected "YES."

The words disappeared and seven blank boxes took their place. He had no clue what they meant.

Robinson stared at them, confused. But then it hit him. He reached in his pocket for the thing his father had given him. It was his mother's locket. He opened it and found the piece of paper inside.

Could it be so easy?

He unfolded the paper and entered the numbers 3-8-5-3-7-7-2 and hit ENTER.

A half second later, the words "COORDINATES ACCEPTED" splashed across the screen and the flyer banked toward the ocean and sped into the night.

PART TWO

"The gates of hell are open night and day;
Smooth the descent, and easy is the way:
But to return, and view the cheerful skies,
In this the task and mighty labor lies."

-Virgil's Aeneid

Chapter Eleven
Into the Unknown

The flyer was speeding one hundred meters above the ocean surface when he woke. At first he had no idea where he was, but then he smelled the smoke on his clothes and felt the dried blood on his face and the memories of last night returned. He had fled the only home he had ever known like a thief in the night and now he could never go back.

He rose unsteadily. The only sound he could hear was the subtle thrum of the engines and the rush of air outside. Out of the view screen in front of him stretched the great, blue Atlantica, boundless and free. He had smelled it his entire life but never dreamed it would look like this.

His mouth tasted of dry blood, so he went in search of water, finding a meager ration in the back. It tasted flat and dull, but he didn't waste a drop. There were also satchels of pre-packaged food stacked in cloth containers that were affixed to the rear wall. His stomach cried in protest as he handled them, but he refused to eat any until he had a better grasp of his situation.

In the pilot's chair, he was careful not to touch anything lest he send the flyer plummeting from the sky. The sun was low at his back, the ship's shadow blazing a course on the water in front of him. Rainclouds lingered on the horizon, but they were quickly evaporating under the morning sun.

On the screen before him, several words stood out: Altitude. Speed. Gravity Displacement. Only one was blinking: Fuel Cell Capacity. He touched it and saw it replaced with a long rectangle, half filled with small, drab blocks. The image left no room for interpretation. He had passed the point of no return.

The flyer sped west, but he had no clue what awaited him. All his life he'd dreamed of escape, of bounding over the Wall on a quest for adventure. But he was reminded that all children shared such fancies because most were made at night under the cloak of their covers, only to evaporate in the morning like dew in the grass. But from this journey, he would not awake. To survive, he knew he needed to keep his wits and put everything else behind him.

When the sun finally overtook his position, Robinson gave in and ate his first box of rations. It was gone in an instant. Just when he felt the most alone, a spray of water burst from below. He leaped to his feet to peer over the nose of the ship as a school of giant sea mammals breached the water's surface. He was awestruck. The creatures were oblong with oily black and spotted coats with fins and forked tails that helped them move gracefully with each stroke. Robinson searched his mind for some lesson that might name these leviathans but came up empty. He was told such things had died in the Great Rendering. Now that too had been unveiled as just another lie.

As the turns passed, the fuel cell markers continued to dwindle. Robinson tried to keep a brave façade, but it wasn't easy. The sun was falling quickly and the ocean waters, once so playful, were growing still, dark, and ominous.

And then the sun disappeared for good.

Drops of rain pattered against the view screen, illuminated by the flyer's front lights, which had turned on automatically after the sky had gone dark. Under the ocean, angry swells broke in all directions. The surface would plummet away into a vast abyss that seemed to stretch toward the planet's core only to rebound a second later and kiss the runners of the ship.

When the second-to-last meter block ticked off, the chime turned into a buzz and a warning flashed on the screen: 325 kilometers remaining. His eyes fell to the numbers he had found in his mother's locket. 3853772. Had they not been coordinates? Had her calculations been wrong?

When the final fuel cell block ticked away, a warning light bleated and an alarm rang. LOW FUEL CELL WARNING appeared on the screen. He looked outside again, but the storm blinded him to everything. He cut the lights to save power but knew it wouldn't be enough. And then something hard hit the view screen.

Robinson quickly turned up the lights only to see that the glass was covered with blood. He was utterly confused until he saw a small, white feather wedged into a crack in the glass. It could only mean one thing: land was near.

Unfortunately, Robinson was so busy watching the kilometers click away that he barely saw the giant structure right in his path. He torqued the yoke hard and missed the gnawed metal edifice by a hair. His action came with quick consequences as the flyer went into manual mode and shook violently. He fought as hard as he could to keep the nose up and straight, but it wasn't easy, especially when more steel structures appeared. They were unquestionably towers, many larger than the Crown itself. Most had been worn away to skeletal frames while others had toppled into the sea.

A second shudder ran through the ship and the warning he'd been dreading appeared: FUEL CELL DEPLETION IMMINENT. The kilometer display blinked twice before the screen went entirely blank with a spark. Smoke filled the cabin. Robinson wanted to scream.

Then he saw the silhouette of land in the distance.

Unfortunately, the flyer was losing altitude and speed. It had gone from thirty meters over the surface to ten. The engine was trying to compensate but didn't have the juice. When the ship dipped again, the boy knew in his heart he would never make land.

Almost as if he were being punished for the thought, a final shudder shook the flyer. The rear thruster sputtered and the vessel lurched. The boy grit his teeth and wrapped both hands around the yoke to hold the ship up, but its engine's gasps were unrelenting.

It's impossible to say why he called out to his mother in that moment. He knew she was dead, but he still found comfort in her spirit. He'd set his course by her numbers but never considered that she might be his true north. Even as the ship fell to a meter above the water, he smiled at the thought, *If only she could see me now.* With a deep breath, he threw both feet onto the instrument panel and pulled the yoke with all his might.

The nose rose just as the first wave clipped the bottom of the flyer. The ship bounded across the surface of the water several times like a rock skipping over a pond. The boy fought to hold onto the yoke, but it was ripped from his hands as the next wave met the ship flush. His body was thrown with incredible force, the leather straps cleaving at his flesh as his head sprang forward with a snap. The ship tumbled and spun, its bones and body breaking, but when it settled, the cabin was intact.

A single blinking light revealed it was also upside down.

He was alive, but the ship was quickly sinking. He groped for the locks of his straps and fell in a painful heap to the inverted ceiling. And then he heard a pop.

It came from the view screen at the point of the bird's impact. The glass had splintered under the pressure of the crash and water had begun trickling in. Robinson shook his head, pleading for it to stop, but the fissure inched its way toward the outer edges of the view screen. The trickle increased. With no place to hide, Robinson did the only thing he could; he strapped a carton of rations across his chest in the hope that they might help him survive.

The view screen exploded.

The wave hit him like a thunderbolt, slamming him against the back wall. He felt little of the impact. His body was too shocked by the freezing cold water to register anything else. The cabin filled so quickly that he barely managed a single gulp of air before the water closed in around him, the swirling deluge tossing him around like a toy.

Weightless and dazed, Robinson knew he had to move quickly, but in the torrent of water, he had lost all sense of direction. His mind floundered and debris spun around the cabin, caught in a vortex of underwater eddies.

The oxygen in his lungs quickly dissipated and the fear of drowning sent waves of panic shooting through him.

And then he felt a slight tug at his neck. At first, he thought it was debris, but as his hands touched his mother's locket, he knew his prayer had been answered. It was pulling upward, the air inside of it defying gravity in its own quest for escape. He let its buoyancy guide him.

As he passed through the view screen, Robinson felt the sting of glass bite into his leg, but the pain was nothing compared to the fire in his lungs. He kicked and the pressure lessened, but then his chest started to convulse from the carbon dioxide building in his lungs. With each stroke, the underwater tide pulled him farther out to sea. Just when he was certain he would drown, his head burst through the surface of the water.

Robinson managed one great intake of air before a wave struck him. Saltwater flooded his mouth and he retched, but he kicked hard for shore until his feet struck sand. Exhaustion overtook him. He lumbered up the beach and collapsed as the night closed in around him.

Chapter Twelve
The Forbidden Continent

Time returned in a flash as the frigid surf washed over Robinson's legs. His eyes vaulted open and he gasped. He was alive. He tried to sit up, but every muscle in his body screamed in protest. The pain was so intense he feared he might pass out again.

It was morning, but the sun was obscured by fog so he couldn't guess at the time. His clothes were wet from the high tide. Not surprisingly, his shoes had been torn from his feet. The pain there was intense. Only when he dredged several small pieces of coral from the wounds did he understand where the pain was coming from.

He looked for the flyer, but it was nowhere to be seen. What did fill his vision shocked him. On a reef, several kilometers from the shore, was a graveyard of ancient sea vessels—hundreds of ships of incomprehensible sizes and shapes. They congealed like driftwood, spines exposed, innards spilt out, noses jutting hundreds of feet into the air while others lay splayed at odd angles or felled like trees. All bore the scars of salt and time. It was a daunting sight.

Robinson saw another curious thing not far from the waterline. There were two metal markers atop a rusty pole peeking out of the sand. Both were greatly eroded, but he could still make out one faded word: Avenue. It wouldn't be until much later that he remembered the sign was written in his own language.

Farther to the north, scores of buildings protruded from the ocean like broken teeth in a waterlogged mouth. Most were rotted and had collapsed in on themselves. Man might have tamed this area once, but nature had reclaimed it.

Robinson was too dazed and weak to process the devastation around him. He felt starved and searched the beach for the rations he'd strapped to his chest. He found them bobbing near the waterline. To his relief, they were dry. He opened the first pack and inhaled three servings of sour biscuits.

Afterward, he attended to his feet. Saltwater was one of the earth's great antiseptics, so he went back to the surf to scrub his feet clean. Then he took off his jacket and tore long strips to bandage them until walking was bearable.

When he was done, he looked around to decide his course. In that moment, he felt a terrible loneliness. The sight of so much destruction—of a mighty empire so hastily felled—made him feel small and insignificant. For the first time, he wondered what chance he had of surviving here. Civilization had been undone. This continent stood in ruin. Had the victor that had wrought death by air and engineered diseases survived? Could water or food contaminate him? Or had the disease already invaded his lungs?

He started west across the hot sand with his rations strapped to his back and his mother's locket securely around his neck. After a while, the dry sand became wet marsh, with soggy earth, verdant grass, and tall reeds. Through the ankle-high water, he saw all manner of life existing below the surface. There were snakes, insects, tadpoles, and frogs. Since he didn't know what was poisonous, he avoided everything.

In time, the marsh became a bog with shallow water falling away to indeterminate depths that rippled, bubbled, and churned with unseen life. Several times he was forced to double back, crossing levees and narrow peninsulas only to realize he'd come that way before. The sun continued to rise—the heat along with it—until he was winded and soaked with sweat.

Mosquitos feasted on his skin and the husks of long dead trees bit at his feet. The bandages continued to unspool, forcing him to stop and retie them again and again. Finally, when he was certain he would never escape the wetlands, he saw a broken chip of road dangling limply over the far side of an embankment. He skipped the remaining way through the shallows and scaled his way to the top of the incline.

Standing atop the hill, he'd have never known the bog existed. Storefronts lined both sides of the road with faded signs Robinson was surprised he could read—the writing of the One People. Most of the windows were broken out and weeds overran everything. Other than an occasional bird passing overhead or a rodent foraging in the shadows, little else stirred.

When he reached the far end of town, Robinson found an old log to rest on. He gauged by the sun that it was mid-turn. Thirsty and tired, he opened his bag of rations. Thankfully, whoever was in charge of the emergency provisions had thought to include several candles and a piece of flint with an instruction booklet. Unfortunately, there was no water, so he went searching and found a small pool between the roots of a gnarled tree. Only then did he realize he had nothing to collect it in. He sifted through a number of ancient items until finally kicking a corroded cap off one of the old carriages.

The cap made the water taste of rust and earth, but it went down like wine. He had to force himself to stop after several liters to avoid getting sick. Then he took inventory of his rations. By his count, he had a three-day supply.

He needed a plan. His mother's numbers might have led him to this continent, but not to a specific destination. He needed shelter. He also needed a weapon. He had no means of procuring either, so he stalked around until he found a dead branch that could double as a walking stick or a spear before setting out again.

The two-lane road led to one with four lanes, which surprisingly led to a military base, its name still discernable on a rusty sign. The fence surrounding it had a heavy lean, but the rusty wire protruding everywhere still looked treacherous. Rather than risk cutting himself further, Robinson continued along the perimeter of the fence until he found a section that had fallen away entirely.

The base was flat and sprawling, made up of large areas of paved stone blemished by a handful of trees and shrubs that had erupted through the rubble. Sunlight reflected off something in the distance. He moved toward it.

Squadrons of flyers in a profusion of shapes and sizes littered the area, though many seemed capable of supporting no more than a pilot or two. Looking closer, Robinson found most were outfitted with weapons, though how they worked was beyond him. Still, this brought up the questions he'd been pondering again and again: How had a civilization so replete with advancements failed to stave off its own extinction? Had the Great Rendering spread so quickly that not a single one of these flyers had gotten off the ground?

At the far end of the tarmac sat a number of cavernous hangars and the main body of the base itself. Waves of heat radiated off the pitch as the sun reached its apex. As Robinson passed the last hangar, he saw the doors were half open. Inside was another flyer that was four stories high. This one was unique. He could still make out the multiple shades of blue and white surrounding its two-dozen oval windows. It also bore a strange circular sigil with prominent words underneath. Unfortunately, they were too faded to read. Robinson wanted to step inside for a closer look, but the heat was rising and he was already out of water. His feet had also begun to burn through his wrappings, forcing him to jog the last one hundred meters to the main building.

The moment he passed through the door he froze in his steps. He was seeing the face of evil for the first time.

Chapter Thirteen
When You Quit, You Die

The metal doors had been rent open, their glass surface long gone. Inside the enormous vestibule, the walls were stained black with streaks of old blood. Mottled discolorations also covered the floor. A great many people had tried in haste to raise two fortifications to block the entrance, but it was clear by the mountain of refuse scattered around the room that they had failed. The walls and roof were peppered with holes and brass casings were scattered across the floor. Not a single skeleton had been left behind.

As much as Robinson was hoping to make this his shelter, there was no way he could spend one night inside. As he turned to leave, his foot struck the edge of the fortification, causing a rumble from above. He leaped back, narrowly avoiding the avalanche of metal chairs and boxes as they slammed into the ground with a deafening clamour.

When he regained his footing, Robinson saw that something cylindrical and metallic had spilled out from the debris. He grabbed it and gave it a shake. It felt empty and light. He tried the top, but it wouldn't budge. He banged it against the floor. This time the cap opened. The smell inside was pungent but not entirely unpleasant. He tucked his new drinking goblet into his bag and left, relieved he wouldn't have to drink from the rusty cap any more.

The base's main entrance had also been heavily barricaded with carriages, but it too had been overrun. He was ready to be free of this place.

Outside the base, he entered a field of high grass and sunflowers that swayed lightly with the wind. Bees buzzed by, searching for blossoms to pollinate. For a time, he imagined if he closed his eyes, he might wake up in the tangled wolds back home and to the sound of Vareen calling him for supper.

Instead, he heard the running of water and after a spell, he came to the bank of a wide river whose waters flowed unhurriedly but looked clean and devoid of refuse. He knelt to cup some in his hands, but just as his lips parted, a fish passed by, sporting two tails and twitching spastically. His thirst quickly left him.

After a brief rest, Robinson pressed on. He was tired, but stopping felt like quitting. His father once told him that, "in the wild, when you quit, you die."

Eventually, he came to a roadway larger than any he'd seen before. The husks of carriages dominated one side while the other was oddly empty. Not for the last time that day he wondered what had happened to the people driving them.

The roadway rose until it reached an elevation that allowed Robinson a view of the entire city. It sprawled out in all directions as far as the eye could see. Vast tracts were utterly vacant, as if a great flood had come through and wiped everything above ground away. But pockets here and there inexplicably remained.

Off in the distance, he saw a collection of enormous structures. There was no question these marked the city's capitol. Standing center amongst them was a single, colossal obelisk rising high into the sky. How men had built such things was beyond him. How they endured centuries of neglect was another matter. He knew in an instant he had to see that monolith up close—to touch it with his own hands—to be certain it was real.

Unfortunately, the sun was rapidly descending. There was only a turn of light left at best. So when he spied a neighborhood of what looked like family dwellings, he quickly made his way to them. Most had caved in on themselves like ill-timed cakes, but one two-story residence remained intact. It was perched on a high cliff, its sunny side the battlefield of a languorous war between ivy and trumpet creeper, the outcome of which wouldn't be determined for eons to come. Despite its weathered, pale exterior, there was something warm about the place that reminded Robinson of home. He moved in for a closer look.

The front of the house was dominated by a robust tree with spindly branches that jetted in all directions. The largest bore two rusty link chains that swayed in the breeze, emitting a painful, rasping ode to the seat and rider who had long ago deserted it.

After rooting the front door from its diseased moorings, Robinson entered the house, only to feel like he'd been transported to some other place and time. For every rustic piece of furniture that harkened of home, there was an article of technology with no discernable purpose. Most were crafted of black, moldable material with cords that fed directly into the walls. Bulkier furniture bore scars of termites and rot, though some were well preserved. He wiped the dust from a glass case and found a bevy of crystal figurines inside—lithe female dancers caught in resplendent repose. When a ray of sunlight caught them just right, they exploded into a kaleidoscope of colors.

A bookshelf full of titles had also escaped decay, but the dense pages held not words but abstract photos of what Robinson took to be art. The images were mystifying.

Discolored family photos hung crooked on walls decked with patterned paper that dangled in wilting spirals and gathered chipped and broken on the floor below. Robinson's fingers traced over fine china and countertops, light fixtures and curtains. In the parlor, he found the carcass of a piano, which he had read about but had never seen. Coils of wire struck by black and white dowels were used to summon its melody, but what few times he depressed them, he was rewarded with a harsh, discordant sound or no sound at all.

As the light waned, that familiar kernel of fear began creeping its way back to the forefront of Robinson's mind. He peeled back the curtain to look out at the street. Nothing moved. Not even the chains on the tree or the grass in the yard. Time felt suddenly leaden as if everything were withdrawing from the coming night. He assured himself that nothing was out there—that he was utterly alone—but his assertions rang as hollow as the fleeting wind. He felt like something was coming.

Building a fire was too big a risk, so he picked a warm corner to sit down in and rest. After changing the bandages of his ailing feet, he unpacked his rations. But before he ate, he realized he'd forgotten to check the second floor.

He was halfway up the stairs when the wood beneath him gave. The steps crumbled away with a deafening roar. The only thing that saved him from going with them was the newel post in the baluster. He used it to pull himself up. Water damage had been the cause, though this realization offered little relief. His narrow escape only illustrated the obvious: there were no healers here. One fractured bone or untreated wound could end his life for good.

The first bedroom on the second floor lay open to the stars. Mold and rot covered everything in sight. As he approached the second bedroom, he heard a deep, pulsing drone inside. He couldn't identify the sound. He should have turned away, but curiosity prompted him to reach for the door. He was shocked by what he found inside. In one corner of the room was the largest beehive imaginable. The room seemed covered in honeycombs and the smell of honey was so strong it brought tears to his eyes. Sensing the invader, several bees turned in his direction. He quickly slammed the door, hoping they had no other way through.

The last rays of sunlight were fading when Robinson approached the final door. Faded yellow tape had been strung across it with a strange symbol beneath.

He didn't know what it meant, but it looked ominous. Still, he was too tired to turn away and there wasn't enough light left to seek another place to hide.

So he opened the door and felt his breath catch.

Two beds had been hastily pushed together against the far wall. Lying atop them were the remains of the family he'd seen in the photographs downstairs. Two hundred years might have robbed them of skin and flesh, but the three smaller sets of skeletons intertwined with the two larger ones left little doubt. They were knotted together under deteriorated fabric, spider webs, and dust. A bedside table was strewn with small, cracked, amber containers and cloudy glasses. Had the family taken their final refuge here together in the face of death? Or had they hastened death themselves?

Robinson spent that night in the hallway, but he never touched his provisions. His appetite had abandoned him. He lay there long after the sky had turned dark, thinking not of how far he'd come, but how little he'd accomplished. He tried to convince himself there was nothing to fear. Then he heard the first cry.

It was loud and raw and seemed to carry over the entire city. It was quickly matched by another, and then another, until the night was full of thousands of such voices. Robinson was instantly paralyzed with fear. He had heard that sound before in the East Room of the Crown, but it was nowhere near as robust or infinite as this.

Renders. The renders were here.

Chapter Fourteen
Out of Many, One

The next morning the sky was drab and gray, but to Robinson, it was a glorious sight. The previous night had been a harrowing experience spent balled up on the floor of the upstairs hallway as he listened to the monsters skulk around outside. Every gust of wayward wind was a fiend looking to crack the cloak of his sanctuary and feed on his flesh. Every unholy cry was a knife to the chest of a boy born of worldly blindness.

The creatures had left under the presage of dawn, but signs of their presence were everywhere. Torn fabric caught on a tree limb. The blood of some animal that had been tilled from the soil. A malformed handprint staining the side of a fence. And above it all, a pervasive stench that befouled the air Robinson breathed.

Robinson set off in the direction of the capitol, eager to test the ancient shoes he'd salvaged from a closet. His compass was fixed on the monolith he'd seen the night before. As the morning passed, the buildings grew larger and larger. Several times he heard the telltale signs of life: the chirping of birds and the bustle of animals. Once, he passed the broken window of a darkened store and spied two small rodents inside, battling over the carcass of a third. Both were afflicted with pustules and moved skittishly. Robinson hurried past.

The oddest sight came when he heard the trickle of water and found a stream flowing through the center of a building and out its doors before plunging into a sinkhole in the street. He was reminded that even the most formidable of human endeavors were transitory. In the end, nature would always have her way.

Crossing through a small park, Robinson's breath instantly caught in his chest. Before him was a massive building, held aloft by innumerable stone columns that stood like mighty sentinels, invulnerable to time. Atop the building was a dome of such ornate design that it put the Crown and Seven Spires to shame. As he drew closer, he saw the dome sported a bronze statue of a woman atop it. She was dressed in full-length robes and wore a helmeted headdress with a crest of feathers. In one hand she held a sword and in the other, a wreath. She stood atop a globe that read, "E Pluribus Unum," which Robinson knew to be Latin, because the Second Law forbade learning it (which was why his mother had worked diligently to ensure he learned it). "E Pluribus Unum" meant, "out of many, one." This woman must have been a mighty warrior to receive such an honor.

He climbed the immense steps that fed the building and passed through an entrance devoid of doors. Dirt, grime, and refuse had been tracked inside the first twenty meters or so, but beyond that, the building was surprisingly unscathed.

Beneath the dome was a great rotunda with windows that fed in copious amounts of light, casting everything in a golden, glowing hue. Aged yet masterful canvases adorned each wall in golden frames, and intricate friezes were cut into the stone walls. Straining to look up, Robinson saw a cracked and faded—but incredibly beautiful—fresco of men and women riding a whirlpool of clouds. He grew dizzy just looking at it.

After he'd seen enough of the building, he went back outside to sit on the steps and wash down a share of rations with the last of his water. It was mid-turn and the day had become humid. He wanted to explore further, but he needed better shelter and a source of food. Already, he'd grown weary of boiling water by the pint. He needed to devise a way to purify multiple liters at once to save time.

After a short span, Robinson finally reached the monolith, which towered as high as the clouds above. Near the top were two holes on each side, though they didn't appear to be windows. Still, he wondered what the view might be like that high up and lamented, not for the last time, that the flyer had run out of fuel too soon.

To his left was the river, across which he saw yet another large rotunda, this one half-collapsed into the water in ruins. Downriver there were a pair of bridges that had both been shorn in two. In this case, the damage appeared manmade.

On the opposite side of the obelisk was a long, rectangular pool filled with brackish water. In the far distance was another great columned building, within whose protection sat the towering sculpture of a seated man. Like the woman above the dome, he had been afforded a most remarkable view and Robinson made a mental note to visit that place and learn his story when he had the time.

First, he wanted a closer look at the monolith itself and began walking its circumference. To his surprise, the structure did indeed have a door, but it was locked and would not budge.

Up until that time, Robinson's exploration had done much to raise his spirits and keep his mind off the renders and being stranded here alone. But when he turned the corner and found his second surprise, all the fear and worry of the past twenty-four turns came crashing back again.

On the westward side of the obelisk was the residue of several large fires that had blackened the wild grass to its roots, leaving ash in its wake. But it was the grisly spectacle at the base of the obelisk that left Robinson's stomach churning. There, someone had hammered a dozen iron shackles deep into the stone, half of which held human remains. Most were bones, the forearm or lower leg. All had been stripped clean of flesh. Old blood had stained the earth and stone black, but unlike the scene from the military base, this blood was relatively fresh, no more than a month old.

Robinson grew instantly nervous. Had his own naiveté once again lulled him into complacency? His mistake wasn't in believing renders only came out at night, but that they were his only threat. The shackles were a sign of intelligence, but what kind of creature was capable of such savagery? Only one that he knew of:

Human.

His head snapped around, scanning the buildings and the streets. Nothing moved. Not even the grass in the breeze. Still, someone could have been out there, watching from the shadows, waiting for him to let his guard down. He swore it would not happen.

The afternoon was moving quickly. Robinson needed to get out of the open. He glanced around for a suitable structure.

The one he found was positioned at the far end of the park, behind formidable black gates and a host of other defensive fortifications that suggested, at one time, the compound held some importance. Like so many other structures in the city, it was an impressive sight. Though only two or three stories tall, it bore columns that secured a great, rounded portico. The most distinct thing about it was that it had once been painted white. Despite years of neglect, it had retained a strange vibrancy.

The walk across the park took almost half a turn. By the time Robinson crossed the final street—Pennsylvania Avenue—blisters from his new shoes had become companions to the previous ones. He took off his shoes for a spell to cool his feet in the clover.

The gates bore signs of some violent ingress with a number of carriages strewn upside down, lying in ruins in the rotting weeds. Many were pocked with holes like the ones at the military base, making it painfully clear that some kind of battle had taken place.

Of all the curious sights, none matched the one Robinson discovered on the lawn. Hidden under a blanket of flowers was the cracked shell of an ancient flyer, its gangly rotor appendages bent and snapped, with a number of oval windows looking up from the earth and with several distinguishable letters: —ITED STA—. A tail section hung in scorched pieces in a nearby tree. Had this ship been fleeing *to* this place when it had fallen, or *from* it? And had Robinson escaped their fate or had they escaped his?

A gust of wind kicked leaves across the yard. The breeze felt cool, but a prickling sensation struck Robinson once again and told him he was not alone.

Robinson felt an odd sense of excitement as he approached the twin doors beneath the portico. Maybe inside he would get a glimpse of this mighty empire before it had fallen. If he was truly lucky, the building might prove a capable shelter in which he could strategize what to do next. He tried the door and it clicked. *Maybe the stars aren't aligned against me,* he thought. And as he pushed them open, he heard the whine of cables and gears as a weighted pulley sent a metal plate swinging down from above. He barely had time to turn his head when the booby trap cracked him flush on the ear and catapulted him backward in an explosion of stars and pain. The last thing he remembered was the sting of gravel and the warmth of his own blood before everything went dark.

Chapter Fifteen
Visitors

The animal was chewing on his face.

Robinson screamed and scrambled back on his haunches.

The animal also leaped back and began baying in sharp, staccato bursts. The sound was foreign to Robinson, but somewhere in his mind, he knew it had a proper name that was intrinsically tied to the animal itself.

It was called a bark. And the animal was a dog.

He had never seen a dog before. He'd been told, like so many other animals, that dogs had gone extinct in the Great Rendering. But this dog was real. It was strong and lean, between four and five stones. Its muzzle was extended with a protruding jaw under dark eyes. It had a brindle coat that bore the distinct scarring of rendering infection.

Robinson's hand went to his face, which was slick with blood, but to his relief, he found no bite marks. The blood stemmed from his brow, brought about by the booby trap. The dog, for its part, hadn't been biting him, but *licking* him. His immediate fear was that he'd been infected. But he remembered his mother telling him that the disease could only infect a person when it entered their bloodstream. Could a dog's saliva do that?

The dog continued to bark. Robinson sat up, confused as to why it wasn't charging. He was easy prey. Maybe it feared him. Or maybe it was waiting for others of its kind to arrive. His walking stick lay just inside the front doors, out of reach. He considered running, but the dog must have sensed his intent because it whined and padded closer.

"Back!" Robinson shouted. "Get back!"

To his surprise, the dog obeyed. There was no way it could have understood him. It must have been responding to his tone. Then it lay on all fours and whimpered.

The ringing in Robinson's head sounded like the tinkling of brass keys. He had taken the kind of blow that would put a man in the House of Healers for a week, but he hadn't a week to work through this and no healers to call on. He needed to get away. But something stymied him, like a tick buried beneath the surface that continued to itch.

When the truth finally came, it arrived in three realizations.

The first was that there was intelligence in the dog's eyes. Though it watched Robinson, it never attacked. Its mouth never curled into a snarl. It wasn't angry or defensive, but agitated. There was no dripping saliva, flaring nostrils, or upturned hackles. This dog bore the signs of the Rendering, but his actions suggested otherwise.

The second realization occurred when Robinson discovered the tinkling sound was not a ringing in his ears, but came from a small medallion attached to the dog's collar. A collar suggested domestication. Domestication suggested Man. But what man would domesticate a diseased animal? And did that mean they were nearby?

The third and final realization happened with a literal whimper as the dog looked not at him but up at the sky. Robinson followed suit and felt a new flush of dread.

Night had arrived.

The first render's cry almost made his legs give out. He turned back to the dog, but it had taken off like a shot. He considered following, but to where? More shrill howls filled the air as additional renders emerged from their slumber. He thought about darting inside the white building, but the booby trap persuaded him otherwise. Plus, he had caught scent of an odor he was growing familiar with—renders.

The half-moon loomed just above the river, but it would be no friend tonight. At that moment, Robinson would have given anything to be back in the safety of the house where he'd spent the previous night, but it was a world away. He turned for the river but halted immediately in his tracks. Twenty meters away was the largest render he had ever heard of, and it was staring straight at him.

He wouldn't have thought for a second such creatures were capable of stealth, but there it was, close enough for him to see its chest rise and fall. It was a towering creature, easily taller than him by half, but stooped with rows of densely packed muscles. It wore tattered rags that glistened with ulcerations that oozed with every twitch. A second, smaller creature emerged from behind it, bearing a second mouth that protruded from its neck, its gnarled yellow teeth beckoning in the night. These were not like the creature he'd seen in the Crown. These beasts were hardy and thick, with calcified bone borne like armor and distended muscles that leaked from every crevice.

On instinct, Robinson leaned back, but the movement was enough for both creatures to charge. He turned to run but slipped on the grass. He realized he'd never put his shoes back on. He had no time to retrieve them now.

The renders were not fast runners. In fact, they were sluggish and clumsy, likely due to the body mass they carried, but if their gasping howls and frenetic movements proved anything, it was that they would not quit once they'd begun tracking their prey. They would pursue him until the sun rose, or they caught him.

Robinson ran with pure abandon, following the path the dog had taken around the back of the white building. He slipped through a narrow gap near the rear gates. More renders emerged from the tree line and as he ran past, he felt a heavy hand full of claws cut through his jacket and tear his skin. With no light to guide him, he was quickly lost. Several times he turned into a street or alley only to find more renders emerging from doorways and sewers, each frothing from a rictus full of razor-sharp teeth.

The city blurred together. Twice Robinson circled back onto streets he'd already run down only to find more pursuers amassing. The streets now seemed full of the creatures when turns before there had been none.

His luck went from bad to worse when he turned down a road and found it blocked by a barrier of rusted carriages. They were stacked together haphazardly but had stood for some time. As he drew closer, Robinson saw bones littered at its base.

With a render on his tail, Robinson leaped up to scale the blockade. A meaty hand locked onto his leg. He wrenched it free just as the rest of the horde hit the blockade like a battering ram. He nearly lost his footing. Even worse, the structure started wobbling badly. It was only a matter of time before it toppled. Several renders tried to climb after him but fell back into the crowd where they were swarmed and torn to pieces.

The horrific scene made Robinson's stomach churn. But as he reached the top of the blockade, his foot flew out from under him and he fell down the other side, landing hard on his shoulder and hip. Pain flared up his legs and spine, so excruciating he couldn't move. Just when he thought he might pass out again, he heard the breaking of glass and the shattering of wood. A render had circumnavigated the blockade through a storefront. The beast rose up on two massive legs and let out a piercing howl that Robinson knew would be the last sound he ever heard. But just as it took a step in his direction, he heard a snap of metal. The creature never saw the barricade as it toppled over and crushed him.

Robinson limped off again, but the pack stormed after him. His hip was hobbled and he was beyond exhaustion. It wouldn't be long now.

As the creatures closed in on him, Robinson's only path was a small park on an adjacent hill. He burst through its gates as the creatures closed in behind. He limped along until he stumbled from the path, his feet submerged in mud that felt like cold, viscid gruel. He fell and scuttled on his back up the hill until he could no longer move. There he waited for the renders to descend on him in unison.

They never did.

The beasts lingered at the edge of the path but would venture no farther. A few still had sight of him, but the majority had been turned away by the scent of something stronger than blood. Robinson looked down and felt the stuff coating his skin. It was black and thick and smelled vaguely sulfurous.

"Oil," he said in comprehension. "You won't go near oil."

The renders thrashed and howled at the sound of his voice, but none would enter the wet part of the field. Robinson scooped up a handful of crude and slung it at them. They quickly scattered. His anger suddenly boiled to the surface as he rose to his feet, screaming for all his worth. There, he fell to his knees, too tired to sob or to celebrate that he was alive. It should have felt like a great victory, but all he could think of were the days ahead. Twice in two days he had faced death. Twice he had persevered. To survive here long term, he would need more than blind luck. He would need help.

The answer came like a thunderbolt. Not from the sky but from the earth. There, in the mud before him, was a boot print.

And it was fresh.

Chapter Sixteen
Contact

The next three days were a soul-numbing experience of limited sleep and limitless despair. He had run too long on adrenaline. All he had left was vapor.

The day after the attack, Robinson returned to the white building only to discover the damn creatures had ravaged his belongings and scattered them to the wind. Of the few possessions he could scavenge, he found only two rations of food, half a candle, and his flint. Everything else was gone, including his shoes. Even if he scaled his already paltry meals back to a few rations a day, he had no chance of them lasting out the week.

Each day at dawn as the renders crept back into the shadows, he was left to face the city alone. He traveled through empty streets, across broken roads, and down to the river where he gathered materials for a fire. Two turns each day were spent purifying water. It was never enough.

Foraging was not a skill he had learned in school. He had little idea what he needed or where to look to find it. Since he was too afraid to travel outside the city, he mostly walked the residential areas, peeking over fences for an occasional tree bearing fruit or nuts. Both were hard to come by and of those he found, the birds and animals had often gotten to them first.

Animals were surprisingly abundant during the day, although they cut

Robinson a wide berth. The sight of rats, squirrels, and the occasional rabbit became a common thing. It shouldn't have been a surprise. They too feared the night.

For every healthy animal that walked the day, there were twice as many infected ones that emerged at night. Like the renders, they amassed in packs, always going after smaller prey in larger numbers. Mutations ran rampant through them—multiple heads and limbs. One bulbous marsupial looked to have been mixed with a feline, its fur matted with mange; it dragged its legless body across the street, leaving a wake of gore. It was so ugly and so damn pitiful he almost felt sorry for the thing. But then a render bounded out of nowhere, snapped it up, and ate it in several gurgling gulps.

How long had such madness been going on? Since man had walked these streets? Or was this some ugly evolution that had followed? Where had the renders come from? How had they been infected? Had they been human once? Were they fellow travelers who had unluckily stumbled upon this city? Or had this same madness spread across the continent? Robinson tried to concentrate on the tasks at hand, but the questions kept coming.

If his days were full of exhaustion, his nights were full of terror. He had built an improvised shelter in the middle of the oil rich park, but that didn't stop the renders from stalking outside the gates, taunting him with their cries. They spoke no words, but the message was clear: we know you're there and one day you will be ours.

The mistake they were waiting for came on the fourth day as Robinson expanded his search of the city. He was passing by something called the library of congress when his head turned just in time to see a silhouette in one of the windows. At first he froze, convinced his eyes were playing tricks on him. Then he heard the sound, like a shuffling, followed by the rapid padding of feet.

It could have been a render. While they mostly came out at night, he had seen them during the day, swathed in tattered clothes to brave the power of the sun, presumably driven mad enough by hunger to root them from their hovels. Still, he had to know.

Robinson ran into the building, hustling through a turnstile so quickly that its rusted guts snapped under his weight. The room was enormous, large enough to fit his entire school under its eaves. The windows above were long gone, but the intricate designs remained.

For the moment, he was too awed to move, but then he heard another noise from above and he continued for the stairs.

Everywhere he looked, there were stacks and stacks of books. The elements had rotted most of them. Paper spilled out like so much porridge gone to seed. But a few remained. There was no rhyme or reason why one book amongst so many should have survived, but the ones that did stood out like trees in a barren field.

On the third floor, Robinson heard the movement of a single form, and through the remnants of these paper skeletons, he saw the figure dash southward. He ran parallel, angling for a better look, but he was blocked by some kind of reading room. The figure was smaller and faster and was running on pure desperation.

As he approached the final bookshelf, the shadow darted by Robinson, so close his fingers felt the rush of wind. But as he turned the corner, he saw a dirty hand whip a metal door closed. He slammed against it, breathless, only to find it locked.

"Wait!" he screamed. "Please! I'm not going to hurt you! Come back!"

He pounded on the door for what seemed like forever. When he finally stopped, his hands felt swollen. "I'm alone here! Please! Please don't leave me!"

His cries went on for some time, but the door never answered.

The combination of exhaustion, starvation, and a mind stretched near the breaking point proved too volatile a concoction. Robinson fell asleep. When he finally woke, it was to the sight of dusk and the sounds of terror that had accompanied each night of this nightmarish land. He wanted to flee, to find an escape, but there was nowhere to go or hide.

He tried looking for weapons, but there were none to be had. When he ripped the leg off a chair, it disintegrated in his hands like kindling.

Only when he felt his legs go weak did he realize he'd given up.

Robinson's mind ventured to simple things. The last time he saw his mother. How she'd cupped his face in her hands and kissed him on both cheeks. How that final kiss still lingered with the sting of its hidden goodbye.

He remembered other kisses. The ones that bore him to sleep like lullabies and unrequited dreams. Of Tessa. Her mouth. Her hands. The blush his smile brought to her cheeks whenever he dared to glance in her direction. Her final look in the Crown before his world fell apart.

But mostly he thought of his father and siblings. What must they be thinking, half a world away? Did they suspect he was dead like his mother? Or did they lay awake at night, wishing they, too, could flee and join him on his grand adventure?

Dusk was hot. Sweat trickled down his skin. The howls surged closer.

Downstairs, he heard the doors crash in and heavy footfalls plod up the staircase.

In the growing darkness, his mind reached for something to grasp, but it was not escape it found. Nor rescue or love. But raindrops and their familiar pattering on the windowpane of his bedroom back home. Their furtive flight down the limbs of the trees in the yard outside. Footfalls in the grass. Dampening lichen on stone. The smells of the earth as she opened herself up to drink.

Robinson's eyes flickered open to see his hand extend, hungry not for the books before him but for the sweet sting of water when brought to his lips. In his other hand, he held tightly to his mother's locket and wondered again what was so important that his parents had risked everything to hide that little disk.

When the lumbering shadows approached from behind, Robinson slid down and laid his head into the bosom of books, wondering if their words would have brought him any more comfort had he the time to read them.

He smelled the hot breath before he felt it. On his neck and back. The books were thrust aside. A hand reached through the shelves. Claws tickled his skin.

He closed his eyes for the last time.

And then the metal door flew open and someone with astonishing strength pulled him through.

Chapter Seventeen
The Widening Gyre

Robinson hit the back wall hard with barely enough time to turn and see the man wrench the door shut and bar it as the wave of renders descended. The concussive force of their attack shook the walls as they charged again and again. In complete blackness, Robinson listened to their frenzied howls as heavy fists rained down and talons gouged the metal outside.

Through it all, the door held.

They stood in silence, listening to the assault as it reached its crescendo and then slowly dissipated. Robinson tried to remember what he'd seen of the man before the door had shut. He'd been wearing some kind smock, patched together with a variety of fabrics that smelled of sweat, dust, and something else. Defeat, maybe. His hair and beard were thick and unruly, more grey than black.

"*Zu cair*," he said once the renders had gone.

"I'm sorry, I didn't—"

Something hard struck Robinson across his outer thigh and he cried out.

"Zu cair," he repeated with a grunt.

"I don't understand," Robinson said.

He hit him again. Twice. Both strikes came close to buckling

Robinson's legs. Both would bruise.

"Zu cair," he said impatiently. This time, he cuffed Robinson on the shoulder, turning him to his right. He wanted him to walk.

"I-I can't see where I'm going."

The man made a noise of disgust before striking him across the back. The instrument felt long and hard, like a piece of wood.

Robinson's hands groped for something in the darkness. They found a railing at the head of some stairs. A hollow echo delved downward.

"You want me to go down—?"

Again he felt the sting at the back of his legs, placed with remarkable precision.

"Okay, okay. I get it. You want to go down. I'm going down. Just don't hit me anymore, all right?"

He was struck again and Robinson stumbled down the steps, grasping onto a railing that wobbled precariously. The man followed in silence. If it weren't for the sound of wood striking each step as he walked, Robinson wouldn't even have known he was there.

After the first floor, his nerves were once again on edge. He had no idea where he was being led. It didn't seem logical that the man would risk saving him earlier only to kill him now. But for all he knew, the man might be a flesh eater too. Or a slave trader. Or the kind of monster his parents warned him about—the kind that had a weakness for boys.

Only when the second set of steps turned into the third did Robinson's panic turn visceral. He started imagining scenarios by which he could overtake him, disarm him, and flee. But it was almost as if the man read his very thoughts. He suddenly felt the sharp point of his staff press against the center of his back. Not hard enough to cause pain or draw blood. Just enough to let him know it was there.

His feet continued to descend. Robinson became certain he was being marched to his grave. Then a dim light appeared below. As they turned the fifth and final stairwell, he saw faint words scratched on a heavily barricaded door that read: SUB LEVEL 3.

The stairwell eventually emptied into a stone room no bigger than six meters square. The source of the light was a small, brown candle that flickered from a rusty tin can. Next to it was a larger can, over which someone had perched a blackened metal spit with some kind of meat on it. A mound of small, delicate bones was strewn across the opposite side of the room—the same area where the man signaled Robinson to go.

He walked over and looked down at the bones.

"*Sentar*," the man said, motioning for Robinson to sit. He remained standing. The edge of the man's mouth curled cruelly as the staff began to twirl.

Robinson sat.

The man huffed and then sat on a mess of blankets that made up his sleeping area. His eyes never left Robinson as he reached up and set the staff on a shelf behind him.

He took a heavy breath and closed his eyes for a second. Then he opened them, reached down, and lifted the tin with the animal on the spit. Underneath were a few half-burned twigs. He pulled out a tattered book, tore its last remaining pages out, and stuffed them under the twigs. He then used the candle to rekindle his small fire.

As his meal cooked, Robinson studied the man. He was older than he had imagined. If he had to guess, he would say no younger than sixty. And yet there was a strength to him—a vitality. His skin was bronzed from a lifetime in the sun, but as he peeled off his smock, Robinson saw a multitude of white scars that shone against his skin. Some were as small as a gnat's bite, while others crisscrossed his entire body. Back home, such disfigurement would make a citizen a pariah, but here, in this context, the man was a god.

When his meal was cooked, he took it off the fire. That's when Robinson saw what he'd missed earlier. The man had no right hand. It was gone just below the wrist, replaced by an angry sheath of raw flesh that could have only been fashioned by fire. Robinson imagined a dozen stories that might account for that missing appendage but doubted any could rival the truth.

Just below the shoulder of that maligned arm was another wound, but this one was some kind of tribal marking or brand. It was in the shape of an inverted V, like the gable of a house. *Did he put it there himself?* Robinson wondered. *Or had someone else?*

The thought of food made Robinson's mouth water, but his host offered none. When he was done, he tossed the bones, hot and smoking, against the wall to his right. The smell was both repulsive and intoxicating.

Next, the man withdrew a reservoir of water fashioned from some kind of skin and drank from it. Once he was done, he leaned back and stared into the fire. In the quiet that followed, Robinson thought he might have heard a render's cry, but it could have been the wind.

Time passed slowly. The morning was still far off. The heat in the stairwell turned stifling. Robinson's eyelids grew heavy. When his head bobbed the first time, he looked up and found the man watching him. The Old Man had saved his life.

He suddenly remembered himself. "Thank you."

The Old Man didn't answer. He simply nodded to the stone floor on Robinson's left and said, "*Kun sono.*"

He didn't have to speak his language to understand. He stretched out on the hard stone and put his pack under his head. Despite the lack of blankets or cover, for the first time in a week, Robinson Crusoe slept like the dead.

Chapter Eighteen
Blood and Tears

The next time Robinson woke, it wasn't from a dog licking his face, but the Old Man's staff slapping against his blistered feet. He had risen early and was now wearing clothes that looked like leather, with several satchels wrapped around his neck and a hunter's knife in his belt.

Robinson was still drowsy as he followed the Old Man up the steps. Twice the man stopped to hit him with his stick. Only after the second time did Robinson realize it was because his footfalls were making too much noise. He apologized but was met with a look of disgust.

When they reached the third floor, the Old Man put his ear to the door, then carefully removed the metal bar and pushed it open. The renders were gone but had left quite a wake. Stacks of books were overturned and torn pages were strewn everywhere. Walls were gouged and great arterial sprays of blood colored the walls; there were no carcasses to trace them back to.

Outside, the Old Man looked upward, presumably to gauge the time. Then he turned to Robinson, grunted, and walked off.

Robinson waited a few moments before following. Robinson's limp had become more pronounced. The debris of the road ate at the scabs on his feet, but the pain was nothing compared to the Old Man's staff as its dull end struck him in the gut. Robinson gasped for several seconds before he looked up. The Old Man pointed down the road.

"But I want to stay with you," he said.

The Old Man shook his head and walked off. Robinson hobbled after him.

"Ser, please—" he began.

The Old Man stopped and raised the staff again, pointing back toward the river. "Zuo," he said.

Robinson shook his head. The staff cut through the air and struck his thigh in the exact spot as the night before. It burned like fire, but he refused to go down.

"I'm coming with you," Robinson said.

The Old Man spun with unbelievable speed and struck a crushing blow to his other leg. This time his knee buckled, but he bit back the pain and stood again.

"Zuo!" the Old Man barked.

Robinson shook his head again. The Old Man grit his teeth and stalked off at a quicker pace. His athleticism continued to surprise Robinson, as his stride became a jog. A man his age should have never been so fleet of foot. But even with the soles of his feet burning, Robinson was determined not to lose him.

"My father once told me," he yelled, ten meters back, "that in certain cultures of the ancient world, when you save someone's life, it becomes yours to care for. Isn't that interesting?"

The Old Man ignored him.

"Look, I'm more than willing to carry my share of the load. Hunting. Foraging. Whatever you require. I'm not even above cleaning. And trust me, that hovel of yours? It needs cleaning!"

He picked up even more speed.

"You know this is ridiculous, right? I mean, I know where you live!"

Still he continued, down roads and through a tunnel. Every time he pulled away, Robinson pressed himself to catch up with him.

"Fine!" he yelled. "You want to run away? You want to leave me? Then go! But don't act like it's because I'm a kid! Don't act like I'm too big a burden and I'd put you at risk! We both know the truth is that you're too big a coward *not* to go at it alone!"

The Old Man stopped. Words were meaningless, but he understood tone. He understood respect and this insignificant boy whose life he had saved was showing him none. Robinson expected a quick attack when he walked back to him. Instead, he stopped a few short feet away and held his staff out.

"I don't understand," Robinson said. "You're giving me your staff?"

He thrust it forward again.

"Ah. You want me to *take* it. So this is what? A test? I take the staff from a one-armed man, and I get to stay?"

The Old Man nodded.

"Okay. Let's do it."

The Old Man circled away, his eyes never leaving his target. Robinson knew he was outmatched, but he'd made a habit out of getting lucky. He was counting the times in the last two days when the staff had exploded across the top of his left leg. The Old Man grinned, but there was no humor in it. He was set to teach the boy a lesson or kill him.

The staff spun and continued to bite, each strike more painful than the last. Remembering his fight with Brapo, Robinson decided to charge, only when he swung at him, the Old Man was gone. The staff plowed into his stomach a second later, and then across the back of his legs. He tumbled to the ground.

Robinson watched his abuser walk a few feet away, turn, and nod again. This time, the boy circled toward the arm with the missing hand. He saw a subtle nod of appreciation before the Old Man attacked again.

The staff came from every angle and he could do nothing to avoid it. His placement was perfect. Soon, Robinson's legs, arms, shoulders, and back were all numb. The staff seemed to spin in a complex rhythm, casting a spell on the boy. He never saw the crevasse until he was falling over its edge.

The Old Man watched him scramble for purchase. His supple fingers were all that was keeping him from plummeting into the deep hole in the street. The Old Man held his gaze and then brought the staff down inches from the boy's hands.

"Zuo," he barked.

Robinson crawled out from the hole. He felt an incredible rage. He looked around and saw a piece of metal rebar sticking out of the broken earth. He wrenched it out, kicked the dirt from one end, and held it in the air. The Old Man's eyes narrowed. He turned, walked two steps, and waved the boy forward.

Robinson rounded the crevasse and swung the rebar with everything he had. He hit nothing but air. He swung it again and again and came up empty. Each attack, he put his whole body into the swing but never got close to hitting his target. The Old Man never appeared frightened or winded. Why should he? Robinson was defeating himself.

Only when the boy stood gasping in the street did the Old Man answer. He expected it on the shoulder or leg, but the first swing hit him flush across the mouth. Blood sprayed across his shirt and he fell to the ground just in time to put a hand up as the second blow followed. It struck him just above the elbow. He felt his arm crack on impact.

Robinson rolled to his right, groaning with pain, just as the next strike hit the ground inches from his face. He tried to rise but the flat end of the staff slammed into his stomach with so much force he thought his guts would explode. The next shot came down on his clavicle. The one after that pounded his calf.

He struggled to his feet, but a strike to his ear had his entire body off balance. He felt blood streaming down his cheek and chest, but the pain only followed in thuds, dull and blunt. Sound faded until there was only a slight ringing and the Old Man's exhalations that accompanied each strike.

For his part, the Old Man went about his task with grim proficiency. When he'd started, his thrusts had moved faster than the eye could see. But with each strike that followed, Robinson began to see the art of it all. His body moved fluidly, using the inertia of his weapon to lead him. Each route spurred by the impact of its predecessor. His body mimicked the boy's, as if caught in a dance—leader and follower, puppeteer and marionette—so that every direction his energy flowed, his staff would be waiting to meet it.

The final blow struck Robinson just above the temple. The ground rushed up to meet him.

"*Gousufi*," the Old Man said.

When he was certain the message was delivered, he turned and walked away.

"Well, Rabbit," he heard Jaras say. "You know how it's done."

Robinson strained to look up, but all he saw were stars and sun.

"Just give us a whimper, yea? A little snivel and it'll all be over."

He tried to smile, but all that came out was blood.

"Come on, Rabbit," he said before drawing closer to whisper into his ear. "It's who you are."

Of course he was right.

He'd always been right.

The Old Man was halfway down the block when the scrape of metal halted him in his tracks. He was slow to turn, certain his eyes would confirm his ears' mistake. But he did turn, just in time to see Robinson rise unshakably to his feet.

He remained motionless for what seemed like forever. But when he started walking back, Robinson knew it was to finish him off. The question wasn't whether he would succeed, but how the final blow would come.

Then he stopped in front of the boy, his face unreadable. Robinson hadn't realized he was crying until the Old Man wiped a single tear from his face. Then, with his handless arm, he maneuvered his staff to the rivulet of blood running down the boy's leg. He raised both the staff with blood and his finger with tears.

He was asking the boy to choose.

There was no option.

Robinson chose blood.

Chapter Nineteen
Drums

He thought things would get easier. Or that by earning a modicum of the Old Man's respect, he might also earn his favor. But neither was the case. The only courtesy Robinson received was a single nod before the Old Man turned and headed back in the direction of the library. Following was the longest, most painful trip of his life.

Once back in the safety of his haven, the Old Man pulled the blankets from his bed, revealing a cache of weapons, both scavenged and forged. Unlike the rest of his possessions, these were kept in perfect condition and were neatly arranged.

Beneath the weapons were several small satchels of herbs. He drew them out and used them to fashion poultices that he applied to the boy's wounds. When he rubbed a particularly nasty balm deep into the cuts on Robinson's feet, the boy cried out. A backhand split the bridge of his nose.

He never cried out again.

Four days passed before he was allowed to leave the stairwell and venture back into the light of day. By then, the Old Man had scavenged a pair of boots and some clothes for him to wear. They fit surprisingly well. His body was bruised and tender. His elbow was swollen and bloody. But it worked, so the boy didn't complain.

Robinson's biggest surprise was that the Old Man was not a great hunter. Or, at least, he wasn't an *active* hunter. He preferred to trap and snare instead. He had made cages out of old wire and deposited them around town, usually in the areas where larger renders had trouble getting to. Each morning, they would set out in a circular route to check them. When one had an animal inside, the Old Man would kill it, strip it, and put it in his bag. If a trap had a rendered animal inside, he would kill the animal, then take the trap to the closest source of water to clean it thoroughly. Afterward, he would replace the trap and leave a dollop of paste made of nuts, mushrooms, and insects as bait.

The Old Man also carried netting. Whenever he heard birds chirping from a bush, he would approach carefully to toss the net over it. His hand would then dart in, grab hold of the bird, and snap its neck between his thumb and forefinger. The first few times he did it, Robinson jumped and won a stick across the legs for his squeamishness.

Atop the library, the Old Man kept several large drums to collect rainwater. When it was hot, he would cover them with a tarp to keep it from evaporating. He had other reservoirs along the food route too. Robinson once tried to explain the dangers of bacteria. Pain taught him silence was more important than cleanliness.

On days too hot, they would head to the river where the Old Man would drop a fish trap into the shallows. They would rarely net a prize—at least one that was edible—but he refused to leave the shore.

At night, or on those days darkened by storm, they stayed inside the hovel, where the Old Man critiqued his charge on his skinning skills. Clip the skin near a squirrel's tailbone, earn a nod. Cut too far across the tailbone, get a slap on the ear. Rid the skin in one neat, uniform pull? You get to eat! Forget to remove the arms and tear the skin? You starve. Robinson got so good he was allowed to do it full time. He loved the feel of the knife and how easily it slid through muscle and bone.

In the late afternoons when they had gathered enough food, the Old Man took Robinson around the city, showing him what areas to avoid and how to determine if a building was likely to shelter renders. Scent was always the first clue, but there were others. Blood was one obvious sign. Scratches were another. Bones were a fourth. The absence of visible animals was always a good clue too.

When they ran short of supplies, they delved into the old stores, though never any place that wasn't well lit or bore an overpowering scent of infection. Sometimes the Old Man cut swaths of clothes off wooden human forms, but more often he trudged through stocking areas where pre-wrapped fabrics might still be found.

Along the way, Robinson saw many relics of the past. He collected them for a while, but the Old Man would smirk with disdain until he gave up.

The one thing he couldn't stop Robinson from doing was reading books. With a library at his disposal and little to do at night, he sat in front of a candle and read whatever relevant subjects he could find. American history was interesting to a point, but the books stopped just short of its final story and it was the only story he really wanted to know.

He had a fascination with science. Half of the discoveries that men had made seemed like rudimentary applications of common sense, while the other half were so revolutionary that it hurt to ponder the extrapolations. Of all the studies and disciplines, his favorite was the one called horror because it most closely resembled the life he was leading.

Even as the weeks passed, the one thing that never eased was Robinson's sense of loneliness. The Old Man only taught him about survival. He rarely spoke. Even when he did, it was no more than a few words at a time. The boy tried to engage him, offering to exchange the names of things, including their own, but he always refused. It soon became clear to Robinson that not every scar a man bore was exposed. Some—perhaps the most damaging—lay deep within.

On occasions, he'd see the dog. They'd be walking the food route or scavenging supplies and he'd see him sitting in an alley or under a tree, watching him. It should have made him nervous. The dog was afflicted after all. But those eyes were so aware. He wondered what stories they could tell.

It was late summer when everything changed. The day was hot and muggy and they had just finished collecting food when they stopped at a hidden reservoir for water. As usual, the Old Man sunk his head deep under the surface and groaned with relief. But when Robinson tried to cup his hands for a drink, the Old Man swatted him. Robinson leaned close only to feel his face thrust underneath. When he came up, the Old Man was laughing. Robinson splashed the water at him. It was the first time he'd seen him smile. But just as quickly as it appeared, the smile faded, replaced by a look of horror.

At first, Robinson thought he'd seen something at the bottom of the reservoir. But then he realized it wasn't what was *in* the water, but *on* it. Across the surface, the reflection of the moon took shape.

"What?" he asked lightly. "Don't tell me you're afraid of a full moon."

"*Chanvamo,*" he yelled. "*Na-ora!*"

The staff clipped Robinson against the back of his shoulders, but he was already in motion. If something was dangerous enough to make the Old Man afraid, the boy knew it was to be avoided at all costs. Unfortunately, they were still twenty blocks from the shelter and the sky was already growing dark.

They were running as fast as they could when they arrived at the bridge to the north. Usually they made their way around it, but this time the Old Man kept going. They both leaped the gulf easily enough, but when Robinson landed, the satchel of food slipped off his shoulder. He slowed to retrieve it, but the Old Man screamed, "*Ladiexe!*" and they kept going.

They were only a few blocks from the library when the drums sounded—deep, thunderous reverberations that rolled through the city like a tidal wave, echoing off the steel facades and growing in volume. The pulsating thrum boomed again and again, shaking the streetlights and dislodging glass that rained down from the towers above.

The Old Man's head snapped around. His mouth was open, tongue lolling. At one point, he threw up his stunted arm to cover one ear. Robinson was afraid he might be going mad.

Two blocks from the library, they heard the first render cry. It emerged from a sewer grate that exploded outward and landed with a clang. It wasn't even dusk, but the drums were rousing them. They weren't waiting for night. Something had come calling and the renders were answering.

Sunset was half a turn away when they spun onto the library's street. Like a starving man bounding toward a feast, the Old Man spurred forward, a desperate snarl in his throat. Only when they reached the final block did Robinson glimpse it out of the corner of his eye. His feet slowed and his mouth fell open.

The crimson sigil billowed stout with air, riding along the surface of the river. The drums echoed up and over the arcade, through the corridors of towers, and across the entire city. His mind raced to catch up with what his eyes were taking in.

"A ship," he said breathlessly. "A ship!"

Chapter Twenty
Waiting on the Moon

The Old Man screamed, but Robinson was powerless to heed his call. A ship meant people. People meant civilization. Civilization meant a way home.

He was already turning toward the water when the Old Man's movement drew his eye. The windup came in a blur. Half an intake of breath was all he managed when the staff flew just past his ear and impaled the render behind him. The Old Man snatched his stunned charge by the shirt and pulled him into the library.

When they reached the third floor, Robinson stopped.

"I want to see," he said.

The Old Man shook his head vehemently.

"Who are they?" he asked. "What are they to you?"

Pain lit the Old Man's face and for the first time, Robinson saw something vulnerable in him. But it quickly turned to anger, as he grabbed the boy with his one strong hand and shoved him toward the stairwell door.

For a turn, Robinson stayed busy making a meal of their emergency supplies and cooked it over the fire. But his mind was elsewhere.

After supper, the Old Man stared blankly into the fire. When the flames dwindled, he lay down and faced the wall. Even in the deep recesses of their haven, they could still hear the drums pulsing like the heart of a great beast as it lorded over the city, hypnotic and suffocating. What did they mean? Who was behind them? And how could they terrify the fiercest man Robinson had ever known?

As the fire ceded to embers, Robinson noticed something in their dying glow. With each pounding strike outside, the Old Man's fingers traced the inverted V scar on his upper arm. The movement was subtle, surely subconscious, but it said something.

Robinson had always understood that in the natural world, contrary forces were interdependent. Light and dark; hot and cold; life and death; two sides of the same coin; none could exist without the other. But only here had he begun to understand that there were a few, rare forces with the power to both attract and repel. One of these was the unknown. The unknown could be a thing, an influence, an area, or a factor. It could inspire men to great deeds or strike them frozen with terror. In his heart, he knew those drums to be evil, but he needed to see its face. He needed to know its name. This was his home now. For better or worse, the next time they called, he would not turn away.

When they headed out the next day, the ship was gone. The Old Man was not surprised. Still, he gave the river a wide berth. The pair fell into their routine, but the Old Man's heart wasn't in it. Something had changed. For one thing, he had lost his staff. It had snapped in two when he'd skewered the render, saving Robinson's life. Also, his smock had torn during their flight and he didn't seem the least bit interested in repairing it.

The task of checking cages and snares fell to Robinson, but unlike before, he was never disciplined when his knife ran afoul. Infected animals were cast aside rather than destroyed. Even the birds the Old Man craved now sang with impunity as they passed by. The only time he ever spoke was when Robinson dallied too long while collecting fruits or nuts, and even then, his rebuke was little more than a harsh grunt.

The days grew longer and hotter. They stopped for water more often, but the lack of rain was quickly shrinking their supplies. Even bathing was a luxury they couldn't afford and their haven soon adopted an intolerable stench.

On the rare days when they still ventured into the city to scavenge for goods, the Old Man was increasingly careless, often bounding into stores or buildings that only a month before he never would have entered. Robinson found it ironic that somehow their situations had become reversed; he almost felt as if he were taking care of the Old Man. His hope was that this fugue state would pass and he would see a glimmer of the man he'd known before the full moon.

Robinson's own transformation was no less significant. He felt comfortable in his own skin. He might not be cut from the same cloth as his companion, but he now believed if something happened to the Old Man, he could survive. He could find food, water, and shelter. He even had a rudimentary understanding of herbs and how to find them. He still had much to learn, but he no longer felt like a child. He might not be a man, but when he walked by a dirty storefront window one day and saw his reflection, he blanched. Gone was the fat from his face and midsection. He now had ribs and cheekbones. His skin had gone from the paleness of a babe to a dull bronze.

At the same time, Robinson knew his body was being deprived. His hair was oily and snowflakes from his scalp dotted his shoulders. His skin broke out in acne. His teeth and joints hurt. Even his urine had become a troubling shade of amber.

But he was alive. He was alive and he intended to stay that way.

Life became rote for the next few weeks. And as the brunt of the work fell on his shoulders, Robinson saw an opportunity to prove his worth. Hopefully, the Old Man would recognize the progress of his teachings, and if luck favored them, it might also buoy his spirits.

In the mornings, Robinson would draw him from bed at the break of dawn and they would set out to hunt and gather. In the evenings, he would prepare the meals and oil and whet the blades until they were razor-sharp. At night, he would lie in bed and read books from the library aloud by candlelight. The Old Man might not have understood the words, but they seemed to give him comfort as he sat and listened without complaint.

One day after a rare September shower, the Old Man came back early and lay down for an afternoon nap. Once he was asleep, Robinson raced out of the library to the edge of the nearest park and brought down a branch that he'd been eyeing for days. He took it back to the stairwell where he hid it on the second level. Each night after the Old Man fell asleep, he would sculpt and shape it. Finally, when the deed was done, he presented it to the Old Man. He took the staff with his one good hand and looked it over. It was a crude thing—of that there were no illusions—but it made him smile.

Unfortunately, the sentiment didn't last. Each morning as they walked, the Old Man's eyes were cast down, his mind lost to the demons of his past. Each afternoon, his head was in the clouds, looking for a future that would never come.

In some ways, he sympathized with the man. Despite the loss of Tessa, he couldn't get her off his mind. At times, he imagined her stepping around the corner of one of these desolate streets, having crossed the ocean on her own accord in search of him, and they would swear to never be apart again. But he knew dwelling on such things was folly and that it betrayed a weakness of character that shamed all those he had loved and lost.

And then one night an inflamed orb as deep and dark as a ruby cast in fire appeared in the eastern sky. Back home they called it the Gatherer's Moon, but here, as Robinson had read, it was called the Harvest Moon. It came shortly after sunset, quickly taking its place high in the sky. But it did not come alone. With it came a panorama full of stars, the turning of leaves, and the return of the drums.

Chapter Twenty-One
Savages!

The Old Man refused to leave the haven that day. He knew what was coming. Sometime around noon, the day turned chilly and the animals retreated like fog. It seemed they knew what was coming too.

The full moon rose just before sunset, but by then they had stockpiled enough supplies for the night. The late afternoon moved agonizingly slowly. When Robinson could take it no longer, he built a fire and started cooking raccoon meat on a spit. The meat was dark and gamey, but when he cooked it properly, it was delicious. The secret was to strip away every speck of fat. He was just encouraging the Old Man to eat when the drums started.

A month before, those deep, booming strikes had rumbled like thunder. Now they sounded like the world was splitting in two. Surprisingly, the Old Man didn't cower or bury his head beneath his blankets. He simply closed his eyes and started to hum. The tone was too soft to decipher a melody, but it ran counter to the beat of the drums, as if by singing his own song, he might beat back the one that haunted him.

While this battle raged, another sparked inside. Part of Robinson wanted to stay there in the security of the haven and support the man who had saved his life. But another part of him needed to go outside to see what mysterious circumstances surrounded those drums.

Turns passed. The Old Man put up a valiant fight, but the moment Robinson stood, he knew the battle was lost. Robinson expected to be scolded or held back, but he had to do this for himself. The Old Man's expression seemed resigned, making clear more loudly than words what he thought about youth and curious minds in general.

When Robinson had donned his darkest clothes and started for the stairs, the Old Man called out, offering his staff. Robinson knew his chances of needing it were great but taking it felt like a violation. Instead, he said simply, "I'll be back."

Outside, night had come, and with it, renders. The parade of flesh moved down Independence Street but also split around the library, like river water around a rock. Robinson slipped out through the western exit overlooking a wedge of wild grass through which he could crawl.

He worked his way toward a narrow ravine split from a vale of concrete and quietly slid down, careful to watch his footing at the crevasse's edge. The rift itself was three meters deep and dark enough for him to go unnoticed as he looped the arcade. After a few short steps, he heard a pack of renders pass. Mercifully, they never saw him.

The full moon filled the streets with shadows, which he used to slip to the northern side of Constitution Avenue. There, he snuck through the foliage of several large buildings. As he neared the last one, he saw the glow of fires illuminating the top of the monolith and the park where the renders were swarming. Unfortunately, his view was blocked. He needed to cross the street to find a building with the perfect vantage point.

The stroke of drums came faster and harder, each pounding, rhythmic call answered by a thousand tortured voices. But then the most horrific sound of all rose above the din—a single human scream. The roar that followed was an explosion of bloodlust and fury. Robinson knew he should go back, but it was too late.

The roadway was momentarily clear when he stepped out of the shadows and ran hard for a carriage shell in the center of the street, hunkering down seconds before a four-legged render passed. He was halfway across the street when he slipped and fell.

The fall wasn't the bad part. It was that he had crashed into a faded blue, metal box that crumpled under his weight. The noise stalled the four-legged render in its path. The creature turned, its nose palpitating. When it began plodding back, Robinson knew it was only a matter of time before he was discovered. His luck went from bad to worse as four more mutated creatures appeared on the grass in front of the building.

Caught between hammer and anvil, Robinson was about to choose which evil might be the lesser when he heard a snarl behind him. He spun to find the dog. It barked at the nearest render, which quickly changed course. The others fell in behind it. The dog sprinted several yards away only to turn back and taunt them again.

Robinson stayed low as he ran for the building. It bore a faded sign that he deciphered as the Museum of American History. Part of its front had collapsed, revealing a number of stone columns, canted and broken. Robinson scaled the tenuous path to an outcropping over a high window. When he looked back, he saw the dog still circling, leading the renders farther away.

At the southeastern corner of the building, Robinson was afforded his first view of the scene below. It was bedlam. The large wooden ship had anchored in the basin, its blood red sail now hanging lax. Its black sigil of a burning dagger shone ominously in the moonlight.

Near the water's edge stood a dozen bronze-skinned savages wearing little more than breeches and jewelry made of shells that shook and rattled as they pounded on the towering drums.

In the foreground were several large fires, their flames billowing into the sky as more savages patrolled the perimeter of the monolith, using torches to incite the renders but also to keep them at bay. When one got too close, a savage would raise a pouch of liquid to his mouth and spit a geyser of fire at it. The immolating creature would shriek as it spun through its kind, igniting any that failed to get out of its way. Only when the creature collapsed and the flames died down did the pack descend to feed on its flesh, eliciting raucous laughter from the cluster of human tormenters.

Among the savages, one towered above all the others. He was a colossal man and wore a feathered headdress over a face painted black and white to resemble a human skull. He held a large, curved blade that he swung with sadistic glee, indiscriminately striking down renders whenever the desire touched him. With each blow, his elaborate breastplate of shells rattled and shook. It was only when he turned and Robinson saw nubs on his vestments that he realized they were not shells, but human bones.

Abruptly, Savage Chief raised his sword and bellowed. The drumbeat fell to a single, slowly paced strike. Robinson's heart thrummed in unison as a savage ran to the ship. There, a half dozen bamboo cages were perched just inside the waterline, each containing a writhing mass of terrified captives. The savage opened the cage and ordered a captive out. When he refused, the savage killed him with a dagger. The other captives wailed as his body fell and more savages raced to claim it. They dragged it toward the arcade and threw it into the mass of renders. It was feasted upon in seconds.

The smell of blood only frenzied the pack as a second prisoner was dragged out, his will broken. Behind him followed two more, a man and a woman. Robinson felt bile rising in his throat. He was sure he was going to vomit, but he couldn't turn away.

Savage Chief ordered the three prisoners chained to the monolith. The nearest never raised his head. His irons were connected to one wrist and he slunk down against the concrete, unwilling to face the death that was coming for him.

In the center, the woman wailed, her tears visible even from afar, but she remained standing, her head turned to see what was coming.

The man at the far end had remained silent, but his head never bowed. His foot was being shackled to the monolith when he suddenly lashed out and kneed one of the savages in the face. A second savage drew his blade and cut him across the chest, but the man disarmed him with shocking speed and hacked the savage twice, once taking an ear, the second cutting him across the mouth. The savage fell in a heap. Then Savage Chief came over. Robinson assumed he was going to help the injured man, but he mocked him and killed him instead. The other savages roared.

Chief then turned to taunt the captive but found no fear in him. He made a joke and his men laughed. His head was turned for a fraction of a second when the prisoner flung the dagger at him. It should have been a lethal strike, but Chief spun with extraordinary speed and batted the blade away.

Chief mocked the man again, but rather than kill him, he ordered the release of three renders. Then he picked up three weapons—the dagger, an axe, and a sword—and tossed them at the feet of the captives.

The drumbeat picked up slowly. Bloodlust was in the air. Robinson saw Savage Chief's chest swell with anticipation, his eyes big, golden orbs in the flames.

The sobbing female grabbed the dagger, her hands shaking as the renders moved in. The third captive yelled at her and motioned to the weapons at her feet. She kicked the blade to him just in time. The first render swept down upon the stooped man, his cry quickly reduced to a gurgle as the beast tore into him. The savages howled with delight as he died. The drums let off a trill blast before resuming their sacrificial pace.

The female captive swung her dagger erratically while the fierce man hacked at the iron around his ankle with the sword but to no avail. When a render charged, he met the attack with one swift slash. The render stumbled and fell.

With the female captive distracted, her render attacked. She tried to raise the dagger, but the creature's massive maw had already locked onto her face. The first render joined in. The fierce man screamed, swinging his blade wildly, but after a few seconds, the woman's body slowed and then ceased to move altogether.

Once again, the drums trilled in recognition of death. The other prisoners wailed. Robinson turned and vomited. He wanted to look away. He wanted to flee, but he knew those images would be there in the dark for a long time to come. He was still hoping the fierce man might beat them back with the fire inside him.

The two remaining renders surrounded their final prize, but he stood tall, sword ready. When their attack came, the blade hit the first render under the arm, but almost simultaneously, the second one sank its teeth into the man's neck. He thrashed and continued to fight, but eventually the blade dropped from his hand and he died.

The savages erupted as the drumbeats rose and fell. The yowling of renders drowned out the cry of the prisoners that were soon to follow. For Robinson's part, he could watch no more. All of his life he had been told the world was full of horrors, but he had never understood that the worst of them was man. He had gone there of his own volition but would leave some part of himself behind forever. He tried to wipe the events from his mind, but two things refused to go. The first was the bravery with which the fierce man had hacked at his bonds before he'd died.

The second was the inverted V scar burned deep into the flesh of his upper arm.

Chapter Twenty-Two
A New Companion

When he returned to the haven the following morning, the Old Man was gone. The only thing he had left behind was the knife Robinson had spent months coveting. Maybe he was ashamed of how he had survived his captivity or how he'd lived afterward. Maybe he couldn't bear the thought of seeing the change he was sure to find in the boy's eyes. Bearing witness to evil scarred a soul too, after all.

But the days rolled forward and Robinson pushed on, sticking to the routine he'd been taught. He rose early, hunting birds or insects for bait. He checked traps for animals, killing ones that were edible, drowning those with blight. The traps that were damaged, he repaired. The empty ones, he moved. All the while he avoided darkened doorways or any place a render might hide. He never ventured into residences.

Three days after the night of the full moon, he went back to the monolith. The grass around the obelisk was burned and the cement was stained with blood. He saw no bones or other refuse. The renders had done their job well.

He came to a decision then. He would not live a life of fear. He began mapping out the city. From the books he'd scavenged, he learned it was called Washington, named after one of the original founders of this country. It had once been the seat of power and had led the free world in many things.

Beyond the realm of towers and glass, the signs of renders lessened. Robinson didn't know if they merely lived where food was more abundant or if they simply lingered where their human ancestors had fallen.

Upriver, he found animals and plants of unknown biological classifications and technologies of indiscernible purposes. To the southwest, he stumbled upon a field of gravestones larger than the whole of New London.

Still he could never quite leave the city. He knew the Old Man would never return, but if he did, he wanted to be where he could find him.

And yet loneliness encroached upon his every waking act. His dreams were haunted by the notion of becoming injured and left to die alone, like being dragged down into some dark abyss, or falling from a high building, or drowning in rainwater as it gushed down the stairwell and flooded the haven.

He went out less often, blaming it first on the rain, and then on the traps when they failed to provide food. He sequestered himself in the library, reading books on history and science, in awe of the gifts the One People had been deprived of and horrified by the plagues they had been spared. Wallowing in memories of Tessa only made those fears more acute. Whenever he passed a reflective surface, he saw how gaunt he had become. Something had to change and soon, but he didn't know what or how. He searched for flyer technology to help return him home, but there was none to be had. Gravity displacement hadn't been invented until well after this republic had fallen.

And then one day he went out foraging for clothes to fend off the cold that had begun creeping in. Only one area of the city catered to such attire. When he arrived at the northern edge of the city, he recognized the faded symbol of a clothing company that matched the inside of his trousers. Unfortunately, the windows and doors were boarded up, making it impossible to see inside. He knew the likelihood of renders living in such a place was thin—they typically avoided street-level areas when possible. But just as he bounded up the steps, a growl startled him from behind. He spun, his hands wrapping around the knife, only to find the dog in the street behind him.

"Crown's sake," Robinson muttered. "You scared the stuffing out of me."

The dog whined but didn't move any closer. Robinson's eyes fell to the afflicted patches on his hindquarters. He was marked like a render, but he didn't behave like one. The contradiction still puzzled him.

"Well? What do you want? Food? I suppose I owe you after the other day."

The dog barked again in two sharp yelps.

Robinson reached into his bag and pulled out a piece of squirrel meat. "You must have a keen nose," he said and tossed it to him. "That makes us even now."

To his surprise, the dog sniffed the offering but didn't take it. Instead, he looked about pensively and let loose another low whine.

"What? Too good for squirrel? That's some cheek. You're rather scrawny to be turning down a free meal."

And then the dog started barking aggressively.

"Whoa," Robinson said, as he held up his hands. "It was just an observation. Nothing to get your tail in a twist over."

Suddenly the dog's ears pinned back and he bared his teeth. The snarl left no room for interpretation. He was about to attack.

"Easy now. I'm just going to step inside. No need to—"

And then the door crashed open behind him, followed by a blood-chilling cry. Seven razor-sharp claws tore through the strap of Robinson's bag as he stumbled into the street. The knife shot out of his pocket and clattered a few feet away.

The render howled, momentarily blinded by the afternoon light. Robinson's hand groped for the knife. The render compressed its legs, and with incredible force, leaped high into the air. Its good leg struck the concrete just by Robinson's hip while its mutated leg smashed into his chest, instantly knocking the air from his lungs. He had just picked up the blade when the creature caught his wrist, knocking the blade away.

The creature's other hand swung straight for his head. He turned at the last second and felt the air bend as its nails passed by and cut into the asphalt. When it wrenched its hand out, chunks of black road scattered. Robinson bucked his hips in an effort to escape, but the render pushed him back down. It howled again and the foul stench that washed out of its maw nearly made him pass out. Its hand went back for a final strike, but before it could launch, a flash of mottled fur slammed into it and sent it flying. Robinson's lungs filled, but his vision still pirouetted. He turned in time to see the render fling the dog away. It tumbled several times before regaining its feet. Its heavy barks were met by the render's howl as they squared off, both prepared to spring at the other again.

Robinson knew the dog would continue to charge. He also knew it had no chance of winning, so he yelled for it to get back. The dog retreated a few steps as Robinson darted by the creature. It halted at the edge of the shadows.

When Robinson reached the end of the block, the render was gone. The dog, however, remained by his side. Curiously, it had saved his life twice that day. Though afflicted with the same disease as the renders, it appeared that the disease had halted its progression. Were all dogs like this? And if so, why weren't there more around?

The animal had been domesticated, that much was certain. So Robinson led him back to the library and to the door of the stairwell. It stood there, sniffing the air and whining. It wasn't because it smelt renders, but because it knew a cage when it saw one. Still, Robinson coaxed it with a soft voice and patient manner. Eventually it followed.

Robinson filled a small pan with water and slid it against the far wall where the Old Man used to sleep. The dog crossed to it and lapped. Twice he filled the pan and twice the dog emptied it. On the third go, Robinson tried to pet the dog to put the little fellow at ease. When the dog looked around skittishly, he knew he wasn't ready.

"Okay, Dog," he said. "Everything in its time."

That night, he read a novel aloud and every time he glanced up, he found the dog watching him from the stairs. The only time he moved was when a draft of wind plunged in from above and the candles flickered. On those occasions, the dog would lift his head and whine softly.

"You know what?" Robinson said, closing his book. "You're right. This is no way to live. What do you say tomorrow you and I go out and find a new home? Something less … *dramatic*. With a view. Would you like that, boy?"

He didn't answer, but he didn't whine again either. Robinson smiled.

"It's a deal then," he said before yawning deeply.

Robinson put a mark between the pages of the book and set it down. Then he bundled his ragged blanket under his head before blowing out the candle. He knew he would sleep well that night. His belly was full. He was safe. And when he heard the dog finally pad over to the Old Man's corner and paw at some blankets before settling down, he had to smile. For the first time since coming to Washington, he had more than a companion.

At last, he'd found a friend.

Chapter Twenty-Three
The Memorial

The next morning, Robinson packed up his belongings and bid adieu to the haven. Before he left, he made sure to disguise the entrance to the stairwell just in case he ever needed to return. He hoped he wouldn't.

He and Dog set out to find their new haven, something that would protect them from the elements and prove inhospitable to renders. That excluded most of the towers and any shop with fewer than one or two entrances. Most government buildings were too large or too exposed. Robinson wanted to be close to the river, not only for its abundant source of water, but so he could see any threat coming. Still, he wanted to be far enough away from the monolith that its ghosts wouldn't haunt him when he passed.

Eventually, he settled on a building at the far western edge of the arcade. It was another commanding stone structure perched high atop a hill with a range of stone steps leading up to some mighty limestone columns that towered several stories high. The structure was devoted to another one of the continent's fallen leaders and it paid homage to the man in the form of a giant statue of him seated in a chair, overlooking an expansive pool of water, the city, and everything beyond. The man wore a grave countenance, devoid of humor or mirth, but there was a stern wisdom fixed on his face that was undeniable. Behind him, these words were etched:

> *In this temple as in the hearts of the people for whom he saved the Union, the memory of Abraham Lincoln is enshrined forever.*

Those words, like his expression, gave Robinson an unexplainable confidence. And he knew in that instant, he wanted to do more than survive. He wanted to live.

A road had once encircled the memorial, but the river had overrun it long ago and now lapped up against the southern edge of the building. An old bridge spanned the river, but it too had succumbed to the steady flow of time. To the north was a barren field with nothing but the husks of old, dead trees and a marsh teeming with mosquitos. To the south, the darkened river flowed steadily past.

"Well, boy? What do you think?"

Dog yapped once and looked suspiciously at the building.

"You're right. I guess we should see what's inside first."

Inside the atrium, they crossed pink marbled floors to find a gold-flecked door marked "elevator," but no knob to open it. On the other side, they found a regular door, which after much prodding gave way to some sort of custodial room at the back of the building. It only had one physical entrance. A ladder framed to the far wall gave access to an exit panel adjacent to the colored glass ceiling. Not every panel was intact and some rainwater had gotten in, but for the most part, the room was undamaged and well lit. Robinson wanted to see the view from the roof, but when his feet hit the first couple of rusty rungs, Dog moaned to make it clear what he thought of this undertaking. The risk paid off when Robinson rose into the clear morning air with a view of the entire city. The husks of towers and web of roads, once so terrifying to him, became identifiable from on high. The fact that he could see threats coming helped alleviate his many fears. If this were to be his kingdom, he would need a perch from which to lord over. And this one even had a throne.

When he made his way back down, Dog had curled up in a corner underneath an old, dusty desk and wagged his tail when Robinson's feet hit the ground.

"Yeah," he said, "I like it too."

For all the strengths their new home afforded, security still came down to a single door. Any creature or aggressor determined enough would eventually get in no matter how well it was reinforced. So Robinson decided to build a barricade. While the columns outside were too big and too numerous to secure on their own, the three interior columns at the atrium's entrance were each under three meters apart. The question then became what to barricade them with. The answer sat on the street outside.

The metal carriages that littered the city would no longer move and Robinson didn't have the strength to lift them by force, so he set out to find something that would. A dozen blocks away, he stumbled across a grocery store and found many stacked metal carts inside. Dog watched as he drew them out one by one, testing the wheels to see if they turned. When Robinson was satisfied with four of them, he drew them down the street.

Two blocks away was a garage that catered to carriages. He added as many tools as the carts could carry, including hammers, saws, chisels, and pry bars. Lastly, he dismantled two hoists used to raise engines and the chains attached to the sliding doors of the garage.

After returning to the memorial, Robinson cut the box portion from every cart and used the long pry bar to slip each four-wheel base along the rusty carriage frame. He then secured the hoist and chains to pitons on the roof before maneuvering the carriage to the foot of the steps. Using makeshift sandbags on a pallet, he used the hoist to pull the carriage into place between the interior columns. Exhausted but thrilled with his progress, he settled down to supper with the last of his rations and Dog at his feet.

"A good day's work, Dog."

Dog barked twice, his eyes on the food in Robinson's hands. Robinson split what he had and tossed it to him. After gobbling it down, he looked up, expectantly.

"I'm afraid that's the last of it. Maybe if you spent more time hunting and less time playing, we could both fatten up some."

Robinson chuckled and turned back to stoke the fire. Then he felt the oddest thing. Dog had crossed over and begun licking the grease from his fingers. Very slowly, he reached out and set his other hand on his head. He didn't stop licking, but when he scratched him behind the ears, his eyes closed and he knew they had turned a corner.

"Man's best friend," he said. "It's a tough moniker to live up to. Still, if we're going to be pals you and me, we'll need to find you a name more suitable than 'Dog.' A proper name, yes?"

Dog barked.

"I'm glad you agree. Now, it should be something representative of who you are—that is to say, your character—but also something with style."

Robinson offered several suggestions, including Patches, Shadow, and even Renderbane. Perhaps he sensed a change in tone, but when Robinson said "Jaras," the dog growled.

"I was just teasing!" he said with a laugh. "This is harder than I imagined."

Dog groaned and lifted his leg to lick his nether regions. With each swipe, the tag on his collar tinkled.

"What's this?" Robinson asked.

Dog went still as he reached for the tag. It was bronze and much worn. One side had an image of what looked like shooting stars escaping a clutch of clouds. The other side was almost entirely faded except for four raised letters on the outer edge: RESI.

"Resi," Robinson said. Dog picked his head up. "Is that your name?"

Dog licked his hand again.

"Well, I can't say I know what it means, but it suits you. 'Resi' it is."

Resi barked and Robinson scratched his ears again.

For the next two weeks, they followed the same routine. In the mornings, they traversed the food route, collecting game from the traps that were still fruitful, while moving the barren ones closer to the memorial or wherever Resi's nose signaled there were animals to catch.

In the afternoons, Robinson returned to the fortification of the sanctuary. The work was grueling, but he developed a system that got easier with each attempt. By the end of the week, he was stacking one carriage every afternoon. Many of the vehicles were corroded with brittle frames that bent or snapped under significant weight. As he stacked them, he was forced to make repairs to keep them from toppling over.

But eventually, the barricade took shape. To fill all three entranceways, he had amassed the shells of twenty-nine vehicles. Each row stood five meters high with only a few small fissures that he filled with whatever recycled materials were at hand—discarded baskets from the carts, half the shell of an old school bus, and rusty road signs. When he was sure no significant-sized threat could burrow its way inside, he broke down spades from wrought iron fences and built a stone grader to sharpen them. He positioned these lances pointing outward to fend off any enemy that got too close.

As an extra measure of caution, Robinson retrieved four drums worth of oil from the park, using a stirrup pump fabricated from vehicle parts and an old garden hose. He used the crane to lift them to the top of the roof where he could push them off any of the building's four corners at a moment's notice.

Lastly, he made an addition to the crane that raised the wooden lift from one side of the barrier to the other. When they were within the structure, the lift was inaccessible to anyone outside. When they ventured out, the lever to release it was hidden in a small cleft laden with oil and broken glass.

Next he began work on a water system that fed directly from the river. Thankfully, he had done a report on hydrodynamics in school, so he understood the basic principles. All it took was the construction of a small waterwheel with support beams, an axel, and rotating glassware that fed to a series of old pipes that ran into the memorial. It emptied into a boiler tank heated by firewood.

This allowed him another luxury: he could bathe. The Old Man had refused to clean himself for fear the odor would make him more identifiable to the renders, but Robinson wasn't worried, being surrounded by so much foliage.

Robinson had also made tallow candles from the fats of animals, but those with high lipid counts were hard to come by. Still, when he heated his last batch, he found some left over in the double boiler. He decided to mix it with oils distilled from eucalyptus, lavender, and sunflower seeds in the hope of making soap. But somewhere along the way, the mixture got screwed up and he woke with a terrible rash. Even worse, the smell of the stuff was so bad, Resi slept on the other side of the memorial for three days and always walked upwind of him when outside.

One morning, Robinson woke to find a chill in the air and he knew winter was around the corner. Twenty-two days had passed since the Old Man had left. Although his new home was secure, he'd put off two of the most important tasks for too long.

The first task was to stockpile food. Since his primary diet was animal protein, he knew it would be hard to come by during the winter months, so he built a smoker that he used to dry thin strips of meat at a low temperature for over six to twelve turns. This would preserve the meat for weeks, if not months, though the burning smoke did draw a few renders during the daylight hours.

The other task was to find a source of heat for the memorial, since the wind came straight off the river and might otherwise turn their new home into a block of ice. Robinson returned to the library. From parabolic boilers to geothermal heating, to stoves that burned propane, gas, or corn, there were a myriad of options. The one he ultimately decided on was a wood-burning stove since it would be easy to maintain. To prevent the smoke from identifying his location, he decided to only use it at night.

While these projects did their best to distract him during the day, nothing could soothe the loneliness he felt at night. When he wasn't reading books aloud to Resi, he was sitting atop the roof, staring through an eyeglass he had discovered in a museum. His eye was set to the stars, hoping each passing meteor was a flyer whose light would grow brighter and brighter until it touched down outside the memorial, where his father would stumble out. He would look around, see his son, and smile, saying, "I knew you'd be all right." But the stars never halted. Nor did the night. And Robinson knew, as surely as he knew anything, that he would never see his loved ones again.

When the nights were too cold to venture outside, he lay in bed, holding his mother's locket. If he closed his eyes, he could almost smell her scent ingrained in its links. When those memories became too much to bear, he took it off, wrapped it carefully in a rag, and pushed it into the recesses of some old pipes and tried to forget about it for a while.

The day that changed everything began with rain and ended with fire. In between, the sky was blotted with smoldering clouds across which flocks of birds trudged silently south against prevailing winds. Ill omens were plentiful when he looked for them. Robinson had done everything in his power to avoid these signs. And yet there was no denying the one portent he had been dreading for twenty-nine days: the killing moon. It had returned, wholly waxed and blush—so foreboding that by late afternoon, it had driven everything else from the sky.

Robinson tried to stay busy. He clung to routine. But in the end, nothing could ease the sense of dread building inside him. Resi also seemed tense.

They retreated early and fortified the barricade. They blocked every door. They sealed every window. But nothing could keep the darkness out forever. There was only the wait and the silence before the storm.

When he could take it no longer, Robinson took his eyeglass up to the roof, ignoring Resi's cries. And as surely as the world turned, his worst fears were confirmed.

It came with a crimson sail and black sigil. It came with the paddling of oars and the beating of drums. But this time, it also came with the one person who would change the course of his life forever.

Chapter Twenty-Four
The Girl

She was pulled from the ship with a group of prisoners, hustled in leather bonds toward the cages that sat just off the river's edge. Had she gone meekly like the rest of the chattel, Robinson might have never noticed her. But this girl had fight.

She refused to enter the cage willingly, so a savage captor struck her across the back with a staff. Her legs buckled but only for a second. Then she spun and hit the man as hard as she could. Her wrists were bound together, so it was her elbow that struck him across the bridge of his nose. He went down screaming.

A second savage swung his staff at the girl, but she stepped effortlessly out of its way before leaping forward and butting the brute in the head. He too went down. Unlike his friend, he did not get up. Unfortunately, before the girl could run, three other savages tackled her and forced her to the ground. Punches and kicks followed. A spear went up, but it never came down. At that last moment, a meaty hand had wrapped around it, staying the killing blow. It was the hand of Savage Chief.

He said something to his men and they laughed. He then grabbed the girl by the hair and dragged her, kicking and yelling, into the cage. Once the door was closed, Savage Chief headed for the monolith, but his eyes stayed on the girl.

She had black hair and dark skin. Even from afar, Robinson could see the tone of her muscles and the fire in her eyes. Her head spun around as she tested the lock on the cage and the corners where it had been tied. The savage whose nose she had broken came over to taunt her but leaped back when her hands shot through the bars.

The drums drew out the renders. The first pair appeared out of the park, lumbering together in a strange unison. Only when they leaped over a small gorge did Robinson realize they were not a pair, but two renders fused as one. The beast writhed and howled as it maneuvered around the fires to where the first of four prisoners was chained to the obelisk. Each held a weapon but none had any fight. The creature attacked. The prisoners died.

Like the previous bloodletting, Robinson could not turn away. But this time, he was no longer willing to just stand by and watch. The sight of the girl and her continued struggle prompted him to act.

Without thinking, he rushed down the ladder and stripped to his trousers. In the corner was a vat of crude oil that he had used to make resin. He opened it and slathered the black liquid over his face and body until he was covered. Then he recovered a small bag of tools. Resi barked his disapproval, but he refused to let it dissuade him.

He crept along the riverbank, keeping watch of both the savages on shore and those aboard the ship. Two men sat atop the bow, drinking some intoxicating concoction and howling at every gory death.

As Robinson moved closer, he saw a wave of renders try and attack from the eastern side. One of the savages tossed several small clay pots of flammable liquid into the fray. A companion slung a torch in seconds later. The conflagration instantly lit up the creatures and the night. The chorus of inhuman shrieks was deafening, but it was the stench of burning flesh that rolled over him seconds later that nearly had him spilling his guts. When he stumbled in the water, the nearest savage turned toward him. He ducked behind some reeds, heart thundering, hoping he hadn't been seen.

The drums picked up in tempo as the savages chanted some evil verse over and over. Near the ship's edge, Robinson could see two of the savages caught in some frenetic dance, their eyes stark and white, their mouths lolling open, screaming in ecstasy as they writhed. Some had sharpened their teeth to points while others had pierced their bodies with human bones. All bore black tattoos in patterns across their chests and backs.

Three more prisoners were hauled out of the cages. They were so thoroughly traumatized that the savages did not even bother tying them up. One was given a spear. Another a bow and arrow. The third ran for a sword on the ground just as his wrist was caught in the claws of a render's foot. The man screamed as others closed in. His companion tried to string the bow but fumbled it. A second later, he paid for the mistake with his life.

As Robinson neared the ship, he dipped into the water, swimming beneath the gangplank as feet stomped overhead. The cages were strung along the waterside, the girl's cage closest to him. From this distance, he was able to see her more closely. One eye was swollen shut and blood coursed down the side of her face. But she wasn't wallowing in fear or getting caught up in the spectacle. She was biting the leather bonds wrapped around her wrists.

Near the monolith, one prisoner was putting up a good fight, fending off two renders with a spear. Tears spilled down his cheeks, but he never cried out. When he managed to stab one of the beasts through the neck, the savages cheered. Savage Chief forced the other render on him, hoping for even more excitement.

That's when Robinson made his move.

The girl spun in shock when he hit the cage from behind. She must have thought a demon had come for her the way he'd slunk out of the river, white eyes on a body that was as slick and as dark as night. He put a finger to his mouth just as a savage grabbed an older female prisoner from another cage and dragged her away.

Once he was gone, the girl turned back to Robinson, but he was already trying to cut the straps from her cage. Unfortunately, the punch he was using was blunt. He cursed his luck for losing the Old Man's knife those weeks before.

"*Quem ni?*" the girl spoke, her voice raspy but clear.

Robinson motioned for her to be quiet. He went back to work on the straps, this time stabbing them with the tool. The girl shook her head and thrust her hand through the bars.

"*Diasa*," she hissed. "*Di-a-sa!*"

He handed her the punch. She slid it through the leather straps, holding the lock in place. She rotated it until the leather groaned. Another cry pierced the night. At the monolith, the two remaining prisoners stood back to back, both gravely wounded. The head of one had already begun to dip. It wouldn't be long before he fell, followed by his companion. When that happened, Savage Chief would signal for more prisoners to sacrifice.

Robinson nodded for her to hurry and she motioned for help. He crept to the front of the cage, keeping low to avoid attracting those on the ship. He reached in and pushed the top of the punch as she pulled from the bottom. The leather bindings stretched and then snapped. The lock fell into the grass and the door cracked open. He waved her toward the water, but when he glanced back, she was heading for the other cages.

"No!" he hissed. "They'll see you!" But the drums drowned out his words.

A young, muscular savage with human skulls capping both shoulders stood in front of the cage. When the last prisoner at the monolith buckled, he cheered and swung his dagger as if he were caught in the throes of battle. Behind him, the girl stalked closer. Unfortunately, the other prisoners couldn't contain themselves and one cried out. The savage turned, but before he could raise a weapon, the girl was on him, plunging the punch deep into his neck and catching his body as he fell.

Robinson thought the deadly act had gone unseen, but then he heard a shout from above as one of the savages on the bow pointed frantically in her direction.

In an instant, all eyes turned toward them and the drums went silent. The savages were confused, too preoccupied by the curtain of renders to immediately process what was happening. But then Savage Chief burst through the fray. When he saw the girl, a murderous rage filled his eyes. He pointed to her and yelled.

"Run!" someone screamed and then Robinson realized that the voice was his own.

Chapter Twenty-Five
The White Building

The savages let out a blood-curdling roar, pursuing them with weapons poised. Robinson's watery escape was now cut off, so he headed for a narrow channel between the ship and the easternmost bonfire. Just as he was passing the gangplank, he saw a dozen of those clay pots stacked on the ground. He scooped up two mid-run, flinging the first one at the savage leading the charge from the monolith. The pot hit the man flush in the chest and disintegrated instantly, the liquid blinding him. But it was the collateral spray, catching the edge of the bonfire, that turned him into a whirlwind of fire.

A swarm of savages also spewed from the ship, some holding large drum sticks the size of hammers. As the girl caught up with him, Robinson threw the remaining clay pot at the ground and a wall of fire went up, momentarily blocking their pursuers.

He signaled the girl to follow him toward the memorial, but a second later, he felt something whistle by his ear. It was an arrow. It was not alone. Several more zipped into the grass, prompting them to turn toward the city.

"This way!" he called, directing her back toward the park's center. He ran faster than he had ever run before, but that didn't stop the girl from flying by him. Her body was lean, her gait effortless. Running was something she had done her entire life.

While the drums had been silenced, the savages' cries had not. Their bloodthirsty shouts were a constant reminder of what would happen if they fell. A brief glimpse back revealed a dozen warriors breaking through the shroud of trees as they sped over a street and into the northern park. There, they broke right, skirting around the edge of a small pond toward the nearest building, when renders appeared out of nowhere.

Robinson jerked to evade the creatures, but the girl pulled him back. He didn't understand why until he heard the screams of the savages that had followed them straight into the pack. More savages stopped to kill the beasts before resuming the hunt.

But the girl started to fade. In the full light of the moon, Robinson could see captivity had wrecked her. Her eyes were sunken from lack of sleep and her lips cracked from dehydration. She gasped for breath. He had hoped to lead the savages into the city where only he would be familiar with the territory, but the girl was not up for it. And for some reason, the savages seemed intent on not letting her go. So he led her toward the building he had long stayed away from: the white building at the top of the park.

They ran through the crumpled wrought iron fence and crossed the graveyard of carriages until they reached the building itself. The door he'd gone through weeks before was still half open, the booby trap unrepaired. That gave him some reassurance that whoever had set it was no longer there.

Unfortunately, the smell of renders was still acute. Looking back, Robinson saw the torches of the savages closing in. It was too late to run elsewhere. His only hope was that if any creatures still lived inside, the drums had drawn them out earlier in the night.

The first floor was cavernous and dark with a number of rooms and partitions. Robinson pulled the girl into the third room as the savages entered behind them.

The room was full of broken furniture, but the wall to their right glistened as moonlight was reflected off a wall of dishes. Robinson turned for a second door, but the girl stopped him and pulled him behind an overturned table in the corner of the room.

Both sat mutely behind the table, listening as the men stalked through the building. Briefly, Robinson thought their pursuers might pass them by, but then light filled the room as a man bearing a torch entered. His pulse pounded in his ears. He looked at the girl, expecting to see fear etched on her face, but she was composed, her good eye steady. In her hands were two pieces of broken china, poised like weapons.

As carefully as he could, Robinson peeked around the table. The savage wore leather pants and no shirt, but had a string of something around his neck that looked like teeth. His chest was thick and riddled with those odd tattoos, extending from the bottom of his ribcage to the top of his throat. His face was painted white and his hair was shaved, save for a single tail on top.

The savage turned for the open door, a massive cudgel in his hands. He poked it open, but just as he was about to enter, Robinson's leg twitched, and the table shifted. He winced. The girl's face was bridled with fury, but then she nodded toward a broken table leg near his feet. He grabbed it.

The shadow stood still. Then the door slowly closed. Robinson looked at the girl. She nodded for him to be ready. The savage's breath grew steadily louder as he approached. Robinson watched his shadow approach, the smell of sweat and blood stifling. He tensed his muscles, ready to spring, when a voice called from the corridor.

The savage hesitated for what felt like forever. Then he turned and stalked away. The pair breathed sighs of relief, but both knew they wouldn't be safe there for long. They scuttled to the adjacent room, a private office, before reaching for the hallway door.

The hallway was clear, but the moment they exited, they saw more silhouettes approaching from outside. Down the corridor, the overturning of furniture could be heard. Above the far door, Robinson saw an old camera pointing directly at them and for a second, it felt like they were being watched. But he knew it was paranoia. These buildings had been powerless for centuries.

The girl nodded to some stairs across the hallway and they hastened, passing underneath the solemn eyes of a suited man in a portrait.

The corridor of the second floor was even gloomier than the first, but movement below spurred them on. They passed something marked "Treaty Room," and turned right into another large hall. The smell in that hallway was acrid and pungent, far worse than any render's scent Robinson had experienced before. He couldn't imagine any creature capable of emitting such an odor, but if one existed, he didn't want to meet it.

A set of double doors was open to their left, revealing a large oval room with yellow walls and curtains stained black. There was no place to hide inside. So they turned right instead, straight into the mouth of the abyss.

It was trimmed in gold with doors that had been rent apart. Several cables ran from the roof down through the open cavern and into the darkness. This was where the terrible smell was stemming from. Robinson urged the girl to go back. Before he turned, however, he thought he saw something move.

The girl shoved him out of the way just as a savage's axe struck the wall. Although she was unarmed, she moved with ease, punching him in the throat and ripping his weapon from his hands. More savages arrived, but the girl spun with unexplainable precision and staved the first savage's head. Robinson yelled for her to run, but she refused.

The girl stood her ground, fighting off her attackers, but she was outnumbered. Just as one of the savages stripped her of the axe and readied his killing blow, a large, mutated tentacle exploded out of the shaft and took hold of him. The savage howled as it was pulled into the abyss, his fellow savages swarming after him. But as more tentacles appeared, covered in blood, Robinson grabbed the girl and dragged her into the room adjacent to the oval one. It was a study full of books, chairs, and couches. Beyond were two glass doors and a balcony outside.

"Here!" Robinson yelled, breathless, not knowing how long the creature from the elevator would distract the savages.

The door opened to the sound of fighting on the front grounds as savages battled the renders that had followed them from the park. When the last two were dispatched, Savage Chief ordered his men inside.

When the girl saw Savage Chief, something in her face turned primal. It went beyond hatred. Robinson watched as she squatted down to pick up a large sliver of windowpane glass to use as a weapon.

"Don't," Robinson said, grabbing her arm. Quicker than he thought possible, the glass was at his throat.

"*Nao pengchu*," she hissed.

He slowly raised his hands.

Behind them they heard voices. Below, two savages carried out a third, dropping him at Savage Chief's feet. He had several large wounds in his chest. Savage Chief used his spear to turn the man over, revealing a grisly bite mark on his back. The man pleaded, but they both knew he was infected. In a flash, Savage Chief raised his spear and killed him. Then he howled for the gawkers to return inside.

Before another word could be spoken, the girl vaulted the railing.

The chief must have heard something, because he turned just as she plowed into him. Both hit the ground hard and even from up high, Robinson heard something crack. When the chief rose, his hand went to his head, finding a deep gouge that spilled blood from his ear to his chin.

Despite the excruciating pain he must have felt, Savage Chief sneered. The girl responded by springing to her feet, but then she lurched. Her leg was injured. Chief mocked her, but before he attacked, he tossed her the sword from the savage he'd just killed. She picked it up and they began circling each other.

The girl was a fighter, but Robinson knew she had no chance. He was about to call out in the hope of distracting Chief when he heard voices behind him. Torchlight filled the room. It was only a matter of time until they found him.

On the ground, the girl lashed out with her sword, but Chief easily batted it away. He spun his spear, using long, balanced attacks to toy with her. Only when she stood again did he strike out, slamming the spear into her shoulder, and then her back, followed by the knee of her good leg. With the last strike, she finally went down, but when Chief raised his spear for the killing blow, she spun out of the way and swung the sword at his front foot. He barely lifted it in time.

Chief continued to stalk his prey, but even she knew she couldn't hold him off for long. The frustration showed first on her face and then in her attacks. Each successive strike looked more and more desperate.

Robinson knew he had to do something. Looking around, the only potential weapon he could see was a small pipe fitted to a security camera pointed right at him. He leaped up, grabbed hold of it, and pulled with all his might. The crack echoed loudly as he dropped to his feet. Inside the room, the savages approached the doors. It was now or never.

The girl made one final effort to kill the chief, but he easily dodged her attack and knocked the blade from her hands. The following strike hit her on the side of the head and sent her reeling. Bloodied and dazed, the girl reached for the sword. Chief must have been impressed by her courage, because the words he spoke were soft. Then he raised the spear to finish her off.

The pipe collided with his shoulder just as Robinson slammed into him. The chief went sprawling. The balcony doors above were blown open with a crash as the savages appeared. When they saw the chief down, they howled, and several raced back inside. Robinson knew it would take a few seconds for them to emerge below.

Robinson grabbed the girl under the arm and tried to pull her away. Though bloodied and dazed, she was still intent on finishing off Savage Chief.

"We have to go!" Robinson screamed. This time the girl didn't have the strength to fend him off.

As they pulled away, Robinson heard a guttural snarl and looked back, surprised to see Chief rise to one knee. His eyes were glassy, but they found them in the dark. When he spoke, blood spewed from his mouth. But to his surprise, the threats were not directed at Robinson but at the girl.

"*Nuer Aserra, gui seiva divida wo me.*"

These words almost buckled the girl, but Robinson had no time to contemplate their meaning. The other savages were coming, so he helped her turn as they fled into the night.

Chapter Twenty-Six
Strangers

The trek back to the memorial took even longer than anticipated. The savages were scouring the city. Those they had fled from at the white building had met up with reinforcements. Despite his injuries, Savage Chief had rallied well enough to organize several small parties to cover as much of the city as possible.

Equally concerning were the renders; they had been worked into a frenzy. Denied their monthly feast, they too were looking for any spot of flesh to dine on. Time and again, Robinson and the girl heard clashes between the two forces. They kept moving.

At one time, he considered returning to the library, but it was too far to the southeast. He also knew the girl needed medical aid and as limited as his abilities were, he had far more resources available at the memorial than anywhere else.

So they clung to the city streets, avoiding darkened buildings and alleyways while doing their best to stay in the shadows. The girl was exhausted. Several times, she nearly collapsed. But she trudged on, never once crying out or signalling for rest.

For Robinson's part, the distraction of caring for someone else was a welcome change. He was surprised by his own resilience, relying often on his cloak of oil to throw renders off the scent.

Just when they thought they might have evaded the savages, they heard dogs baying. The girl's former captors were pulling out all the stops to find her. But for as much as those high-pitched cries haunted them, the renders also heard them. They came out en mass to eventually drive the savages back. When the drums started up again, their tempo had changed. Several mobs of savages flew past the duo as they hid in a doorway to a shop. A retreat had been signaled. This allowed a narrow window for the duo to return to the arcade by way of an underground furrow made of black marble stenciled with names. Once on the other side, it was a straight shot back to the memorial.

The girl was reluctant to step into the basket that would lift her over the barricade, but they both knew she had no other option. She was too injured and too tired to leave now and fend for herself. At the same time, Robinson was incredibly nervous allowing someone inside his sanctuary. He had invested so much time in creating it that the thought of risking it for a veritable stranger was daunting.

She was staring at the seated statue when Robinson secured the basket and chain before directing her toward the door. The moonlight spilled through the colored glass above, casting the ancient hero's stern face in a golden glow.

She uttered something, which he thought was, "Who is he?"

"I don't know," he answered. "But he's with me."

That's when Robinson noticed a dark patch of skin under the torn fabric of her upper arm. He recognized it immediately.

"What is this?" he asked, unveiling the inverted V brand. Her hand latched onto his quicker than a snake.

"*Aserra*," she said as if the word contained some great power.

And then her eyes fluttered as she fell unconscious into his arms.

She vaulted from her bedroll with uncanny dexterity for someone who had been unconscious for the better part of three days.

Resi barked and the girl's eyes snapped from him to Robinson as he boiled river water on the opposite side of the room.

"Good morning," he said.

She stared at him for a full three seconds before lunging for the pipe leading inside to the spigot, her closest weapon. Unfortunately, the moment she put weight on her foot, she went down in a heap.

"I'm no healer, but your foot doesn't appear broken, only sprained. I hope you don't mind the boot. I thought it made a pretty good splint."

She stared at the plastic boot on her leg as if it were the most foreign thing in the world. He'd found it in a store after two days of searching. Apparently, the ancients used to wear them when playing games on the snow.

Resi continued to bark until Robinson called his name and said, "Be still."

The bark turned to a growl, but he padded back to his bedding.

"That's Resi," Robinson said. "He won't hurt you." But he added under his breath, "Unless you kill me in my sleep and then maybe."

Robinson offered her a jar of water and a can of dried pigeon meat. "Are you hungry? Thirsty? It's not much, but …"

She looked like a trapped animal, so he set the stuff in front of her.

"Well, it's there if you want it."

He went back to the food prep area to clean. After a few seconds, she slid over to the water and food and ravenously gulped both down.

"I hope you don't mind, but I took the liberty of patching you up some."

He touched his forehead, gesturing where he had stitched up her largest wound, plus the ones to her shoulder and knee. She felt them and her eyes narrowed again. Then she smelt the wound on her shoulder and scowled.

"*Queye zhi uso?*" she asked accusingly.

"Sorry?"

"*Zhi. Zhi!*" She pointed aggressively to her wound. "*Queye zhi uso?!*" Then she rubbed her fingers together like she was pouring salt on a meal.

"Oh, you want to know what medicine I used. Hold on."

Robinson retrieved his can of herbs, showing her the mixture the Old Man had taught him to use on open wounds. She spat out an angry stream of words.

"I don't understand. You're saying I did something wrong?"

She rolled her eyes and took a heavy breath before referencing the herbs one at a time. First, she pointed to the yarrow, and mimed the halt of blood from a wound.

"You're saying it's a coagulant," Robinson said. "To stop blood flow."

She pointed to the second, white willow's bark, and winced.

"And that one relieves pain. Go on."

She pointed to the third, marigold, and then pointed to a scar before "wiping it away."

"Does that mean it speeds up healing or prevents scarring?"

She rolled her eyes, but never clarified. She next pointed to a garlic balm.

"Garlic. Yeah, I know. Back home we use it as a natural antibiotic too."

Her issue was with the next one, a daisy-like plant for which he had no name.

"It shouldn't go inside the wound? You're saying it's for external use only?"

She then angrily motioned for him to smell her shoulder. He winced. It smelled rotten. Then she unleashed another slew of curses, pointing to the stitching he'd done.

"Wait, you don't like my stitching? All things considered, I thought I did … Oh! You want to know what I used. Hold on."

He went to retrieve the needle and thread he'd gotten from the textile shop a few blocks north of the capitol building.

"It's thread. Cotton, I think. But I definitely sterilized the needle."

She looked at the thread and lit into him again, tossing the entire roll away. She then used the needle to rip the stitches out as if she were pulling a few errant hairs. She didn't even blanch when the blood ran down her leg. When Robinson winced, she shook her head with contempt. It was a look he was familiar with.

"Sorry," he said. "I did the best I could."

Afterward, she scrubbed the wounds in water and mixed her own salve.

Robinson watched closely until she signaled for a bandage and he tracked down some clean fabric, which she only used after determining it was clean.

When she was done, she rubbed her eyes wearily. To give himself something to do, Robinson fetched more pigeon.

"*Eryi?*" she asked.

He shrugged. "That's all I have."

She sighed and looked at him and then around the room. She did not seem impressed.

"*Lao hua er furioso?*" she asked quietly, but he didn't understand. "*Furioso,*" she enunciated slowly before making small X's across her chest and miming the action of a ship.

"The savages? They left yesterday. Uh … gone. Do you want to see?"

She followed him outside. Even through the barricade, she could see the arcade and basin were empty. She tested her leg to see how much weight she could put on it.

"We're safe here," Robinson said. "You can stay, if you want."

She scoffed, but there was no anger in it. She had come from a world far more severe than his and had survived, perhaps even flourished. He knew what she saw when she looked at him. To her, he was soft, something less than a man. He was far more likely to hinder her than keep her alive.

And yet he had done just that.

"Aserra," he said. She looked up sharply as he pointed to the brand on her arm. "Is that your people?"

She nodded curtly. "*Observar qian?*" she asked, signaling outside.

Robinson raised a finger. "Once."

Her head tilted toward the obelisk. "*Nali?*"

He shook his head and pointed toward the city. "Out there."

She looked out over the city. "*Hezai ja?*"

He shook his head again. He didn't understand.

"*Gawn?*" she asked.

"Yes. He's gone. I don't know where."

She nodded one last time and then turned and limped from the room. Only when he was alone did it occur to him that he had never asked her name.

Chapter Twenty-Seven
Broken Parts

If he expected her to take it easy—to rest and recover from her injuries—he was sorely mistaken. The first thing the girl did was head inside and grab an old flagpole that she snapped in half to use as a crutch. She then conveyed that Robinson would take her with him as he gathered food. As it was already midday, he tried to convince her that it wasn't a good idea. Not in her condition anyway. That elicited a smile.

In his sixteen years of life, no smile had ever made him feel so small.

They set out to the northwest with Resi in tow, backtracking along the river and the amended food route that had condensed to a twenty-block radius. At each stop, he showed her where he'd set the traps and how he killed and bagged the animals inside.

She stayed silent as he retrieved various forms of bait—worms, snails, and nuts—to make his paste. She never interrupted when he showed her how to rig a snare or flush a bird from a bush. Her eyes took everything in. Only when he collected the final carcasses of two dead rats and put them in his bag did she signal for him to stop.

"Are you tired? Do you need to rest?" he asked.

She indicated that he should hand her the bag. He did. She opened it up, looked inside, and then pitched it over a fence. Without warning, she swung the stick at him as furiously as she could. Robinson swore in pain and tried to avoid the strikes, but they seemed to target every place the Old Man used to hit. All the while, the girl cursed him in her own language, punctuating the various blows with a finger to her head as if he were crazy.

When she finally grew tired of hitting him, she grabbed his ear and dragged him to an open yard where she pulled several squat, maroon roots up by their umbels.

"Are those carrots?" Robinson asked.

She dragged him to a bush, collecting a handful of berries that she thrust under his nose.

"I didn't think those were edible—"

Her tirade continued as she pointed to other plants and his traps, and to the blunt punch in his belt and even to the shard of glass he'd used to strip the animals. Just when he thought he was in real danger, she went silent, shook her head, turned, and walked away.

"W-where are you going?" he yelled.

She never bothered to reply. Robinson stood there, feeling like a fool with the carrots in his hand, wondering what other types of food had been around him all this time.

Then Resi groaned.

"Don't even."

Robinson grabbed any other carrots that were in the vicinity before heading home.

"Man's best friend," he scoffed. "Is that what you call watching my back?"

Resi barked twice.

"It's a little late for apologies. I'm not saying you had to maul her or anything, but maybe just draw a little fire next time?"

He barked again.

"Easy for you to say. You're going to be walking normally tomorrow."

When they got back to the memorial, it was empty. Robinson wasn't concerned. There were still a couple turns of daylight left and really, how far could the girl get on one leg? He stowed his gear, cleaned up, and made another piddling meal for himself and Resi. He lay on his bedroll and pretended to read as the threads of light rose higher on the wall. Only when he was forced to light the candle by his bedside did he consider that she might not be coming back.

And then he heard the basket chain unfurl outside. He leaped up but stopped halfway across the floor. He didn't want to appear relieved by her return, so he busied himself with repairs. Resi barked once when she opened the door, but Robinson didn't even glance in her direction until she dropped a thirty-pound dead sow on the table in front of him. He looked at it, stunned, and then at her. In one hand, she held a rusty old axe and the limb of what looked to be a hickory tree. In the other was a canvas bag full of old clothes and a pair of leather boots.

Before he could ask her how she'd managed to accomplish so much in under three turns, she pulled out a narrow, black-handled knife and slammed it into the table.

"*Tufu porco*," she ordered before walking off to stow her gear.

Robinson had never butchered a pig before, but he wasn't about to argue. He decided to approach it like he had any other kind of meat. He inserted the knife just below the ribcage and pushed deep, but before he could yank it downward, he heard the familiar whistle of her crutch before it struck him across the shoulder blades.

"Ow!" he cried. "What was that for?"

"Ow! Ow!" She seemed to take pleasure in mocking him. Then she grabbed the knife, pushed him aside, and carefully cut the pig's abdomen before pulling out its entrails. When Robinson moved to throw them away, she spun the knife and hit him hard across the knuckles. He nearly screamed but held his tongue.

"Ow?" she mocked again.

She fingered the entrails and pointed to her bandages. "*Categute*." She followed up by miming the action of drawing a bow and arrow. "Categute."

"Seriously? That's revolting."

She stripped the fat away before cleaning out the fecal matter. Then she filled a pan with cold water and set it aside. She pointed to the carcass.

"Once," she said.

Then the knife flew. She cut off the head in two quick strokes, sliced along the backbone, separating the shoulders from the ribs and the ribs from the loins. She wasted no energy while she worked. The meat was cut cleanly. When she was done, she pointed for most to go into the smoker but signaled that Robinson should cook the belly.

While he prepared dinner, she washed and redressed her wounds. Then she withdrew a natural whetstone to clean and sharpen the blade of her axe. Robinson had no idea where she'd gotten it, but even her circular strokes seemed effortless. After a few minutes, she stopped and glared at him. He quickly went back to work.

Supper that night was among the finest he'd ever had. Even Resi agreed, since he spent a turn afterward at the girl's feet. Later, he came back with a raw shank bone to gnaw on until a light rain fell and his eyes grew heavy.

Robinson laid down on his bedroll and read from a book. Though he didn't know why, he read aloud. The girl had moved on to sharpening her knife, but her strokes were slow and steady. Even from afar he could tell she was listening, though she didn't understand the words. He had expected her to call out and silence him, but she didn't. These were new lands to her, as were his customs, and she greeted them not with a blunt hammer, but with the silence of one searching for a deeper understanding.

After a quick breakfast of leftover pork and leeks, the girl bid Robinson gather his things and they headed out along the river to the north and west, away from the capitol and deeper inland where the buildings grew smaller and tracts of land blossomed. The morning was cold—winter was just around the corner—but there was still a bounty of vegetation for her to identify and him to collect.

As they moved farther west, paved roads fell to dirt ones, and then none at all. This was where she flourished. She pointed out the tracks of animals, striking Robinson's legs with the stick when he didn't recognize ones she had already named. She showed him the pattern of Resi's gait and compared it to a group of similar prints, which he inferred was from a pack of wild dogs that were to be given a wide berth.

In the countryside, the girl singled out hidden rabbit warrens and a giant, shelled creature that floated in the water. It was too far away to catch, but she seemed to suggest it would make a tasty meal. Fallen trees and lodges also boasted beavers and muskrats, though she seemed less eager to hunt for them. And she refused to hunt anything they did not eat.

Occasionally, they stumbled upon the tracks of renders, but most looked several days old and rarely gave the girl pause.

As the territory grew more bucolic, the girl's step seemed less hobbled, as if the land somehow imbued a power that revitalized not only her body but also her spirit. Again and again, Robinson found himself watching her as she moved fluidly across the terrain with an understanding of its dangers and an appreciation of its beauty. Implicit in this was its ability to sustain them so long as they never took it for granted.

Blood continued to soak the wound at her brow, though her shoulder and knee appeared to be on the mend. Even the boot seemed less cumbersome, yet it frustrated her greatly. The biggest surprise was her face. As the swelling receded, Robinson saw she wasn't as unattractive as he'd previously believed. In fact, her face was quite comely in its own way. Even her strong nose, which had clearly been broken at some point, gave her appearance a character that belied a deeper femininity. And yet it was the eyes he couldn't turn away from. They were a vivid green, deep as a forest and yet flecked with chips the color of the sun. Every time a hawk called or a cloud rumbled, she would look into the sky, and he would look into her. But these moments were always met with the inevitable whistle of wood and the familiarity of pain.

Even then, Robinson thought of Tessa. When the girl's black tresses blew in the chilled wind, he felt his hands running through his betrayer's flaxen curls. When in some unintentional moment he brushed against her bronze skin so laden with sweat and scars, he felt only the cool smoothness of perfumed flesh both pale and luminous. One smelled of earth, the other of sky. One broke his body, the other had broken his heart. Both wounds were transformative, leaving something stouter in their place.

On far away ridges, they saw deer grazing. Once, the girl picked up a clod of dirt and tossed it at a small herd. Even before it hit the ground, they were galloping away. She mimed the use of a bow and arrow when she saw fowl in the sky. Then she would point to the north, implying they would be gone before the first snow fell.

When they crested a small hill, the girl immediately ducked down and waved him over. There, on the opposite side, was a score of bovine—large and hardy—chewing grass and cud without care. She spoke excitedly—this was what she had been searching for. Her head spun around and then she pointed to a small farmhouse on a ridge to the south. They backed away and set out for it.

Robinson wasn't sure what she had planned at the farmhouse, but it was already past midday. Unless they were going to spend the night there, they had maybe a turn before they had to start back for the city. He also didn't want to risk losing Resi, who was digging at a rabbit hole on the other side of the field.

As they crossed the vacant yard, Robinson suddenly felt an ill foreboding. The dilapidated structure looked sturdy enough, but something about its remoteness bothered him. He couldn't say why. And then a curtain in the upstairs window moved.

"Did you see that?" he said, halting in his tracks.

She went still, her eyes scanning every part of the house. But then a gust of wind blew and the curtain swayed again. Her shoulders slackened and she smirked.

When they reached the porch, the girl tested the boards carefully with the heel of her boot. The wood groaned, but it was in no danger of collapse. Still, she pulled the axe from her bag and used its toe to push the door open.

The house smelled of must, but not of renders. Most of the windows were unbroken. If they had to stay there, they'd be safe for the night. The girl knew it too. She was already entering the second room when the front door slammed. They turned and saw the man. He was dressed in dirty rags from head to toe and held a rusty, curved blade in his hand. When he opened his mouth, revealing a handful of blackened teeth, it was not to smile but to whistle.

That's when five other men stepped from the shadows and surrounded them.

Chapter Twenty-Eight
Aserra

They stood silent and ready, all holding weapons. They had done this before. They had no intention of taking captives. The only questions were how long it would take and when it would begin.

The answers came quickly when the tallest one near the stairs made a sound with his tongue. But before the air left his mouth, the girl was in motion, drawing the knife from her belt and tossing it to Robinson. Unfortunately, his hands were shaking so badly, he failed to catch it and it clattered to the floor. When he bent to grab it, he felt the air above his head move with the whistle of something that sunk into the wall behind him.

For her part, the girl didn't panic or hesitate. She took a single step back, twisted under the descending arc of the doorman's blade, and cleaved off his jaw with a single swipe of her axe. He let out an inhuman wail as he tumbled forward, but she caught him under the arm and spun him just as a one-armed foe let a spiked ball connected to a chain fly. It landed with a wet, sick thud in the first man's chest, ending his cries and his life. But before the flail could be drawn free, the girl pirouetted backward with unbelievable speed, her good leg whipping hard across the back of the dead man's knees. As his torso pitched backward, the one-armed man was wrenched forward and in one motion, the girl lopped off his remaining hand at the wrist before flinging the axe into the kitchen, where it struck the head of a man loading a bolt into a crossbow.

The man teetered there for what seemed like an eternity before he fell back with a sickening plop. Everyone in the room suddenly froze. It had taken less than three seconds, but half their party was dead or maimed—all at the hands of a skinny girl.

The most astonishing part was that she was barely breathing. When she glanced at Robinson, it appeared as if all the green had gone out of her eyes, replaced by something black. She didn't look surprised or affected by the fact that the leader now had his hand wrapped around her companion's mouth or his blade positioned at his throat.

Truth be told, Robinson didn't understand why he was still alive. And then he heard the man whisper the word.

"Aserra."

It was tinged with awe and reverence, but mostly fear. When the assailants in the kitchen heard it, both seemed to wither as if the air had been let out of them. Robinson looked at the girl and saw the brand on her arm was showing, but by then, the men knew what they were up against. He even thought that the one in the kitchen might run when he turned and looked at the back door. But that hesitation cost him.

The second half of the battle came as quickly as the first, but this time it was on the girl's terms. One moment she was standing empty handed, the next she had a blade in it and was racing across the room. To his credit, the leader didn't bother killing Robinson. He knew it would only cost him time. Instead, he pushed the teen out of the way so he and his companions could attack the girl simultaneously. When Robinson fell to the floor, he covered his head to avoid the scuffle and closed his eyes. The din that followed was pure horror: the clash of metal, grunts and shrieks, the spray of blood, and the rattle of the dying.

When he finally looked up, the girl stood alone, a single stitch of red lining her forearm. He must have gasped because she turned and pointed the blade at him, her eyes momentarily wild.

"It's me," he said, his hands in the air.

The girl looked through him before lowering the blade and turning away.

"Are they … all dead?" Robinson asked.

The girl didn't answer. She was too busy examining their weapons. The leader's blade was by far the best of them, but when she looked at it closely, she saw faults in the steel and eventually put it under her boot and broke it in half. The weapon she was most interested in was the crossbow, but it was in poor shape too. By the way the man had handled it and how it had misfired over Robinson's head despite his being so close, it was obviously worthless. She destroyed it as well.

When Robinson stood up, his heart was still hammering in his chest and he gagged from the smell that had filled the room. And then he heard a whimper and saw the man with no hands sobbing softly, his new stump in the cradle of his old one. The girl crossed to him and he murmured a few words. It was unclear if they were pleas of mercy or something else, but when the girl went to retrieve her axe, Robinson quietly slipped out the door.

Outside, he closed his eyes, trying to forget everything he'd seen, but the void was quickly filling up with such memories and he knew if he was to survive with his sanity intact, he needed to accept that such events were a part of his new life. Only by learning from them might he avoid similar situations in the future. He also knew he had relied on others for far too long. The Old Man, the girl, and even Resi had at some point saved him.

It was time to start looking after himself.

Inside, he heard the girl opening closets and cupboards, but she didn't find what she was looking for. She exited a short while later and made her way to a detached garage. Robinson followed her there only to see her dig out an old shovel and a pickaxe with half a handle.

They made it home just before sunset, but already the chill had seeped in. Robinson started a fire in the stove, but the smoke brought out the renders. He knew the barricade would hold them, but their incessant buzz was like a wooden sliver sunk deep beneath the skin. It grew worse and worse until finally he climbed onto the roof and flung several full cans of oil over the side. The beasts pulled back but didn't fully retreat until morning.

The girl ate mechanically. Resi sat at her feet, having sensed something bad had happened. Robinson tried to think of something that would make her feel better but nothing came to mind. Only when she made for her bed did it hit him.

"Teach me," he said.

She turned, her face wary but curious. Robinson pointed to the brand on her arm.

"Aserra," he said before pointing to himself. "Teach me."

Her grim expression softened, but he didn't like what had replaced it.

She stepped close—closer than they had ever been—and tapped him on the bicep and said, "Aserra." She tapped him lightly on the head and said, "Aserra." She tapped her own stomach and said, "Aserra." Then she touched his and shook her head.

He didn't need to speak her language to understand. She was saying he didn't have the stomach for it. He didn't have the heart. It was a blow that rivaled Tessa's deception. It might have hurt even worse because this one wasn't born of some petty cause or political strife, but of his own failings.

He wanted to run away. He wanted to hide. He felt an incredible sense of shame, but when his gaze fell, she lifted his chin with her hand and then walked over, picked up a book, and handed it to him.

"*Nian*," she said.

"You want me to read this?"

She nodded. "Read."

Robinson read well into the night, his voice echoing lightly under the glass that bore a star-laden sky. They were separated by the breadth of the room, but that night, they felt closer. His words and her presence were a comfort to each other where nothing else would do.

How strange, he thought, that she could be so proficient at killing and yet feel so low because of it. She was like a beautiful flower whose stem was riddled with thorns. Robinson knew that nature often secured its greatest treasures in hardened shells, making sure any that valued them won their prize only with patience and considerable effort.

Chapter Twenty-Nine
Friday

The next day he found out what the shovel was for. They returned to the field near the farmhouse and crossed over the low cliff where the bovine fed. The girl walked the circumference of a ravine, eventually settling on a section of narrows where she tossed Robinson the shovel and ordered him to dig. It was backbreaking work, but Robinson came to enjoy the strike of the blade, the weight of the earth, and the cadence of his swing. Resi watched from the lip of the trench as the girl hobbled off. He heard the crack of wood as she swung her axe. Only a few turns later when they broke for lunch did Robinson see that she had cut several small tree limbs and shaped the ends to a point. He knew then they were building a deadfall and if her plan worked—as they almost always did—they'd have beef that night. The idea made his mouth water.

After the spears were set, Robinson climbed from the hole as the girl dragged branches and leaves over the top until it was well disguised. She then drew up a plan of attack in which they would chase the bovine down the ravine, into the narrows, and toward the deadfall. When she was finished, she looked to him for confirmation and he shrugged. Mistake. The stick whistled. He howled. Resi's yap sounded surprisingly like a laugh.

The plan did not go quite as expected. They managed to get behind the

146

bovine and chase them into the ravine, but as they neared the narrows, they'd forgotten about Resi. The minute he saw the creatures, he charged. The bovines knotted up and quickly turned toward the pair. Robinson was lucky enough to scramble up the side of a hill to escape the stampede. The girl, unfortunately, dove into a pond full of mud. When she emerged sodden and simmering, Robinson bellowed. She immediately went after him. He ran down the ravine laughing. He was afraid the hobbled girl might skewer him with her spear when she yelled. Down the ravine, one bovine was returning with Resi hot on its tail. Together, Robinson and the girl waved their arms, driving the animal into the narrows. A few seconds later, they heard a crash and a cry. When they arrived at the trap, they looked down to see the bovine was dead.

Robinson let out a triumphant roar and hugged the girl. She hit him three times with the stick, but for the first time, she smiled.

Getting the meat back to the memorial would be no easy task. The girl indicated that Robinson should find two large branches on which they would drag the carcass, but he ran back to the farmhouse instead and returned with the molded canoe from the garage. She looked it over and gave a curt nod of approval.

"Aserra," he said lightly. "Teach me."

She grinned but shook her head again.

"No?" he asked.

"No," she answered.

Robinson shrugged and started transferring the butchered meat.

The next two weeks went on the same. They rose early and hunted, fed the smoker in the afternoon, and he read after dinner.

After each meal he would ask, "Aserra?" And she would shake her head and say, "No."

The snow finally came around the first week of December. The city was bathed in a pastoral white.

They had amassed enough meat to make it through the winter, but it was still bitterly cold in the memorial. Steadily, the girl's leg got better until one day she took the boot off and tossed it into the river. She then constructed a pole to fish the river with, collecting only those that weren't blighted.

With the weather came one welcomed dividend. The renders seemed to vanish from the city. Robinson soon learned they were only hibernating. When he and the girl stumbled upon a warren of sleeping renders while hunting for supplies, she prepared to kill them, but he reminded her of her own words: people should only kill what they eat.

With the rivers frozen over, the savages could not return. Robinson never asked the girl about them and she never volunteered anything, but several times, when she thought he was busy, he would catch her looking toward the monument with that forlorn look that said, like him, she had a whole other life waiting elsewhere.

His duties fell to collecting firewood and reading bedtime tales, but he also kept the roof clean of snow and patched the areas where rain seeped in. When the weather was really cruel, he repaired the pipes that led to the indoor privy. When he showed the girl how it worked, she made the sign of evil but eventually used it, albeit grudgingly.

The wood stove burned well enough, but it proved too small to heat the entire room, so Robinson went back to the library and began reading up on various energy sources. He was shocked how many there were and by their complexity. He was surprised that the previous civilization could engineer such things as thermal, chemical, radiant, nuclear, and electric power. Most were beyond his understanding. But he did understand that at the height of the previous civilization, petroleum was one of the chief sources of energy and that it was the same stygian oil he had gathered from the park to fend off the renders.

Processing it would be no easy task. Theoretically, it all came down to boiling. By using superheated steam, he was able to run the oil through a distillation chamber that, at different temperatures, separated the hydrocarbons into various groupings: petroleum gas, naphtha, liquid gasoline, kerosene, diesel, lubricating oil, fuel oil, and some residuals. He collected these in old bottles, most often slender and colored white, green or brown with names like Coca-Cola and Budweiser stenciled across them.

He scavenged tubing where he could find it and polyester sheeting for filters. Lastly, he boiled moldy rubber tires for seals.

Again, it was trial and error learning to collect the individual hydrocarbons, which was why he built his small refinery downwind and only ran it during the day. On the third day, while he was out retrieving tubing, he heard an explosion and knew the distillery had blown. Thankfully, he had built the refinery in the rubble of a burned building, so nothing else could be destroyed. He was not deterred by this failure, no matter how often the girl made her gestures to ward off evil.

The following week, he succeeded at gathering a healthy sum of liquid gasoline, kerosene, and oil. The oil he used for lubrication. The liquid gasoline, he discovered, was incredibly volatile, and although he did not want to lose it, he decided to store it in barrels near the river, far enough from the memorial to stay safe, but close enough that, should the need arise, he could get to them. He chose the kerosene as his method of every day fuel since it burned cleanly and seemed the easiest to store. He then fashioned a small boiler from an old steel sink, which he connected to the building's old furnace. Although it smelled terrible for several days, it did keep their home quite toasty.

Resi also seemed to thrive, although he spent more and more time with the girl despite the fact that Robinson fed him and let him out when nature called. One day, the girl invented a game by which they chased Resi with curved sticks and the one who could grasp his collar and bring him down into the snow was the winner. The girl almost always won, but Robinson thought it was mostly due to Resi feeling sorry for her.

The fiercest storm came at the end of December and for two long weeks, they remained confined inside. Robinson was reading through the latest collection of books for the second time when he noticed something hanging from the wall. It was a calendar turned oddly enough to December.

He looked to the girl and said, "You know, I still don't know your name." The girl looked at him strangely. "I mean we are living together. And will be at least until spring. Don't you think we should be on a first name basis by now?"

Her eyes narrowed the way they always seemed to when he'd overstepped himself.

"Fine, I'll start," he said, pointing to himself. "I am *Robinson. Robinson Crusoe.* And you are?"

When he pointed to her, she looked very self-conscious.

"Me, *Robinson Crusoe,*" he said again. "You …?"

"*Yolareinai-esa-tu-shin-zhi-ma-coctera-wal-pan-bayamasay-fri.*"

He shook his head and then asked her to repeat it. She did.

"That's quite a mouthful. Honestly, I was hoping for something a bit shorter. See, me, *Robinson Crusoe.* Short and sweet." He held his hands together. "You, Yobo-sata-singa-whatever." He held his hands far part. "Do you have a nickname?"

"Cru-soe," she said.

"Yes! Like Crusoe. I am *Crusoe.* And you?"

"Bayamasay-fri?"

"Closer, but still …" And then he noticed some words scribbled on the calendar. The ink was faded but he could just make out, "Thank God it's Friday!"

"Fri-day. How about 'Friday'?"

She considered it and shrugged.

"Great. Friday, I am Crusoe. It's a pleasure to make your acquaintance."

He held out his hand for her to shake, but she slapped it away.

"Okay. Baby steps," he said. "But I'll make a civilized girl out of you yet."

He was about to sit back down when she stopped and pointed to the water spigot and asked a question.

"Sorry, I missed the first part. And the middle and the end."

She spoke again, this time pointing to the spigot, then to the pipes that led to the furnace, and then to the privy.

"Are you asking me *how* I built these things?"

She nodded. He turned and grabbed a book, holding it out for her.

"The wealth of the world is inside, milady. All you have to do is open one."

She took the book and paged through several sections.

"Teach me," she said.

Robinson smiled. "And in return, you teach me to fight."

She paused, and then nodded. "Friday teach Cru-soe … *fight*." But then she raised a finger and shook her head. "No Aserra."

"Deal."

He held out his hand and this time she took it.

Chapter Thirty
Fire and Ice

And so began the days of fire and ice, of a boy broken and a man reborn. They rose each morning at the crack of dawn and struck out into the city. The first lessons were of balance and speed and the two were always in motion. They ran along paths slick with ice and atop the rims of the tallest buildings. They scaled stairs and bridges, danced over the rocks on the edge of high falls. They leaped, they crawled, and they climbed and never stopped.

At night, Robinson read aloud to her, enunciating words and ideas while his body soaked in secret salves. He explained the basics of English and math. Whenever some subject frustrated her, she scolded him for not explaining it better. When the light lit her eyes with some new wisdom, he felt his heart beam with pride.

She had an appetite for learning that rivaled any he had ever known.

If the nights were full of words, the days were full of pain. Not a turn went by when Robinson wasn't bleeding from some cut, scrape, or gouge. His hands were nicked, fingers and toes twisted. Every muscle in his body was bruised and swollen. Every patch of skin was scabbed over or worn raw. When they fought hand to hand, she held nothing back. His reward that first month? He touched her once.

When February arrived, they concentrated on efficiency and awareness and how everything that surrounded them could be a tool to hinder or aid. Robinson learned about the power of first strikes and the necessity to always do the maximum damage possible.

She pushed his body beyond endurance. He dove into freezing waters. He walked over coals of fire as her people did as a rite of passage. He bloodied his hands against trees and built up scar tissue on his shinbones. He learned the greatest hurdle in life was pain, and that by mastering it, anything was possible.

Her philosophy extended to her own lessons and she worked diligently to learn as much from this boy as she could. But whereas her physical skills were without rival, her ability to process the more conventional aspects of language and math eluded her. Still, before long, they had developed a kind of pidgin tongue using both their languages. They discussed the ancients, their ways, their politics, and religions. The only subjects that were off limits were their pasts and loved ones.

In March, as the snow melted, they moved on to weapons. Robinson trained with countless types that they had scrounged from the city. Swords, axes, staves, and bows, the latter of which Friday had made herself. He used daggers, hammers, pikes, and clubs. The goal wasn't to be proficient with all of them, but to determine what weapons best suited his body and style. In the end, Friday chose two for him.

The first was a pair of tomahawks that they had found in a war museum. The handles were made from something called ironwood that was, as its name suggested, very hard, but also weather resistant. The blades were alloy steel and impossibly sharp.

Despite his effectiveness with the axes and the damage they could do, Robinson's favorite weapon was the sling. Running as fast as his legs could carry him, he could hurl a rock fifty meters and hit the target almost every time. More often than not, his shots were dead on.

He trained with these weapons at every session. Friday grew more intense but also closer. His determination impressed her, but she had not expected him to display such skill.

One afternoon, she pulled him aside.

"Cru-soe. Come. See for me."

She walked him to a nearby clothing store and pointed to an old mirror.

The transformation was astounding. He didn't even recognize himself. He'd grown six inches in the last ten months. But more impressive was his body, which had developed thick, lean muscles that stretched like leather cords and rippled with each movement. His hair fell to his shoulders and he had some scruff on his face, but his skin was a rich tan that glowed. His jawline stood out prominently, featuring high cheekbones he'd never known he had. They were his father's cheekbones.

"You are man," she said.

He looked at her and for the first time, the disdain was gone from her face. And that's when he realized how truly beautiful she was.

"And you are a woman."

He reached for her hand. To his surprise, she let him take it.

That night, they lay entwined as all lovers do, but they were still strangers in many ways. His heart ached to know her, to learn of her past and ease her pains. At the same time, he was happy. If he had his wish, he would have stayed there by her side forever.

"Cru-soe," she spoke softly. Her English had gotten better, but she still sprinkled it with words of her own from time to time. "Spring comes. The rivers thaw. Soon the renders will wake and black sails will fill skies again."

"Surely they won't still be looking for you?"

"The Bone Flayers, as we name them, believe they eat soul of enemies when they die. And none is greater than *Aserra*. My ... um ... *tao?*"

"Escape," he said.

"My e-scape will bring much shame to Chieftain. He will not sleep until he finds me."

"So you want to go?"

She nodded.

"And you want me to come with you?"

She nodded again, but this time there was reluctance there.

"But there's some other business, isn't there?" She didn't know that word. "Something in the way?" He searched her eyes. "Ah. Not something. *Someone*."

She turned to face him. "I am promised to *Cimoshi*."

"Who's that?"

"Not 'who.' 'What.' Among the Aserra, the Cimoshi is our greatest warrior. It means, he who fights from summit."

"And will he fight for you?"

"After tonight?" She shrugged. "But he fight for honor. Honor is everything to the Aserra."

"How far away are they?"

"The Aserra does not stay long in one place. They will be hard to find. Weeks, months, years. But find them I will. They are my *tun* and *lua*. My sun and moon."

"Then we better pack well."

This time her smile betrayed her youth. When she pulled him close and kissed him, he felt the kind of reckless abandon he had never felt with Tessa.

"How long will it take to get ready?" Friday asked.

"One day, two. We'll need ... how do you say, provisions? And proper clothes. Travelling south won't be easy."

And suddenly the night was rocked by a blast that boomed over the city. Resi leaped to his feet and barked. Friday was reaching for her axe when something bright and loud whooshed by overhead.

"It can't be," he said as he stumbled out of bed. "Not now. Not after all this time."

He ran for the ladder to the roof, scaling it in an instant. When he spilled out into the night, he was oblivious to the bitter cold and the scrim of stars that stretched across the sky. He ran to the edge of the building, shocked by the sight before him.

Friday appeared at his side, wrapped in a blanket, her eyes wide and fearful.

"Cru-soe," she asked. "What is it?"

"My people," he answered, staring at the flyer as it hovered over the city. "They've finally come."

Chapter Thirty-One
Rousings

The flyer circled twice before it banked hard and set off to the east. Even at night, Robinson could see the contrails lit by the pulsing of the thrusters.

"How do you know this is your people?"

"Because the flyers are ours. Friday, it has to be my father. He's the only one who would come this far for me. We have to go find him."

"This moment? But the ice thaws and we have no trail."

"All the more reason to set out before daybreak. We can cross the bridge upstream and stick to the streets. If you've taught me anything, it's how to move safely and trust my eyes and feet. We can't afford to wait."

As if on cue, the first howl cut through the night and echoed over the city. It was high, raw, and full of menace. Others also quickly followed it.

"The sonic blast," Robinson said. "It must have roused them."

"The renders are at their most deadly after long winters. They wake starving. Even the sun will not turn them away."

"Then I'll leave in the morning."

She heard the resolution in his voice, so she said, "I will accompany you."

Neither slept that night. But once dawn arrived, they dressed quickly and grabbed their weapons before heading out into the street. The sky held a smattering of clouds infused with pink and violet colors that would soon blend to gold.

Robinson withdrew a map he'd scavenged from the library.

"Last time we saw the flyer, it was headed southeast—in this general direction. But since the river is impassable all along here, we'll need to head north and cross this bridge here."

"Once we pass, everything is open. We will be … what is word for *exposto?*"

"Exposed. I know, but if we keep moving, we should be all right. Resi! You ready, boy?"

Resi barked, but his ears were up. He could smell the hazards in the air.

"Good. You're our eyes and ears today. Don't let us down."

They had hoped to make the bridge within a turn, but after a few blocks, they knew that would be impossible. Render tracks were everywhere. Not only in the streets, where streaks of grime and decay led from every doorway and hovel, but to the yards and fields where animals had been dragged from their warrens or torn from nests in trees. Even worse, many renders had turned on their own kind. In several places, they saw lumps of clothing soiled with black blood, with the streaks leading into nearby buildings.

Friday had also been right about the renders braving the daylight turns. Twice they were set upon by packs. The first was turned back when Friday let loose two arrows, striking the leader and killing him in an instant. The remaining monsters dragged his body away, some already feasting on his flesh.

The second pack was larger, but after a few short blocks, Robinson and Friday outran them.

They had conditioned Resi not to bark in the city, but his low growls, raised hackles, and flared ears were always a sign that danger was near.

They moved north on Virginia and up 24th Street, but as they passed some kind of university there, Resi stopped.

"Come on, Resi. Keep up."

He didn't move.

"What is it, boy?" Robinson asked. "Do you see something?"

He barked twice and kept looking back at the university.

"He knows this place," she said.

"Well, we don't have the time to stop. Maybe when we come back this way, we'll let him give us a tour. Right now, we need to keep moving."

Robinson patted his leg, but to his surprise, Resi suddenly dotted across the campus and disappeared. He called after him but he never came back.

"We stay or go?" Friday asked.

Robinson was torn, but he shook his head. "We don't have the time to go chasing after him now. Plus he knows how to get back to the memorial. He'll be fine."

"We will miss his nose."

"Thankfully, we still have yours."

Friday punched Robinson and he laughed.

They jogged along an old freeway and made their way to the Key Bridge. The years had worn it down. In places, they had to help each other over sections that had eroded and fallen away, but they soon made it to the other side and continued south along the water.

While they walked, Friday opened up about the Aserra, whom she said translated to People of the Mountain. They had lived in the harsh highlands to the north, back even before the days of the Great Rendering. When the plague first struck, people fled the city in droves, many hoping to find refuge in those hills. But they came too fast and too many and the mountain dwellers were forced to turn them away. Many lives were lost, but the People of the Mountain persevered.

For the next hundred years, they safeguarded their borders and lived off the land, swearing off the technology that they believed nearly fostered the end of Man. But mountain life was not easy. Other clans of survivors wanted what they had. So they became a warrior state, like the Spartans. Robinson had read about them in the library of congress; the Spartans trained their children in the arts of combat from the day they were born. Their ability to defeat any foe—no matter how vastly outnumbered—helped cement their reputation and instill fear in all their enemies.

But reputations were not always a good thing. A few decades before Friday was born, one of the Aserra betrayed his people by smuggling ancient weapons onto their land. These explosives helped lead an attack by the Bone Flayers, the same savages that hunted them today. Only one in ten survived, but those that did made a pact to strike out on their own and reseed the people where they could. When the time was right, it was foretold one among them would reunite the clans and help them rise again.

"I told you the man who first saved me was Aserra." She nodded that she remembered. "He'd been a captive too. I didn't know it at the time, but he had cut off his own hand to escape. The strength it must have taken to do that—"

"This not strength! The Aserra never flee! He should have welcomed death proudly by killing as many enemies as he could before he fell. The Goddess of the Mountain will never open her halls to such man. It's no surprise he lives in shadow and shame."

"But, Friday," Robinson said carefully. "You escaped too."

"Not to run and hide. I will return to my people, tell them what I saw here, and soon we will return and wipe all sign of the Bone Flayers from the earth so the only black that fills skies again is smoke from their ships burning across water. Then and only then will I seek Goddess to atone for my sins. This I swear on the blood of the Aserra."

"Well, let's hope that day doesn't come any time soon."

He thought she might smile, until a string of loud cracks reverberated over the basin.

"What is that?" Robinson asked.

"Weapons of ancients. Not many remain, but from time to time, we run across them."

"They came from the same direction as the flyer flew. Come on."

As they continued down the road, they passed a faded sign on the ground that read: PENTAGON - 2 MILES.

Chapter Thirty-Two
Buried Secrets

True to its name, the pentagon had five sides of equal dimensions. It was a squat, gray building of four or five stories with small windows and heavy fortifications. Friday looked at Robinson and saw they were thinking the same thing: it'll be very dark inside.

There was no sign of the flyer as they drew near. They decided to circle the building to check the other entrances, but the building was secure. They weren't even sure if this was where the cracks had come from or where the flyer had gone, but something told Robinson it was an important piece of the puzzle.

After three quarters of a turn, they returned to the front of the structure where two large doors of glass stood atop a portico. The sun probed only a few meters within.

Friday said, "I am not wanting to go inside, Crusoe. I have—how do you say?"

"A bad feeling."

"Or two."

"Lucky for you, I have these." He pulled out his tomahawks and grinned.

She rolled her eyes and set her bow and quiver of arrows behind a tree.

She then twirled her staff and signaled for him to go ahead.

"Ladies first."

She cracked him across the leg.

"I no lady."

"After last night, we'll have to agree to disagree."

She cracked him again and he busted out laughing.

"Okay, okay," he said and opened the door. "As her Highness commands."

The stench that first hit them confirmed their worst fears. Renders were here.

The initial corridor was decently lit and many faded photos hung on the walls. In one, Robinson saw an aerial photo of the Pentagon itself and it revealed that the interior of the building was once a courtyard. He pointed it out to Friday.

A slew of ancient equipment sat toppled over in the lobby, gathering dust. On the floor were the blackened remnants of this country's flag, its once red, white, and blue colors faded and eaten by moths.

Thankfully, the corridor was wide, but the farther they strode from the doors, the more the darkness consumed. Scant light poured in through the windows in the offices on both sides, but there were more than enough shadows to keep their senses tingling.

They moved cautiously and silently. They had become an efficient team, well versed in communicating by the subtlest of movements. Many of the offices they looked in had been ransacked. Desks were overturned, books torn apart. Here and there they saw claw marks but more often, the rifling looked organized.

In an interior office, Robinson looked out of the window into the central courtyard. The park-like grounds that once existed were now overrun with plant life. Ivy covered most of the walls and trees. High grass obscured the rest of the view. Only one narrow angle afforded him a glimpse of what he'd been searching for.

The flyer was there.

Robinson nodded to Friday and they continued down the hall. He was looking for an entrance to the courtyard when another series of cracks rang out. Both Friday and he hit the ground.

"Does that sound close?" Robinson asked.

"I cannot tell."

They waited until they were sure they were in no immediate danger before they got up and continued down the hall. Eventually, they reached an intersection where a doorway led to the courtyard. Unfortunately, a structural collapse blocked the way. They continued down the next hallway where the stench of renders grew more pungent. Friday touched her nose and Robinson nodded. They moved even slower.

Somewhere inside they heard a shout and then laughter. Part of Robinson wanted to rush forward, yelling for his father, but he knew it would be foolhardy. If such an act didn't draw an attack from renders, it would surely draw one from Friday, who always chose caution first. Still, Robinson believed in his heart that his people were here looking for him and were most likely going room-by-room searching for evidence of his survival.

At the end of the hall appeared a set of steel doors with the words "TOP SECRET CLEARANCE ONLY" written across them. One door was slightly ajar, so they peeled it back and peered inside. The smell hit Robinson like a punch. Friday motioned for him to pull back, but they both knew that wasn't going to happen.

Robinson's palms were moist and sweat ran down the middle of his back, soaking his shirt. As he opened the doors, a loud creak echoed down the hall. Friday's focus reminded him to measure his breathing and take slow steps on the balls of his feet while always maintaining a good center of balance.

To their right was an open door with something on the floor. Robinson bent down to pick it up, turning it over in his hands before raising it to his nose.

"What is it?" Friday whispered.

"Barley bread from Reg5. My favorite."

He felt giddy and nervous as he entered the room, first checking behind the door as he'd been taught. It was a basic room, filled with one upturned desk in the corner and a series of large, metallic cabinets lining the walls. On the floor in front of the cabinets were a few wooden crates with "GRAIN – REG6, Township Shir'ton" stenciled on them.

Robinson realized someone from Isle Prime had been in this very room.

Friday signaled that she would wait outside while he looked around. Robinson waded through the open files that were strewn across the floor but could make nothing out. One cabinet stood open with a number of files removed. The file index read: Security Protocol: Omega 4 / FENIX 1.2.1. / Satellite Imagery [ASIA].

He didn't understand what he was seeing but knew it was important.

"Friday? You're not going to believe this, but someone from back home—"

He stepped out into the hallway only to find her gone.

"Friday?"

A wave of nerves crept up Robinson's spine. He pulled out his tomahawks and scanned the hall. The metal doors to his left remained closed. To his right, the hallway plunged into darkness. He was about to call out again but knew Friday would disapprove. So he walked forward slowly instead, even as the smell of renders grew stronger. The first two rooms were empty. But at the end of the hall, he saw an open door with two rectangular, blacked out windows. He gave the door a wide berth before looking inside.

Friday was standing just within the threshold, deep in shadow. Her sword was out and ready, but she wasn't moving. Something had spooked her and now it was spooking Robinson. He blew air through his teeth to get her attention. Her eyes flashed to him and then all hell broke loose.

The creature, a render of impossible size, sprang out of the shadows, roaring straight at Friday. She raised her sword but had no time to swing it. The beast howled as it swung its enormous arm, slamming into a bookcase that Friday dove to avoid. The bookcase hit the door a fraction of a second before Robinson did, slamming it closed. He rammed it as hard as he could, but it would not give.

The next mighty roar was followed by Friday's call as she was batted into the rectangular windows, bringing their shades down. The render slapped the equipment on the center table and ripped a curtain covering the interior windows, giving the room a modicum of light. Robinson watched Friday drop hard to the floor, only to rise as the behemoth stormed her again.

He screamed her name at the top of his lungs while his tomahawks hit the door over and over. It failed to give. A security mesh ran inside the glass, so the windows couldn't be broken either. Inside, Robinson saw Friday duck a blow and slice the render across the hamstring. It stumbled back. He thought that would give her the time she needed to finish him off. Then the second render appeared, boxing her in.

Chapter Thirty-Three
A Familiar Face

"BEHIND YOU!" Robinson screamed.

Friday spun just as the smaller render attacked. This one was quicker and Friday had to barrel roll across the center table to escape it. Robinson looked around for another entrance. He found one in an adjacent office, but the windowed door was also locked.

His heart was thundering in his chest. He knew Friday could handle a single render, even two, but not in such an enclosed space. When one of the creatures slammed a chair into the wall, dust and debris rained down from above. He looked up at the ceiling planks, which were chipped and cracked.

As the renders circled the table, Friday went on the attack. She went after the big one first. The creature raised its arm and her blade sunk into its flesh. Trouble was, when Friday tried to remove it, the creature yanked her around and slung her across the room. She slammed into the far wall and slid to the floor, dazed.

The smaller render was moving toward Friday when Robinson tumbled through the ceiling and landed on top of the big render, wrapping his arm around its throat. It gasped, and the smaller render ran to its defense. Robinson reached for his tomahawk, but the big render slammed him back against the wall, pressing him until his chest felt like it would implode. It had him pinned and was waiting for his companion. Robinson felt the creature start to slacken and knew it was seconds away from passing out. But he didn't have seconds. So he dug fingers into both its eyes. When the big render's arms came up, Robinson slammed the pommel of Friday's blade into its arm. It slid through the larger render's forearm, straight into the brain of the smaller one.

The big render howled as its companion toppled to the floor, dead. It leaned forward to slam Robinson against the wall again, but he rolled off. The beast was blind, and it started thrashing around. Robinson was scrambling across the floor when Friday gasped for air.

The instant the creature's head turned, Robinson knew Friday was in serious trouble. The beast had pinpointed an easy target. Just as it was about to rush her, Robinson screamed, "No! It's me you want! Me!"

The creature roared and they ran at the same time. It must have weighed four hundred pounds. When it leaped, it filled his vision. But Robinson was already sailing through the air, tomahawk raised high. They hit each other with a staggering impact. Robinson was blown back under its weight. He fell to the floor with the creature's mass landing on top of him. Every molecule of air he had in him exploded from his chest and the room went completely dark.

Robinson felt something hot and sticky running down his chest and neck. He was about to die. It almost felt peaceful. Then the render's body rolled off him and a shadow filled his vision. It slowly took shape and focus. It was smiling.

"Are you okay?" Robinson asked, reaching up for Friday's face.

She nodded and then touched his wet chest.

"It's not mine," he said. He looked to the render and found his tomahawk buried in its brain. Its nostrils flared a moment longer and then stopped.

"Did it infect you?"

Friday shook her head and asked after him. He shook his head too.

"I don't know what I would have done without you," He said.

Her hand came up slowly and cuffed him gently on the cheek. He grinned.

"Sorry. It's the adrenaline talking. Can you sit up?"

She nodded and he helped her up.

"We must go. Your people …"

"Will wait. That's if they aren't already coming. We made enough noise to raise the dead."

"You mean your screaming like baby?"

"I could have sworn I heard you scream."

"That was war cry," she said. "There's a difference."

Robinson grinned and went to clear the door.

"Wait," Friday said. "First, look." She nodded to an upturned desk. Robinson cautiously walked around it. Writhing in a nest of fabric were two squirming heaps of flesh. He saw eyes, legs, hands, and feet, but they were not human. They were renders. Render infants.

"They breed," he said, surprised.

Friday nodded. "It was thought to be."

That led to a more sobering realization. They had killed their parents—parents who were only defending their young.

"What should we do?"

Her look said everything.

"Okay, I'll handle it."

Her next suggestion surprised him.

"Leave them. If Goddess wishes for them to live, they will live."

The hallway grew brighter as they approached the courtyard. Friday rubbed the back of her head, but she appeared to be okay. Robinson was cleaning the blood from his tomahawks when they passed through the door.

"Your people will not enslave me?" she asked.

"We're not like that. Plus my father has a real affinity for strong women. Once he meets you, he might try and keep you all for himself."

Her elbow easily found his liver.

The plant life in the courtyard was denser than Robinson had first thought, though they found a narrow path to wade through.

He imagined the reunion that would take place. First, a pilot or crewmember would see him and call out. Then his father would come running. They would meet in the middle and he would pull his son into an embrace and say something like, "I always knew you were alive." Then Robinson would introduce him to Friday and he'd suggest bringing her home. Maybe their relationship could forge an accord between their people. Maybe the One People could supply the Aserra with the means to defend themselves and unify their tribe. Maybe Friday and he could—

Voices echoed across the courtyard. Robinson saw the flyer sitting on an empty patch of soil. Then some men emerged in familiar dress from across the park. He was about to call out when the sun reflected off something in one of their hands. His smile fell and he grabbed Friday and wrenched her behind some trees.

"What is it?" she asked.

"Iron Fists."

He shook his head, confused. Could the Iron Fists be working for his father now? The only way that was possible was if he'd somehow become Regent. A glimmer of hope bloomed inside Robinson, when suddenly all hope was dashed. In between the Iron Fists emerged a group of men and women carrying boxes full of documents. And he knew each of these citizens. Their clothes were ragged, their faces dirty, but there was no mistaking them, even from afar. Byron Frostmore, Sienna Pillar, Vonus Cork, Quars Ulay, Fonel Keric, and Palos Moor—all friends of his father. All people who had walked the Red Road or had been marked for it.

They were alive and in chains.

Their executions had been faked and now they were slaves. Seeing each of them broken and weary was like a blow deep to Robinson's soul, but none hurt as badly as the last prisoner to exit the building. Even bruised and battered, there was no mistaking the wizened features of Taskmaster Satu.

Chapter Thirty-Four
A Desperate Call

Satu looked thin and pale and bore bruises along one side of his skull. His beard, so long a fixture that had dominated his face, had been shorn clean and dark circles consumed his once proud eyes. This was not the teacher that Robinson knew. This man was broken. When one of the imprisoned Tiers fell in front of him, Taskmaster Satu set his box down to help him and was lashed across the back for it. He winced but didn't cower or protest. He simply picked up his box and continued on.

Robinson's blood was boiling, but Friday held him back. Anything he did would only end up getting them captured or killed.

His thoughts shifted to the Isle. The One People were being deceived. They had no clue the Eight Laws were being subverted to this degree. Crossing into forbidden continents? Salvaging dangerous contraband? Using those sentenced to Expiry as slave labor? What did they hope to gain here? And why was it so important that they needed former Tiers to do their bidding? It was this final point that stymied him. Could his father also be a captive? And which was worse, the image of him broken but alive, or knowing he had died fighting for what he believed in?

Weapon fire suddenly erupted, followed by a series of familiar shrieks. A pack of renders—numbering at least a dozen—flooded out of the western doorway, frothing and snarling under the light of the sun as they spread out in a coordinated attack. The Iron Fists moved efficiently, forming a two-line rank while calmly firing their weapons. Forgotten in the madness were the prisoners cowering between the two forces.

When one of the renders vaulted over the ranks and slashed an Iron Fist's face, the rest of the squad scattered, giving the monsters a small window to launch a blistering attack. For a moment it was bedlam as two of the faster renders leaped into the fray. One tackled an Iron Fist who was reloading his weapon while the other tore into Fonel Keric. The former Tier of Water Resources opened like a spigot, spraying blood all over his companions before his attacker was shot through the mouth.

From the flyer, two more Iron Fists aided in the defense, laying down a covering fire that momentarily halted the render attack. While they pushed forward to reform the line, Robinson grabbed Friday and said, "I'll be right back."

As the bloody skirmish played out in front of the flyer, Robinson raced behind it. With the Iron Fists reforming a perimeter around the prisoners, he knew he had no chance of rescuing Taskmaster Satu. So he ran to the flyer instead.

The dashboard had undergone extensive changes, including the installation of a pad with a blinking hand icon that read: BIO AUTHENTICATION.

Instantly, a voice beckoned from the panel.

"Aerial One-One-Three, report. Has the attack been neutralized?"

Robinson stared dumbfounded at the screen. He had no idea if the voice on the other end was coming from the Isle or somewhere else.

"Aerial One-One-Three, report!"

Outside, two more renders fell, but others were using the foliage to mask their attack.

Robinson had no idea what he was doing when he hit the ACTIVE button and said, "Hello?"

After a brief silence, the voice returned. "One-One-Three. Identify yourself."

"This is ... Tier Keric. Fonel Keric. Uh ... the Iron Fists have been overrun. The survivors have fallen back to the building. Are reinforcements available?"

There was a brief pause and then another voice sounded. "Reinforcements are en route but will take some time to arrive. Can you hold out?"

Robinson asked him how long and was told less than a quarter turn. That meant there was an outpost somewhere nearby.

"How many in your party are alive?" the voice asked.

Robinson's mind was scrambling. "A few. We've fallen back to the ship, but there's something wrong with the controls. The bloody thing won't start! I need to speak with a repair person, now!"

"Calm down, *Ser* Keric. The flyer can only be operated by an authorized pilot."

"No, no, no, listen! It's not that. The bloody thing is dead. I need to speak with someone quickly. We have ... two wounded Iron Fists here, including the commander—"

"Has he been infected?"

"What? No. No. He fell, but if we don't get this flyer moving quickly, he'll most certainly die! Isn't there anyone I can speak to? Tier Crusoe, perhaps?"

His hands were slick. The silence was interminable.

"You know that's not possible," the voice said.

And then a third, huskier voice came on. "Ser, identify yourself."

"I told you, this is Tier Fonel Keric, from Regen 1! We need help immediately!"

"I'm from Regen 1," the voice said. "And I can tell a New London accent when I hear one. *Now, who is this?*"

Robinson cut the radio off. There was nothing more to do.

Outside, the Iron Fists took down another pair of renders with loud cracks. Most of the Tiers continued to cower, except for Taskmaster Satu, who was busy doing compressions on Fonel Keric despite knowing it was a lost cause.

As the weapon fire dwindled, Robinson looked around and saw an unattended bag on one of the seats and grabbed it before springing for the door. Just as he was exiting, he caught something flashing on the screen but had no time to process it.

The Iron Fists called out when the final render tumbled and the prisoners gathered together to lick their wounds. The Iron Fist who had been gored writhed on the ground. When the others gathered around him, he held out his hand for help. No one took it.

"I'm fine," he said. "The bloody thing never touched me."

But from Robinson's vantage, it was obvious no one believed the man. When the commander nodded, the wounded soldier mouthed a protest, but it died when a bullet blew through his heart.

Robinson quickly made his way back to Friday, who was pulling her knife out of the chest of a small render.

"He came through grass and met me by surprise." She nodded to the bag. "Did you find what you seek?"

You know that's not possible, Robinson thought.

"Yes," he lied. "But we need to go. Once they reach the flyer, they'll know for sure someone else was out here. Then we'll be the hunted ones."

Friday was leading them away when Robinson took one last look over his shoulder as Taskmaster Satu and the other prisoners were loaded into the bay. His former teacher paused, and for a second, he thought he might have seen him. But the idea was ludicrous. How could he recognize Robinson when he couldn't even recognize himself?

As suspected, the flyer didn't immediately lift off. From the doorway of the Pentagon, Robinson saw one of the Iron Fists climb onto the flyer's roof to scan the courtyard. His transmission had raised a red flag, but this crew was in no position to handle a search by themselves.

Nevertheless, he and Friday knew they had to get as far away as possible. They exited the building as quickly as they could. Just as their feet hit the freeway, they caught sight of two more flyers approaching from the east and they were forced to hide in the reeds along the riverbank.

They remained there for the afternoon as flyers circled overhead and

Iron Fists searched both the interior of the Pentagon and the outside. Friday's apprehension grew as the daylight turns burned. Only when dusk approached did the flyers rise in unison and return to base. Once they were gone, Robinson and Friday rose.

"Almost dark," she said. "They will be coming soon."

She didn't have to elaborate on who *they* were.

"Any chance we can swim across? If we had to, we could stop on the pilings of that old bridge."

"We will freeze before then. And there are worse things to fear in the water. No, we must run. Now."

He knew better than to argue. They ran fast but cautiously. By the time they reached the Key Bridge, the sun had nearly disappeared. Already the city was pulsing with the cries of renders emerging to feed. Robinson looked to Friday and she nodded. It was time to leave caution behind.

When Friday leaped on the hood of an old car, the concrete deck beneath gave way and a large chunk of bridge plummeted into the river, taking the car and Friday with it. Robinson raced to the barrier just as Friday reemerged, flailing in the water as the fast moving current pulled her quickly downstream.

"Friday!" Robinson yelled.

His first instinct was to jump in after her, but he wasn't a great swimmer either, so he raced to the end of the bridge and tore down the embankment a hundred meters downstream. Friday thrashed against the current, but when she saw an area cluttered with debris, she swam toward it and grabbed the branches of a half-submerged tree.

As Robinson scrambled down the bank, he saw her gasping for air after taking in a mouthful of water. Her position was precarious, but looking downstream, he saw the river fed into a wider tributary. Should she reach that point, there was little chance of her making it back. Even worse, the water was nearly freezing. He was only in it up to his ankles and already both legs were nearly numb.

"Hold on!" he yelled as he peeled off his coat and the Iron Fist's bag. He looked around for something to toss her. He spotted an old stretch of rope, gummed up with mud. When he grabbed it, it disintegrated in his hands. He knew panic would sink them both, so he gathered his focus, aware they'd only get one chance.

"Cru-soe," Friday called weakly. "Hurry!"

At last he saw a long, rusty guardrail hidden in some brambles. He twisted it free and thrust it into the water. The cold metal bit into his hands. It wasn't long enough by half to reach Friday where she was, but he was out of options, so he ran a dozen meters downstream and walked out until the water reached his knees.

"Okay!" he yelled. "I'm ready when you are!"

Friday barely managed a nod before letting go. Robinson was stunned how quickly the water took her. He had an instant to react as the brief shock of black hair approached. He knew instantly it wouldn't be enough. Then he saw Friday's long arms and legs stroke ferociously until, at the last moment, her hand broke through the surface of the water and grabbed hold of the guardrail.

The impact nearly pulled Robinson off his feet as the guardrail swung toward open water. He wasn't sure how she held on, but he quickly pulled her in and dragged her to shore.

Despite gasping, her teeth chattering, and her skin turning blue, her grip was like iron. Robinson wrapped his jacket around her.

"I've got you," he said over and over.

"Mu-st go," she replied, her voice weak.

She was right. Night had fallen. The river might have masked this near fatal event, but they were still in the open.

He wrapped the Iron Fist bag around his neck before loading her onto his back. At any other time, she would have protested, but she must have known there was no other choice. He struggled up to the roadway and started jogging back toward the memorial.

They had barely cleared the bridge when the howls rang like a chorus, echoing from every building along the street. Robinson stopped, chest heaving. Once again, they were trapped.

Chapter Thirty-Five
Tracks

"We have to find somewhere to hole up," Robinson said.

Friday was shaking badly. They were at the edge of the campus Resi had run onto earlier. He felt her nod.

"If it's good enough for Resi, it's good enough for us."

Robinson ran onto the campus, passing a faded sign that read, "GEORGETOWN UNIVERSITY," just as a number of lumbering shadows appeared in the street. The school itself was made up of gothic, brick buildings with towering steeples and a number of overrun gardens and brick walkways. He could almost picture how beautiful it must have looked and how students his age had once freely pursued an education with no restrictions.

As darkness descended, there was little choice but to make for the nearest building. Then Friday's trembling hand pointed toward the ground.

"L-look," she stammered.

There, in the mud, were a number of paw prints leading away. Robinson followed them across the quad to a glass building wedged into the grass near the center of the school. Resi had entered the building through a broken windowpane near the lobby. He carefully set Friday on her feet and pried the window open so they could slip inside.

The hallway was expectedly dark, so they stood still, listening for sounds of life. Outside, the wind had begun to pick up and the leaves rustled in the breeze. After a few minutes, they heard the approach of a render outside, but because of the river water or their good fortune, it failed to catch their scent.

When the torch clicked on in his hands, Friday blanched.

"Sorry, it was in the bag. I meant to show it to you earlier."

"W-hat is it?" she asked, her voice trembling.

"It's a torch. Meant for seeing in the dark."

"C-can it w-w-w-arm?"

"No, it doesn't put out heat, but it can help us find something that does."

He went to pick her up again, but she signaled that she could walk.

The light was bright, so he pointed it at the floor. There, they saw Resi's paw prints leading down the corridor. They led to a stairwell and then up to the fifth floor and to an area marked "GENETICS." They had detected no odor of renders along the way.

When they reached a T-junction at the end of the hall, Friday let off a soft, trill whistle. A moment later, a low whine sounded within one of the rooms.

They followed Resi's tracks to a set of double doors that had been wedged slightly open. Friday drew her knife and Robinson his tomahawk as they peered inside. Resi was lying on an old couch. His tail thumped when he saw them.

"Look at him. I don't know whether to kiss him or skin him alive. You all alone in here, boy?"

Resi jumped down and trotted over, nuzzling up against both of them.

The room was filled with lab equipment, but it wasn't nearly as neglected as the others. Robinson checked the closets, but they were empty. Friday was already stumbling toward the couch. There was an old blanket atop it, covered in dust and hair. Only when Friday stripped off her clothes and had the blanket wrapped around her did they huddle on the couch for warmth.

"Should I start a fire?" Robinson asked.

Friday shook her head. "Hold me."

A moment later, Resi leaped onto the couch next to them and wormed his way into Friday's lap. Robinson scratched behind his ears. When Friday groaned, his nose rubbed up against the food satchel. Friday pulled out some meat and gave it to him. He didn't seem to mind that it was soaked with river water.

They lay there for a good turn without speaking, both beyond exhaustion. Only when Friday's coloring returned did she start asking questions.

"The *bing yuan* ..."

"Soldiers."

"They come from your homeland?"

He nodded. "They're called Iron Fists. They're a special unit assigned to protect the Regent, our leader."

"And the slaves?"

"Political prisoners. Dead men walking."

"But you know them?"

He thought of Taskmaster Satu. "Some better than others. What I don't get is what they're doing here. Or if their objective is somehow connected to my mother."

He could see she didn't understand.

"The flyer I stole was directed by coordinates she'd written down but kept hidden in the locket I keep. Today, when I stepped inside the flyer, I saw a similar set of coordinates. Similar, but not exact. Two of the numbers were off by one."

"What does this mean?"

"I'm not exactly sure," he said. "Only that there was something important enough here that was worth her risking her life for."

"Like paper? The soldiers carried much away."

He nodded.

"What was it?"

He shrugged. "Relics, I think. *Ruinas.* Information. Technology, maybe.

Things long ago banned." She didn't understand the last word. "It's our version of …" He made the warding gesture she so often used. She nodded and then shivered violently. He pulled her close and held her tightly, brushing the hair from her eyes. "You took a nasty fall back there. And I don't know how you survived the river."

"You … fall too."

He wasn't sure what she meant until she mimed his fall from the ceiling.

"Hey, you're a hard girl to impress. A guy has to do something."

"You make jokes where there should be none. But I was proud. You did not hesitate. You did not stop. Even when the render *carga*. Charge. You did not fear it?"

"No, I was very much afraid."

"But still you attacked it. This is Aserra. We do not welcome death, but we do not run from it either."

Robinson grinned. "Does that mean we get matching tattoos?"

When her eyebrow arched, he pointed to her brand. She punched him softly and laid her head on his chest.

"I am your *mestre*. Your teacher. I will sharpen you as best I can. But you will never be Aserra," she said.

To his surprise, that proclamation hurt deeply, though he tried not to let it show. She seemed to sense it anyway.

"The Aserra," she said, "are a hard race that has known much pain. Much darkness. You are a child of light. There is hope in you—a fire that lights the dark around you. I do not wish for that flame to die."

Outside, a gust of wind blew a branch across the glass. Friday's eyes grew heavy.

"You need rest. Why don't you stretch out here and get some sleep."

"You will wake me for my turn?"

He nodded as she curled up with Resi. When the dog licked her ear, Robinson felt an odd moment of jealousy. That damn dog never spooned him.

With nothing to do, he walked around the room, touching tubes and beakers. Like everything in this city, it seemed work had just stopped midstream, as if people had simply vanished without a wink. Had the students finished some test before the lights went out? Had the professors conducted their final experiments?

He hoped to find an answer on the chalkboards at the front of the room, but after switching on the torch to read, a strange panic swelled inside him. His throat grew dry and he felt dizzy. He had to sit down; otherwise, he might not believe his eyes.

The sun was barely up when Friday woke, but he was still staring at the chalkboard. She rose and stretched with a yawn, followed by Resi, who scratched, his tag jingling lightly, before he padded to the door to go outside and mark some trees.

"You did not wake me," she said as she drew near.

"No," he said. "You were sleeping so peacefully I didn't want to disturb you."

"You have been awake all this time?"

He nodded absently. She yawned again and plopped down into the chair next to him. Her eyes followed his to the boards.

"What is this?" Friday asked.

"Research. Someone was conducting a series of tests on the antigens of various blood groupings."

She frowned.

"Blood," he said. "They were studying blood."

"Whose blood?"

"Humans and renders."

"For what purpose?"

"This is the biology building. And this floor is actually dedicated to the study of genetics and infectious diseases, including mutations in human DNA. I imagine when the Rendering first hit, this room was full of scientists running around, performing tests, looking for a *cura*."

"But one was not found."

"No. Not before anyway. But these notations are not from *before*."

"*When* are they from?"

"I can't give you a specific date, but gauging by the amount of dust, I would say at least a year ago. But I can guarantee it was no more than sixteen months."

"And how do you know this?"

"Because sixteen months is how long ago my mother disappeared."

"And you say your mother why?"

He nodded toward the chalkboard. "Because *that* is her handwriting."

Chapter Thirty-Six
Seeking Answers

The early morning return to the memorial was met without resistance, but when they reached the structure, Robinson saw signs that renders had done their best to break through the barricade. There was also some damage to the trough leading from the waterwheel inside. Within a turn he had repaired it.

He finally had time to sift through the Iron Fist's pack he'd taken from the flyer. Friday had slept on it the night before. It contained mostly survival equipment. Along with the torch he'd already commandeered, there was a phosphorous flare, a medical kit, a hand-held radio, a bottle of water, three small bars of food, and a map.

It was the map he took particular interest in. It was a pre-Rendering map of the area, complete with the names of buildings, parks, and sections of the city. Only two locations were circled. The Pentagon, which bore the numbers he'd seen in the flyer:

3852773

And to the east, a second location was circled with the numbers:

38477653

That location turned out to be the military base he'd stumbled across when he had first entered the city. Someone had written: BASE OF

OPERATIONS.

Neither of these numbers matched the one he'd found in his mother's locket:

3853772

But the Pentagon appeared closer. Unless he could discover a map that used similar coordinates, he would never determine the exact location she had identified. Unfortunately, the Atlas section of the library had been destroyed under a collapsed roof. If he hoped to narrow the mystery of his mother's actions, he'd have to do it by some other means.

The day spent away from the memorial held an added consequence: the embers that fueled the smoker had died with their largest cache of beef inside. If they were to leave the city on Friday's timetable, they needed that meat ready. He carefully restarted the smoker, but it would be turns before they knew if the meat had spoiled.

Robinson was also determined to keep an eye on Friday. Although she bore no physical wounds from her fall from the bridge, she was moving slower than usual and had developed a cough, which quickly prompted the brewing of herbs. She said it was a precaution rather than a serious worry, but he wasn't so sure.

Over the course of the day, neither spoke much. Both dwelled on different things. For Friday, it was leaving the city before the Bone Flayers returned. If she were there when they returned, she would not be able to resist the call of drums. She would attack and it would mean both of their deaths.

Robinson's mind was troubled over the two people from his past who had intersected with his present. There was no denying he had once hated Taskmaster Satu, but one of the realities of becoming an adult was the realization that some acts that hurt you were done to shape, not scar, and that those responsible often bore the pains just as profoundly. His teacher was such a man. Now Robinson was preparing to leave his former teacher to a fate he himself had set in motion.

The other thorn he couldn't pull out was his mother, but he wouldn't go there yet.

"The smoker is good," Friday said. "The meat is unspoiled."

"That's great news. How are you feeling?"

"Fine," she answered before offering a familiar refrain, "Forever ready."

Robinson smiled, but he could tell she was weary.

"There is no question you are Aserra," He said. "Braver and stronger than any. But you need more rest."

She tried to wave him off, but he gently took her hand. "My mother was a healer. A *curador*. She knew such things were important not to dismiss. You are tired. You have a fever, and your cough is getting worse."

"There is no time to rest. The full moon—"

"Is not for several days. I promise, by then we'll be long gone. And you know the dangers of travelling ill-prepared better than anyone."

She reluctantly nodded, but there was something else bothering her.

"What is it?"

"I feel these past days ... someone watches us."

He asked her who, but she shook her head. Finally, she gave in. "I will rest tonight. First, I *yu lie* to do."

"*Yu lie?*" he asked, the edge of his mouth curling up.

"*Fish-ing,*" she enunciated. "Is a terrible word to the mouth."

"*You lie* isn't so cheery in our language either. Okay, you fish. I'm going to go up top and scout around."

Robinson crossed to the steel ladder and started for the roof. Halfway up, Friday called his name. She hadn't moved.

"To the Aserra, a warrior's word is his *quan*. We will leave the city together, as you promised?"

Her voice was soft, unsure. The first time he'd ever heard it so.

"Yes," he said, but as he headed up the ladder, he knew he wasn't sure.

From the roof, Robinson did a cursory scan of the perimeter and basin. Outside of a few birds and squirrels, there was nothing to see. He took the eyeglass and looked farther upriver where the Bone Flayers would come from, but the water was as still as glass with only a few isolated chunks of ice too stubborn to melt.

In the park, the trees that had only begun to foster buds would bloom into cherry blossoms and turn the killing fields beautiful once again. Bushes would grow fuller and leaves would dance in the wind. He was reminded, once again, how happy he'd been there with Friday. She had become his north star but also the seed that had given him roots. How could he ever have compared what he'd felt for Tessa with what he felt for her?

But those thoughts brought him back to his mother, and for once, he had to face the truth that he didn't know if she was dead or alive. He wanted so badly to believe she was alive, but the city was fraught with perils. The lab where she'd worked had shown no signs of infiltration, but she couldn't have lived there long. Even if her escape had been plotted, the flyer's provisions couldn't have lasted her more than a year. How had she survived afterward? How had she kept the will to live? The mother he knew was hale in body and mind, but she was no hunter. Then again, he hadn't been either, until coming to this continent. The older he got, the more he understood that people changed through necessity, not by choice.

Yet if his mother had set down here intact, where was her flyer? If she had survived the renders, the Bone Flayers, the struggle for sustenance, and the elements, where had she gone? He wanted to believe she was alive, waiting for help to come, but he knew in his heart it wasn't true. For her, this had been a one-way journey and he needed to find out why.

To the Aserra, hope was a coward's word because it meant that you had not taken fate in your hands. Of all the commodities to possess here, hope was last to be rewarded and the first to lead to ruin. But it remained, buried deep inside him, waiting for the narrowest shaft of light to grow. Hope was eternal. It was what made them human.

Behind the memorial, Friday chased Resi with a stick. He had latched on to a fish she'd caught and was now leading her in circles, jumping and barking with delight. Friday groused and cursed but eventually gave up and went back to the water. When Resi trotted over and set the fish beside her, Friday patted him on the head and said, "Good dog." Robinson didn't want to lose this. And up until the minute he saw that chalkboard, he had been ready to follow Friday wherever she wanted to go, whether it was south after the Aserra or to the gates of the Bone Flayers themselves. But now, with the evidence that his mother had been in the city as recently as last year, all that had changed. He still wanted to go with Friday, but could he live with the cost of knowing he would never discover what had happened to his mother? It was the hardest choice he'd ever had to make.

Ultimately, he decided he needed answers—answers he couldn't get anywhere else. To find out what had happened to his mother, he would have to follow his nose, and it pointed toward the military base. He knew he couldn't risk Friday's health by dragging her across the countryside at night. And there was no way she would let him leave on his own. So he came up with a plan, even though he knew there would be a stiff price.

As dusk arrived, the sky turned a golden pink, with small, white puffs of clouds that spirited across the sky and headed out to sea. The river churned loudly as they settled down to supper. Resi snored lightly beneath the table, weary from the day's exertions.

The fish Friday had caught turned out to be succulent, flavored with just the right spices to sate their hunger and put her in an amorous mood. As much as Robinson wanted to reciprocate, part of him felt badly about deceiving her, so he told her it was best if she recovered another day before they resumed their lovemaking.

After supper, Robinson read until Friday was asleep in his arms. He waited until her breathing slowed before he grabbed his gear and crept for the door. Resi whined.

"I'll be back soon," Robinson whispered and scratched his ear. "Watch her for me, will you, pal?" To his surprise, Resi licked his fingers.

Outside, Robinson slicked his clothes with oil and set off to the east, past the monolith, until he linked with Independence Avenue. As expected, there were many renders out, but by that time, he'd learned a great deal about how to navigate around them.

It wasn't until he'd reached the capitol building that he heard a new danger. It began as one lone yowl, slow and keening. And then it was joined by a chorus of others that melded together until the divergent tones became an orchestra of impending death.

Robinson took out his eyeglass and looked out over the city, finding a group of shadows devouring something several blocks to the north. The moonlight illuminated the attackers long enough for him to see they ran on four legs, not two, and were very fast.

He slid the eyeglass shut and slipped it back into his pack. He needed to get as far away as possible. He was pretty sure he'd be safe if he could make it to the Pennsylvania Avenue Bridge. But when he turned, all the air was sucked right out of him.

There, twenty paces away, was a massive mutated dog staring at him with black render eyes. Robinson didn't move. He didn't blink.

And then the creature started to bay.

Chapter Thirty-Seven
The Hunt!

The render dog was used to hunting in a pack. Robinson knew this because the second he ran toward it, it flinched. It took two steps back before it bared its teeth, but by then, both tomahawks were buried in its skull. It managed one surprised yelp before its blood and brains stained the grass.

Robinson pulled out his tomahawks, knowing his victory would be short lived if he didn't get moving quickly. The keening of the dog's mates carried across the park. There was no way to misinterpret them. The pack was now hunting him.

He fled southwest across the capitol grounds, only looking back when he reached Pennsylvania Avenue. From there, he saw the pack flooding around the capitol building, each mutated dog running with a grotesque gait all its own. The throaty yaps were terrifying, but one rang deeper than all the others. The Alpha. Larger and thicker, it directed its horde with big, booming roars.

Robinson knew he'd never make the bridge, so he broke south toward the water, passing under the elevated freeway he had first traveled across nearly a year before. The sound of heavy padding grew behind him and he turned to see the first render dog closing in. To his surprise, it had no eyes, but its long, mutated tongue whipped out every few meters to taste the air for his trail.

Robinson slid his tomahawks back into their straps and pulled out his sling, along with a rock he'd ground to razor sharp points. He spun it until the dog was a few paces behind him and then let it fly. The projectile hit it where its eyes should have been, resulting in a spray of bone and blood. The dog pitched forward, but before it could yelp, its face struck the asphalt and its neck snapped with a loud crack.

Robinson pushed harder toward the water as the bays closed in. He blew through a gate marked "NAVY YARD" and the shape of a boat emerged. It was an older military vessel, a little larger than the savages' ship. It was canted slightly to one side, hanging half out of the water and half perched atop an old wooden pier that had partially collapsed long ago.

Knowing his odds of survival would be greatly improved if he could reach the ship, Robinson ran as hard as he could for its single, strangled ramp. He was a dozen feet away when he felt the attack come from his right. He dove to the ground just as the render dog passed overhead, its fetid breath warming his ear with a loud snap.

When he spun to his feet, the dog to the east was at his flank and a third dog surrounded him. Seeing Robinson had both tomahawks in hand, the dogs postponed their attack. They wanted to keep him there until their pack mates arrived.

Robinson twisted and feinted while the dogs dipped and lunged, snapped and retreated, always keeping the human on his defenses while working to tire him out.

Once again, Robinson fell back on the Aserra's teachings: never expend needed energy unnecessarily; always keep calm and focused; when the opportunity comes, attack first and be decisive; and always, always go for the kill.

When he heard more dogs approaching, he knew he was out of time, so he feinted toward the dog to the east and then spun, catching the one nearest the ship as it lunged. The tomahawk barely left his hand when it sunk into fur and the beast fell dead.

The third render dog latched onto his sleeve, but it had miscalculated the distance to the channel. Robinson spun fast and hard, and propelled it off the ledge and down the steep, rocky incline that led to the water below. The sound of bones snapping eclipsed its cries until it landed in a heap near the water's edge.

Robinson rushed across the twisted gangplank just seconds before the pack arrived. They snarled and barked but stopped short of crossing. Then the Alpha emerged. The pack cowered under its powerful gaze until, at last, it turned its attention to the human.

Of all the grotesque mutations Robinson had seen to date, none had repulsed him like the Alpha. Its form was rife with muscles pocked by bloody abscesses that ran from its front, thin legs to its squat, powerful rear ones. To his surprise, he saw teats lining its chest and belly, marking it not as male, but female. But it was the qualities of her face that really made his stomach churn. They were not canine, but human. What perversion of nature could create a fusion of man and beast? Mythology was full of them, but here was fable made flesh. And as her eyes bore down on Robinson with intellect and hate, he wondered, was man's folly staring across the void at him, or was he staring at his future?

Robinson set down his tomahawks and took up his sling, sliding one of his last three stones into the pouch just as the Alpha snarled and the pack charged. The first dog was halfway across the gangplank when the stone came loose and hit it in the mouth. The render dog bucked sideways, shrieking in pain as shattered teeth flew. It smashed against the railing, which broke away, and then plummeted to the rocks below.

A fearsome bellow erupted from the Alpha's throat. Quickly, Robinson grabbed his second-to-last projectile and slipped it into the cradle. The Alpha stalked just beyond the gangplank but was intelligent enough to stay back while the sling whirled. To Robinson's surprise, the Alpha directed the remaining pair to either end of the boat. The stern was five meters from shore, but the cant of the ship had left the aft section slightly submerged. If the render dog was capable of swimming, it could easily get behind him.

The second dog had the more difficult task, but it seemed less hesitant. It treaded its way to the upheaved dock where it looked to leap onto the bow of the ship. If both creatures were successful, Robinson would be caught between anvil and hammer with the Alpha ready to make it a three-pronged attack. He would have no chance of survival.

Thinking fast, he edged higher up the deck so he could keep all three targets in sight but still maintain the revolutions of the sling that kept the Alpha at bay. Then his foot struck against something that shook with a groan. He looked up and saw it was a tall, rusty radio tower that extended three or four times his height. On the same plane was a bowed cable at least one hand thick that ran along the waterline and was presently suspended over the Alpha.

When Robinson heard the splash to his left, he decided to act. He released the projectile with as much force as he could muster. He knew it wouldn't be a killing shot, but when one of the Alpha's eyes blossomed red, he let out a triumphant cheer. Immediately, he turned and tugged at the tower with all his might. The rusted bolts on the deck snapped and the tower groaned as it toppled forward. The plan seemed to work perfectly when the tower struck and snapped the cable at one end, sending it plummeting straight for the Alpha, but she vaulted back at the last second, allowing the cable to whip by freely. After it passed, she charged. To Robinson's left, the dog in the water was just reaching the submerged stern. To his right, the third dog was leaping for the bow. It came up just short, but its limbs clung to the railing as its rear legs kicked to get aboard.

Robinson was certain he was about to die, when suddenly the cable recoiled toward the dock and tore through the rotting wood like butter. With a roar, the timber tumbled down the incline, smashing into the gangplank and the ship's hull. The ship jolted once more, throwing the dog at the bow into the water and under an avalanche of falling debris.

With the boat bucking wildly under the falling beams, Robinson ran across the radio tower and made for land. The Alpha sprang up and lashed out at him as she passed below. Pain flared through his foot as one of its nails sliced through his boot. The ship started pulling away from the shore, the radio tower drawing back, and he dove at the last second, impacting hard against the incline's edge. Jagged asphalt bit into his chin, but he scrambled to safety.

When Robinson turned back, he was shocked to see the ship was now free and listing away from land. The Alpha stalked up and down the deck, howling and slashing at the last remaining dog that had swum to the bow. Eventually, she settled, but her eyes never left Robinson. Implicit in that stare was a fury that chilled his blood. He hoped wherever the ship landed, it would be far enough away that they would never cross paths again.

Chapter Thirty-Eight
Base of Operations

The remainder of the trip to the military base went without incident. If there were renders this far out of the city, they were hunting other game tonight.

A few blocks from the base, Robinson saw a glow over the airfield. As he got closer, he saw industrial lights set up to illuminate the trees surrounding the base. He wondered why such a display wasn't drawing more predators, but as he neared the perimeter, he saw several mutated animals writhing in pain along an imaginary line.

Only when he neared it did he feel a pinch at his temples that made his teeth buzz. Someone was using radio waves to keep the renders back. The waves weren't debilitating to him, but he didn't know what prolonged exposure would do, so he ran between two abandoned hangers for a look at what awaited him on the other side.

The base had been set up in the central airfield, surrounded by the carcasses of ancient flyers. A dozen glowing tents were huddled just off the main tarmac, with a large group of Iron Fists milling outside. Many sat around fires, laughing and drinking, while political prisoners sat huddled together in the cold, a dozen meters away. They were finishing off some sort of meal and had only thin bedrolls for cover. None bore chains that

Robinson could see, nor was there any kind of fencing, but as he drew closer, he saw each had a device locked around his or her ankle that emitted a small, pulsing light.

It took a while but he finally spotted Taskmaster Satu lying on a blanket near the back. Another prisoner brought him food, but he waved it off, only to reconsider when the man badgered him. It was incredibly difficult to see someone so domineering reduced to such a shell of his former self.

Between the tarmac and the far tree line was a tent, triple the size of the others. Half a dozen flyers surrounded it. Iron Fists came and went from the tent, each carrying boxes of paper that were then either stacked in a flyer or tossed into a bonfire.

Near Robinson were a number of latrines that the Iron Fists used at will, but the prisoners were left to attend to their business in the open. To the west was a large water tank that had been hoisted onto a wooden platform adjacent to a still. Over the course of a half turn, Robinson heard the Iron Fists call out for the prisoners to fetch their drinks and promptly clouted them when they took too long. The situation made his blood boil, but he needed answers, so he crept along a low berm to the back of the water tower. There, he waited nearly a turn before Taskmaster Satu rose wearily and made his way over to fill his cup.

"Taskmaster," Robinson whispered, "can you hear me?"

His former teacher went still for a moment. Robinson was about to call out again when he asked, "Who's there?"

"It's Robinson."

Robinson thought he might have heard the beginning of a laugh.

"Bloody hell, boy. Is it really you? Or have I finally gone mad?"

"You're not mad. Not any more than you've ever been."

This time he did laugh, although it was low and not loud enough to carry.

"I should have known after all the hullaballoo yesterday. I thought my eyes were deceiving me. You used the radio."

"That's right."

He chuckled again. "Asking for your father. That set the hornet's nest up end, I'll tell you. Then again, that was always your forté."

"Taskmaster, I need to know what's happening. Why are the Iron Fists here? What are they looking for? Is my father still alive? What about my brother and sister?"

"So many questions. I see your time away hasn't changed you much."

"Then you're not looking closely enough. Who's behind this? Is it Tier Saah? Is he in charge?"

"It's *Regent* Saah now. And yes, he's had the entire bloody Isle turned upside down looking for you. When he couldn't find you, we thought you might've come here."

"*We?*"

"Your father and me."

"Then he's alive?"

"He was. Locked in the Tower for months. Now, I'm not sure."

"Why didn't Tier Saah just kill him? Or have him walk the Road? Or bring him here with you?"

"Vardan and your father go way back. I believe he views Leodore as his sworn enemy. 'Nemesis' might be a better word. Perhaps he keeps him to gloat over. Then again, he might also fear making him a martyr. Your father is loved by many, you know."

"What about Tannis and Tallis?"

"Alive and in hiding, but again, I can't say for how long."

"I'm going to get you out of here."

"Impossible. They have affixed us with these devices like chattel. Quite irremovable. Twice my fellow detainees have attempted escape only to be recaptured and … well, I'll save you the unsavory details. Needless to say, these conditions do not bode well for our long-term health."

"Is there anything I can do?"

He paused and then said softly, "You've already lost so much."

And then an Iron Fist yelled out from across the field, "Teacher! A glass!"

"Right away, Ser!" Taskmaster Satu responded before grabbing a cup and spitting into it. "Petty and crude, I know. But I've found little is beneath me these days."

"What does Saah want with the documents? And what does any of this have to do with my mother?"

"Your mother was the one who discovered Ser Saah's plot. She was trying to find a cure for the Rendering when she learned of his campaign."

"The campaign to do what?"

"What men do best: *make war*."

"Teacher!" the Iron Fist yelled again. "I am getting parched. And when I get parched, I get angry!"

"Right away, Ser!" Taskmaster Satu responded but the cup fumbled out of his hands and cracked. Across the field, several of the Iron Fists laughed.

"I don't understand. Who would we go to war with?"

"There are seven continents on this planet, Robinson. You know we weren't the only ones to survive."

"But the One People live in peace."

"Peace, war—two sides of the same coin. It is man's nature to struggle. When devoid of natural conflict, we will always turn upon our brother to fill the void."

"That's it!" the Iron Fist shouted and rose. "I'll show you what happens when you keep me waiting."

"Taskmaster—" Robinson said.

"Be quiet and listen. Saah has begun amassing weapons from the pre-Render civilization here but now he is searching for something specific. It is called FENIX. I cannot speak of its capabilities or purpose, but he cannot be allowed to find it. You must do everything in your power to stop him from acquiring it. Promise me."

"Of course, but come with me. I can help you."

Taskmaster Satu looked over his shoulder as the Iron Fist closed in.

"There is no help for me now. Go. Be the man your parents hoped for. Light the wick they can never blow out."

"Talking to yourself again, Teacher?" the Iron Fist said as he pulled out his truncheon. "I have just the remedy for that."

Fueled by alcohol, the Iron Fist swung his truncheon again and again as

Robinson edged back into the night, silently pleading for the rain of blows to stop.

"Careful," another Iron Fist warned. "Captain has a particular fondness for that one."

"As do I. He failed me in all my classes ten years back. Let's see how he grades this performance."

The abuser was raising his truncheon again when the toe of Robinson's axe caught him flush in the forehead. He dropped like a stone.

"Taskmaster? Can you walk?" Robinson asked, but his teacher could only groan.

Robinson reached down to pick him up when something struck the back of his head. His vision exploded with stars. He teetered and fell to the ground as blood ran down his scalp and neck.

A boot rolled him over as a familiar voice sounded: "Looks like we have company, boys. Let's make him feel welcome."

Robinson's vision focused long enough for him to recognize the face, even though he wore a different uniform.

There, standing over him, was Jaras Saah.

Chapter Thirty-Nine
Captain Jaras

"It looks like a native, Captain," said the Iron Fist.

"I can see that," Jaras snapped. "Though Father always said they were formidable. This one fell like a woman with a single blow."

"He might not be alone. Shall I have the unit check the perimeter?"

"Yes," Jaras said. "And shoot anything that moves. We can't have these apes wandering into our camp and killing us in our sleep."

The Iron Fist left just as Jaras secured Robinson's tomahawks to his belt. He had called him an "ape" while his subordinate had described him as a "native," which meant neither had recognized him. It might have been the oil and dirt that covered Robinson's face or the fact that it was night. Then again, he was probably the last person in the world Jaras expected to see here.

Out of the corner of his eye, Robinson saw an Iron Fist check Taskmaster Satu's pulse and shake his head. Robinson let out a moan.

"When that man recovers," Jaras said, pointing to the Iron Fist on the ground, "I want you to disarm him, escort him past the repulsion field, and give him to the renders. And any man that defies my orders in the future will be immediately executed!"

"Yes, Ser," the Iron Fist responded.

Another nodded at Robinson. "What do you plan on doing with him, Captain?"

"I plan on delivering him to my father. He'll know what to make of him."

For some unexplainable reason, Robinson chuckled.

"Find that funny, do you? Let's see if you're laughing after this."

Jaras held something in his hand. Eventually, Robinson realized it was Taskmaster Satu's old lash. One minute it was twirling and the next it was speeding straight for his face. He caught it midflight.

"Let go. Let go, you bloody bastard, or else!"

Robinson grinned. And then he heard the Iron Fist's weapon click. He let go.

"You know what that is, don't you? So you're not entirely stupid. I imagine you'd need some brains to survive out here in this Spires-forsaken land. How ironic then that you're going to die at the hands of someone far more civilized than yourself. Get him up," Jaras said to his men.

Robinson pretended to be wobbly when the two men picked him up and started marching him toward the big tent. Behind him, he heard the third Iron Fist release the hammer of his weapon, but he couldn't tell if he'd put it away.

Jaras had also grown over the past months. Stubble dotted his face and chin, but he still had that impish look that served to rekindle Robinson's hatred of him.

Robinson was already five moves ahead in his mind when a weapon discharge echoed from the far edge of the field. When every head turned in its direction, he pulled out of the smallest man's grasp and whipped the bridge of his hand into the second guard's throat. He felt it collapse as the man fell.

The Iron Fist behind Robinson was trying to raise his weapon when Robinson's thumb clamped over the firing pin. His other hand locked onto the soldier's wrist and pulled. The Iron Fist was thrown over Robinson's hip, landing hard on the ground, where his elbow was snapped with a kick, followed by a punch to the face that put him out.

Surprisingly, Jaras wasn't running. Instead, he pulled out the tomahawks and swung them with obvious strength. Jaras had no experience wielding such weapons, but he was light on his feet. He'd obviously received some kind of training in the months Robinson was away.

The third Iron Fist froze and Robinson spun behind him, wrapping one arm around his throat while he struck the man's temple repeatedly. He waited for Jaras to step closer before kicking his man straight into him, knocking both to the ground.

Robinson scooped one of the tomahawks off the ground just as Jaras grabbed the other. Only then did he hear the downed Iron Fist pull his weapon from its leather purse. Robinson rolled as the barrel came up and felt his blade sink deep into the flesh behind the man's right ear. The man collapsed without a sound.

That was the first man Robinson had ever killed.

The thought was still center in his mind when Jaras swung the second tomahawk at his head, missing by the narrowest of margins. Then Robinson did the unthinkable. He dropped his tomahawk and waved Jaras forward.

Jaras sneered. "*That* was a mistake."

He stormed in, swinging the tomahawk wildly. Robinson pivoted to avoid each strike, and the fight slowed way down. Robinson remembered Friday telling him the Aserra became so attuned to the rhythms of battle that they could see every blow coming.

Jaras grunted, his footwork sloppy with each strike. He charged without balance and he watched his enemy's eyes, ignoring his torso and hips altogether. Finally, Robinson paused and let him come. When the tomahawk rose up, he ducked under the blade and landed a fist behind Jaras's ear. As he fell, the tomahawk shot from his hands.

Jaras struggled to rise. For the first time, there was panic in his eyes. When he regained his feet, Robinson went on the attack. Each punch caught Jaras flush but at half speed. Each kick was poised for maximum pain but not for maximum damage. He wanted him to suffer. He wanted him to suffer as so many others had. The attack was a dance of subtlety and precision. Jaras reeled back, gasping, with terrified eyes.

Robinson smiled. And then he heard the bolts click into place. Two Iron Fists stood ten feet behind him, holding long barreled weapons. They had him dead to rights.

"Kill him!" Jaras screamed.

Robinson waited for the explosion. Instead, one of the Iron Fists groaned and toppled forward, a knife jutting from his back. Robinson recognized the blade an instant before Friday sped out of the darkness and clubbed the second gunman with her stick. She fell to the ground next to him, winded and looking very pale.

Robinson stalked over to Jaras.

"What do you want?" he whimpered. "I'll give you anything."

"Beg," Robinson said.

He nodded shakily. "Please. Please, don't kill me," he sobbed.

Robinson smiled. "Since you asked so nicely."

A flicker of recognition passed over Jaras's face a second before Robinson hit him. His eyes rolled into the back of his head and he ceased moving.

Friday was already struggling to her feet when Robinson took her arm. She wiped the blood from her knife and slid it back into its scabbard.

"You shouldn't have come," he said.

She knew better than to argue there. "We must go."

He grabbed his tomahawks before helping her back toward the airbase's buildings, taking only one last look at Taskmaster Satu lying dead in the grass.

Just as they passed the hangar with the blue seal, a flyer swooped in from the east and landed.

"Wait," Robinson said and Friday pulled up.

A moment later, the flyer door opened and Vardan Saah got out. Robinson wanted to kill him so badly, but his time would come. He would make sure of it.

"Let's go."

The trip back to the city was twice as slow. Friday was wracked with a terrible fever. She coughed and shivered and her forehead was burning to the touch. Robinson knew if anything happened to her, it would be his fault.

Once they were past the bridge, she agreed to rest.

"How did you find me?" he asked.

"You leave trail like child. Plus, I found this." She held the map in front of him. "Did you learn what you want?"

He nodded. "But you still shouldn't have come. Not in your condition."

"Had I not, you would be dead."

"Are you kidding? I had them right where I wanted them."

Despite herself, she smiled and raised a trembling hand to his face.

The streets were still dangerous. Robinson knew he'd have to be doubly careful with Friday in her condition. Soon, the capitol building came into sight again and he felt a little reassured, but then Friday froze in her steps.

"What is it?"

"Listen," she said.

His heartbeat picked up a notch. He was expecting to hear the faraway bay of render dogs. But he didn't.

He heard drums.

"It's too soon," Robinson said. But Friday's look assured him it wasn't.

"Do you smell it?" she asked.

Robinson sniffed the air. "They've lit the fires."

She shook her head.

He should have known what she'd meant.

They headed quickly to the top of the hill of the capitol building, which afforded them a view of the arcade below. The Bone Flayers' ship was anchored in the basin. The renders had gathered around the bonfires. The night was full of carnage and dance.

But one flame shone brighter than any other.

The memorial.

It was ablaze.

Chapter Forty
The People of the Mountain

The Bone Flayers had come early, no doubt to find Friday. Had Robinson not set off on his selfish journey, and had Friday not followed, they would both be dead. But how had the savages learned where they lived?

Robinson's first thought was of Resi. They had left him behind. Friday bore the responsibility mutely, but it was there, forming another scar around her already hardened heart.

As their home wafted into the ether, Robinson knew they should be counting their blessings. Friday's Goddess had given them a gift, but that's not how she would see it. To her, this would merely be proof that her fate was aligned with the savages and that any hope of escaping them was futile.

"There is nowhere to go now," she said.

But he knew a place.

They entered the library cautiously and made their way up the grand staircase. Nothing in the main room looked as if it had been disturbed. On the third floor, Robinson saw the signs of the struggle where the renders had nearly killed him during his first week in the city.

He pushed aside the refuse blocking the stairwell door. The inside smelled of dust and stone but nothing else.

They descended to the subbasement and scrounged a few old blankets and clothes to wrap around Friday. Robinson then found the nub of an old candle and lit it in a tin before taking her trembling form in his arms as they listened to the drums.

"As soon as they're gone, we'll find a new place to live. It doesn't have to be as fancy as before. Just something safe and secure while we hunt and restock our supplies. In two weeks, maybe three, we'll leave and never come back. It's probably fortunate this turned out the way it did since the weather will be better then."

Friday hesitated before saying, "I will not be leaving."

"What do you mean? Of course you will. We're leaving together."

"The Goddess has chosen my fate. Tomorrow, I will wake, go outside, and seek the leader of the Bone Flayers and I will challenge him to a duel to the death."

"Friday, you can't beat him. Not in your condition."

"It is not Aserra to name the future. The Goddess will decide. I must only attend and give what I can."

"And what about me? What am I supposed to do? I love you."

"The Goddess will protect you, Cru-soe. She has marked you her *bright sun*. Your destiny is only beginning to unfold."

"I have no destiny without you."

She looked at him with pity in her eyes and told him her story.

When one of the Aserra comes of age, messengers are sent out to the other tribes to find a mate, since the bloodlines within their tribes had become too diluted. When an acceptable match is found, a party is dispatched, taking the woman to the man's tribe. With her, she caries a single gift.

Friday pulled an acorn from a small bag hidden beneath her garments. Robinson had never seen it before.

She explained how it was a seed of the tree of her people. When those to be mated meet for the first time, there is a brief ceremony, after which they scale the nearest mountain to plant it in fertile earth. Day and night, the two remain to nurture the seed. Each day the man says, "I am the morning sun," and the woman answers, "I am the evening shade," and together they ask the Goddess to bless their union. The tree then becomes a symbol, not only of their ties, but also of the tribe's. If the seedling first appears in the light of day, they return to the man's tribe to be mated. If it comes at night, they return to the woman's.

"And if no tree appears?" Robinson asked.

Friday's eyes narrowed. She told him both are cast out to face the Goddess alone. She was on such a journey when the Bone Flayers overtook her party. Her tribespeople fought valiantly, claiming many lives, but they had been greatly outnumbered. She was the only one taken captive. That in itself is a great shame. But she had heard the Aserra were sometimes allowed to challenge their captor's leader, and if worthy, send him to the everlasting night. This was her only objective.

When she turned to him, something in her eyes had changed. "And then you came along," she said. "I don't know why the Goddess sent you. At first, I thought she was testing me to see if I could survive. But now I believe I failed her test because I chose love over duty."

"That's not true ..."

"Isn't it? We have failed at every turn. We have survived by luck and the evils of the ancients." She made the warding gesture.

"And yet we're still here. That has to mean something. If your Goddess wanted you dead, wouldn't it be so?"

"Not if I was meant to suffer first."

"The Aserra are hardy people, but I know a thing or two about pain, Friday. I know about suffering and loss. And I'm still here, by your side. And if your Goddess or the Bone Flayers or anyone else wants to take you from me, they're going to have to kill me first to do it."

"You would die for me?" she asked.

"Yes."

"And your people? The soldiers? The answers of your mother? You would give them up too?"

"Yes."

She buried her face in her hands. At first, he thought she might be crying, but when she looked up, her eyes were dry and resolute.

"I need water," she said suddenly.

"There's a reservoir on the roof. I'll be right back."

She nodded and Robinson rose quickly, halting at the foot of the stairs. "You won't go anywhere, will you?"

"Oh no," she said. "We have *business*, you and I."

The reservoir was full but had a thin sheet of ice covering it. Robinson broke through it with an old glass bottle, taking a quick swallow to make sure it tasted fine.

When he turned, he saw the glow of the bonfires reflecting off the façade of towers and heard the drums echoing through the empty streets. He never understood why the renders responded to its call. But he understood why Friday did.

As soon as he approached the stairwell, he saw the smoke. He hustled quickly inside, calling Friday's name again. To his surprise, she hadn't fled or done herself any harm. Instead, she sat on her knees, eyes closed, humming while she rocked slowly in front of a small fire. She had tossed everything that would burn into the can until the kindling was red-hot.

"Friday?"

Her eyes opened, but she never looked at him.

"Remove your shirt."

He did as told.

"We are the mountains that stand together. We are the summit and the base. From our forests come the arrow, from our crags, the blade. We are born in shadow and pass in fire. We are Aserra. Blood is our name. Will you stand the mountain with us?"

"Yes," he answered.

"Then may the Goddess give you a death worthy of life."

She stood, the iron glowing in her hand. When it struck his flesh, it took every ounce of his being not to wince or cry out in pain. His skin popped and crackled, and the smell that followed made his stomach turn, but he never flinched or grit his teeth.

When the job was done, Friday swooned and Robinson caught her. She was shivering again and he quickly covered her and lowered her to the ground. Afterward, he used the water to cool the iron and put out the fire.

"Cru-soe," Friday whispered. "Now my love and duty are one. Tomorrow, we leave the city?"

He nodded. "With no looking back."

Her mouth curled delicately and then she fell asleep.

Chapter Forty-One
Betrayal

It was still dark when Robinson woke. The drums had been silenced, but the noise was replaced by something even more frightening—the sound of Friday's raspy breathing. She was wracked with fever and shivering terribly. When he tried to rouse her, she moaned with delirium.

"Friday, can you hear me? I have to leave to fetch you medicine, but I'll be back as quickly as I can."

She shook her head and tried to speak but convulsed with coughs.

"I have to go. If we don't ease your fever, I'm afraid of what will happen."

"The G-goddess—" she managed.

"Can wait. We cannot. I've left water just there and the barley bread from the flyer. Get it moist before you eat it and stay covered, no matter how hot you feel."

She shook her head and whispered something into his ear. It nearly broke his heart. He kissed her forehead and squeezed her hand.

"Of course I'll come back. I'll always come for you."

He kissed her again and left.

Outside, the dawn smelled of smoke and burning flesh, but to Robinson's surprise, the Bone Flayers' ship was gone. The full moon was still two days away. He had no idea what to make of it.

Equally troubling was the number of render corpses strewn over the arcade. They were everywhere. Last night had been no ordinary sacrifice. This had been a call to slaughter. The burning of their home was meant to convey one thing: the leader of the Bone Flayers had not forgotten Friday. The chief's desire for revenge fueled his rage to the exclusion of all else. When he couldn't find her, the city had bourn his fury.

If they didn't leave that day, they never would. But Friday was in no condition to travel. Even if Robinson could find the herbs to reduce her fever, she would still need time to recover.

Thin ropes of smoke still curled from the back of the memorial. Although the structure itself was mostly marble and limestone, the savages had used the gasoline Robinson had refined to torch the interior of the sanctuary. The barricade had been torn away and the murals had been sullied by fire. The savages had even scaled the marble statue of the seated man and attempted to hew his head from his shoulders. There were hack marks at the neck, face, and legs, but the bronze figure had persevered. Like most men, his aura only loomed more powerful bearing those scars.

He would have made a fine Aserra.

The rear of the memorial was worse than he'd feared. The waterwheel had been torn into pieces and cast into the water. The garden was destroyed and the Bone Flayers had somehow rent open a hole in the back wall.

Inside, the room was a smoldering mess. All their possessions were gone and all of Robinson's inventions had been destroyed. Even the stores of meat they had spent so long accumulating had been left to burn. The savages had spared nothing.

Robinson walked slowly through the rubble, searching for Resi's body. He hoped he wouldn't find it. He imagined several scenarios in which he had somehow managed to escape during the chaotic attack. He was a clever dog. He had survived worse things. But, it was not to be.

Huddled in the corner where Robinson and Friday had kept their bedding was a darkened, curled form. It appeared almost to be sleeping.

Robinson wanted to weep, but he knew Resi wouldn't approve.

Nearby, he found a charred blanket and draped it over Resi's body. He saw a glint of gold at his feet. It was Resi's tag. He pulled it from his charred collar and stuck it in his pocket.

Had Robinson known anything of religion or had he a Goddess of his own, he would have said a prayer. The dog had been a good friend, even if he hadn't always liked his human companion. He decided to save his mourning for later.

Robinson walked to the collection of pipes and stuck his arm deep inside. There, he pulled out a tin can, blackened but intact. Inside were the herbs he needed to help Friday heal. Also inside was his mother's locket. He had been without it too long. After slipping it over his head and tucking it inside his shirt, he left his second sanctuary behind forever.

Looking back, Robinson wished he had buried Resi in the garden where he'd have a view of the water each morning and could see the river fowl that flew past at dusk. But the dog had given his life protecting their home, in the same way that the Seated Man had given his. If anyone in this terrible new world deserved a place by the man's side, it was Resi. It would be a comfort to know they rested together.

The trip back to the library passed in a blur. When Robinson heaved through the front door and ran up the stairs, he was already mixing the tonic in his mind. But as he reached the third floor and crossed toward the back wall, he froze in his steps.

The stairwell door was open.

"No," he said breathlessly.

But he already knew what he'd find inside.

He rushed into the stairwell, his feet flying over the steps until he reached the bottom floor.

Friday was gone.

"No! No!"

Robinson ran back up the steps, bellowing Friday's name. But as he spilled out of the door he saw a figure standing just a few feet away. Robinson halted in his tracks.

He wore the same tattered rags and bore the same heavy glower. And yet he looked infinitely older than the last time Robinson had seen him.

"Where is she?" he asked in the man's tongue.

The Old Man sighed wearily, but only answered, "I am sorry."

"Tell me where she is!" Robinson screamed. His tomahawk found its way into his hand. But the Old Man never flinched or prepared a defense. He simply turned toward the window. Robinson's heart lurched.

He crossed and looked out.

Down on the street, two savages held Friday with a noose tied to the end of a stick. Blood ran from her nose, but her captors looked worse. Behind her stood Savage Chief, eyeing Robinson with the haughty sneer that only a victor knew. Then he turned and called someone from the shadows and everything spun askew.

Vardan and Jaras Saah stepped out from under the awning of a building. They were surrounded by half a dozen Iron Fists, all fully armed with ancient weapons.

In an instant, Robinson's world collapsed around him.

Chapter Forty-Two
Fenix

Jaras wore his usual smug smile, marred only by two purple rings under his eyes. For his part, Vardan didn't care to gloat. He wanted this over as quickly as possible. He signaled Robinson to come down.

Robinson turned to face the Old Man, asking him only one question. "Why?"

If the Old Man was surprised that Robinson could speak his language, he didn't show it. His eyes stayed at his feet.

"Eight years I lived here in hiding. Eight years of shame. And then one day you appeared and reminded me what it meant to be a man. The morning you left, I went to challenge the chief, but he laughed at me. There is no honor, he said, in fighting an Old Man with one hand. The Bone Flayers I had escaped were long dead. They would not grant me an end worthy of the Goddess. Instead, I was taken and paraded among their people. Spit on, beaten, and at last … ignored. And then one day Chief returned. A girl had escaped him. He wanted her badly."

"And you agreed to hand her over. For what? Your freedom?" Robinson asked.

"A month of sacrifices and seven Aserra. Surely you see the honor in that."

Robinson shook his head. "I don't pretend to know the ways of the Aserra, but I know right from wrong. And I know you don't sell out your own people for any cost. When we first met, I thought you were a hard but fair man. But now I see it's only your heart that's hard. You speak of honor as if it could be bartered or given freely, but even I know honor can only be earned. The truth is, you didn't sell the woman I love for a month of sacrifices and seven Aserra. You sold her for your soul."

Robinson turned and walked toward the central stairs.

"The Goddess will forgive me," the Old Man said shakily.

Robinson scoffed as he set down the stairs. "Old Man, from what I hear, she's not the type."

The moment he stepped out of the library with his tomahawks in hand, a dozen weapons were trained on him.

"I want the girl," he said.

"We both know that's not going to happen, son," Vardan Saah responded. "So why don't you put your weapons down? Let's talk."

"Call me 'son' again and it'll be the last thing you ever do."

"He's telling the truth, Robinson," Jaras said. "He doesn't want you dead. He has a proposition for you—"

Vardan glared at Jaras.

"Tell your men to lower their weapons," Robinson said.

"No. You will lower yours."

Savage Chief grew pensive and barked at his men. They tightened their hands around their spears and bows, but Vardan waved them back.

"You're making Arga'Zul nervous," Vardan said.

"I'll give you to the count of three," Robinson responded.

"You can't kill us all," Jaras said incredulously. "You're outnumbered fifteen to one!"

"I don't need to kill everyone. Only that big bastard and you. After that, it won't matter who's armed and who's not, because Friday will finish the lot of you off."

"Robinson," Vardan warned.

"One," he said.

"I told you, he's crazy," Jaras swore.

"Two," he said.

Half a dozen rifles zeroed in. Spittle flew from Arga'Zul's mouth as he shouted. Robinson's eyes flicked to Friday and he saw her trying to shake her head, but it was too late. He tightened his hands on his tomahawks, deciding which of the three targets he would kill first before he died, when suddenly, all eyes flew up.

A shadow fell out of the sky and slammed into the road a dozen paces away. It hit with a sickening splat. Blood sprayed everywhere. Jaras gasped and covered his mouth. Everyone else stood stunned.

The Old Man was dead.

Before Robinson knew it, the tomahawks were ripped from his hands and several savages tackled him to the ground. They clouted him mercilessly until Vardan Saah called them off. Two Iron Fists came over and stood him up.

"Why did he do that?" Vardan asked of the Old Man's suicide.

Robinson smirked. "For honor. Something you know nothing about."

"You see, Father," Jaras sneered. "I told you I hadn't imagined him."

Vardan looked Robinson over and shook his head.

"Indeed. Apprentice Crusoe, you surprise me, surviving out here all this time by yourself. I didn't think you had it in you. And my, how you've grown. I believe you're even taller than your father now."

"Let's get to the part where you tell me what you want."

"I seek an artifact. Something the ancients created in the days before the Great Rendering. It is called the FENIX, after the mythological bird that rises from the ashes. Your mother came here to find it. Now I want you to take me to it."

"You want more weapons?" he scoffed.

Jaras threw a lazy punch that hit Robinson on the mouth. It barely turned his head. "This is the listening portion of the conversation."

Robinson spit blood but never looked at him.

"You'll have to forgive Jaras. These excursions get him terribly worked up. He has such zeal for his new position. But to answer your query, it is not a weapon."

"Then why do you want it?" Robinson asked.

Jaras threw another punch, but this one Robinson slipped.

"Touch me again and I'll kill you."

Robinson's voice was soft but firm, leaving no question to the truth of his statement. When Jaras stepped back, he had the look Robinson had waited a lifetime to see: uncertainty mixed with fear.

"The details of the device are my business. Procuring it is yours. Can you do it?"

"Let's say for the sake of argument I know where my mother is and she has what you want. What makes you think she'll give it to me?"

"In the past, your parents have shown their willingness to go to great lengths to keep their children safe. I'm betting that hasn't changed."

"And in return? What do I get?"

"Why, you get to choose, dear boy. You can have this lovely lady on our left. Or you can have your father. But you can't have them both."

This time Jaras couldn't contain himself. "Oh, that's brilliant," he said between laughs. "You should see your face."

"But you must decide quickly. Arga'Zul here desperately wants to take his prize home. Some gibberish about honor, which apparently will require years of physical and sexual abuse to remedy. Though he is not so amenable as to accept a few baubles and blankets for her. He is very fond of guns."

"I'll need a day."

"You have a turn."

"It's not enough time."

"Sundown, then," Vardan offered. "And Ser Crusoe, if you even think of backing out of this deal or working up one of your clever little inventions, I promise you the girl and your father won't be the only ones punished. Tannis and Tallis will too."

The rage in Robinson nearly boiled over, but when he looked at Friday, something in her resolute gaze calmed him.

"Sundown," he said.

"We'll be waiting by the obelisk."

He turned and walked away. As the rest of the party followed, Friday managed a single look over her shoulder and Robinson raised his hand to touch the brand on his arm. She nodded curtly. A few beats later, the Iron Fists released Robinson and dropped his tomahawks in the street before running to catch up with the others.

Chapter Forty-Three
Resi

Robinson had bought himself some time for all the good it would do him. He'd been on this continent for ten months and had never come close to finding his mother. Now he had to do it in the next six turns. Even if he found what Saah wanted and could get it for him, the idea of choosing between Friday and his father was too much to bear. But the people of the Forbidden Continent were nothing to Saah. The FENIX, whatever it may be, was everything. So Robinson had bargaining power.

But the more he thought about *what* Saah wanted, it made him question *why*. If this FENIX was so important that he'd scour an ancient city full of renders for it, it must be truly dangerous. Taskmaster Satu had called it a weapon and Vardan Saah was certainly not above lying. The question then became: if it was a danger to the One People, or to people anywhere, was Robinson willing to trade all their lives for the two that he loved the most?

In the end, he went back into the library to collect his things. He sat by the third floor window that he'd looked out all those months before, trying to imagine where his mother could be. What he knew for certain was that there was something critical enough in this place for his mother to fake her own death and fly across an ocean knowing she would never return home.

He'd also discovered proof that she'd been here when they had stumbled upon her research at the university.

She had been studying renders—or more specifically, how the Rendering virus had affected their genetic makeup. Robinson's former teacher had said she was looking for a cure. He was inclined to believe him, not only because his mother cared about such things, but also because she had never spoken of renders as monsters, but as people.

And yet if Tier Saah was to be believed, she also knew of a weapon—or non-weapon—that might be connected to everything else. It was so much to process. Robinson groaned in frustration, leaned back, and closed his eyes. There was something he was missing. He heard Friday's voice, "Never rush. Never be rash."

His mind went back to the day he and Friday had brought down their first bovine. It was the first time he'd seen her truly smile. He had wanted to take her in his arms then and there. The wind had swept in from the flatlands, so crisp and clean. Resi had barked behind them, his tail wagging furiously from the hunt.

Robinson's hand dug into his pocket and pulled out the dog's tag. He rubbed his thumb over it, wiping away the soot that revealed the name, RESI, in faded script. On the other side were the stars shooting through the sky. He was surprised how keenly he missed that dog and his scolding glances. He even missed his disapproving whine. He thought back to the first time he'd seen him, how scared he'd felt, and how scared Resi must have been. They had found each other in the midst of chaos, two creatures looking for company and comfort.

And then he remembered something.

Resi had been to the lab where his mother had worked. In fact, he had led them there. Had he known her? Robinson closed his eyes and tried to picture the scene, the two of them together. His mother never had a pet growing up and yet there was something important that he was missing.

And then it came to him. The blanket! The blanket he had taken off the couch and wrapped around Friday had been covered with hair. Dog hair. Resi hadn't wandered into that lab by chance. He had gone there because he had spent time there.

What were the odds that a dog his mother had befriended would wind up finding him too? Maybe it wasn't random at all. Maybe Resi had found him on purpose.

And then it hit him like a bolt of lightning. It wasn't the timing of their meeting that was important, but the *place*. Robinson looked closer at the tag. It couldn't be so simple.

He stood and ran through the library, scanning the sections as he passed. By the time he reached the first floor, he was sweating badly. He found it in the history section. *The White House: a History of America's Most Famous Residence.*

Cracking open the first page should have been enough. There was the glorious symbol of this region's highest office: the Seal of the President of the United States. It was the same symbol he'd seen on the floor inside the White House. It had also been on the side of the giant blue flyer at the military base.

In the oval center was an eagle holding an olive branch in one talon and arrows in the other. Two symbols that under the right condition might look like stars shooting from the clouds. Around the top were the words, "PRESIDENT OF THE UNITED STATES." Central among that first word were four letters Robinson had come to know very well.

P-*RESI*-DENT

It should have been enough, but he still needed one more thing to convince him it was true. It was in the back, listed on an old map detailing the White House after it had partially burnt down. The coordinates had been recorded. 38° 53' N / 77° 2' W

3853772

Robinson was running before the book hit the floor.

He should have seen it long before. He had awoken to Resi licking his face on the steps of the White House. He'd met him there because he had just been released from the inside. His mind went back to the cameras and how he'd felt like they'd been watching him. All this time and she'd been right under his nose. Only then did he remember the booby trap that had knocked him out. At the time he thought its construction felt familiar. Now he knew why. His mother had built it. It was a gift he had seen in many permutations at home. It was from her that his love of tinkering had sprung.

The building loomed dark and foreboding when he entered through the side door. He immediately pulled out his torch and turned it on. Blackened blood stained the floor where the savages had fallen months before. The smell of the tentacled render still permeated above all.

Robinson moved through the hallway more cautiously than before, noticing more cameras in the daylight, many already pointing toward him. The oval office was empty, but it was the camera there that he chose to address.

"If it really is you," he said into the eyeless void, "I need your help. Tell me where to go."

For a moment, nothing happened. And then the camera spun right. He gripped his tomahawks and headed in that direction.

He let the camera's movements dictate his path. They led him down the hall, through a doorway, and into a grand ballroom where upturned furniture laid in pieces. A massive chandelier that had once lit the room sat shattered in the corner. How beautifully it must have shone, hanging above a room full of elegant, well-dressed people as they danced.

A third camera was centered above a staircase, but when Robinson stopped in front of it, it swiveled from side to side.

"I don't understand. Did I come the wrong way?"

The camera swiveled more frantically.

"Am I ... am I in danger?"

The camera stopped and its red light blinked once. Robinson spun, but there was nothing behind him. Then he felt the air move. It was subtle and he might not have noticed had the hair on his arms not stirred. It felt like an exhalation.

To his right, the elevator doors had been ripped apart from within. The grip on his tomahawk was slick with sweat, but he held it firmly as he moved forward. The torch exposed the innards of the shaft. It was dark with several cables extending from the roof and into the abyss.

He had seen tentacles explode from the third floor entranceway to assault the savages. He knew whatever was buried there had significant speed. But he also knew time was running out and there was no turning back.

As he stepped toward the shaft he heard a sound like the tinkling of glass. He should have recognized it immediately, but even by then it would have been too late. For Robinson, the realization came when something hot and sticky dripped onto the back of his neck. He slowly looked up and screamed.

Chapter Forty-Four
The Watcher at the Gate

It was suspended from another chandelier above him—a mutation several parts man and Crown knew what else. It had multiple torsos and faces and mouths that howled in unison. It had numerous arms that transformed into tentacles. They shot out and grabbed Robinson, pulling him off his feet. The discharge that seeped from the creature burned his skin, but as it drew him up, he knew that was the least of his worries.

A loud crack emanated from the middle of the beast as one of its torsos split open, revealing a giant rictus full of bloody teeth. As its diseased tongue extended to haul him in, Robinson yanked his arm back and threw his tomahawk at the only place he could.

The blade hit the mooring of the chandelier and the entire thing jolted but didn't come loose. To prevent itself from falling, the creature was forced to release him. Robinson hit the ground hard and his torch bounced out of his hands. The creature roared, its tentacles slithering downward. He rolled and reached for his second tomahawk. Unfortunately, the handle had snapped in two when he'd fallen and was now useless. Robinson groped for his only other weapon, the sling, but the second he twirled it, he thought how pathetic it was that after searching for his mother for nearly a year, he was about to die mere feet away from her as she watched.

He heard the tinkle of the chandelier, followed by the sound of the creature settling onto the floor. It slithered in the darkness. Robinson knew he had little chance of felling the creature with a stone. Even if he could strike it in the eye like he had the Alpha, it had a dozen more. He cursed himself for not asking Saah for one of the ancient weapons, but Robinson knew he would have never given it to him.

When the sound of the creature's movements pierced the dark, Robinson yelled and released a stone in its direction. The stone did not strike flesh, but whatever it hit shattered and the beast stopped. It clearly understood Robinson could hurt it, even if he couldn't kill it.

A hiss of movement came again, this time lighter. Only when a long, skinny tentacle entered the cone of the torch's light did Robinson realize it was headed for the elevator shaft. A second later, it dragged something from the shaft. It was the half-eaten body of a render suspended on a makeshift hook.

When it pulled the cadaver in, Robinson had no idea what it intended to do. He heard the crunch of bone and flesh and a sound like chewing. When it finished, the creature retched several times and that fetid stench hit him like a wave of acid and death as it spit up the regurgitated meat.

Silence followed. Then out of nowhere, a projectile hit his leg just above the knee.

The strike wasn't enough to knock him off his feet, but when the masticated flesh started to sizzle and smoke, he knew he had to get it off.

Robinson used an old candlestick to knock it away, but he could already feel the acid cutting through his trousers. He was reaching for the water in his pack when he heard the second projectile coming. He dove just in time to avoid it striking his face. It splattered against the wall behind him and started eating through the plaster. The stone from his sling rolled across the floor and several globs shot after it.

One fact struck Robinson. The creature was having trouble seeing him too. It lived in almost perpetual darkness, but the flashlight was angled in its direction. When it took another bite of its victim for ammunition, Robinson picked up an errant piece of debris and chucked it across the room. It landed with a crash and the creature slithered in that direction, firing off globular blasts that sizzled and popped as they hit.

Robinson ran in the opposite direction, shielding himself from the regurgitated projectiles he knew would come as soon as the creature realized it'd been duped.

If the creature hated light, he would give it plenty. As the thump, thump, thump of steaming masses hit the wall behind him, Robinson slid and tore the first of three curtains off the large Palladian windows. Half a dozen mouths roared simultaneously as light exploded in. Tentacles spun in pandemonium, trying to cover its multitude of eyes. Robinson stood and tried to kick out one of the windows, but the glass didn't even crack. Even when a glob of acidic flesh hit it flush, the vile substance merely slid off with a wisp of smoke.

The only weapon in the room now sat against the far wall, but the second Robinson leaned in its direction, the creature slithered back to cut him off. With his escape route blocked, that tomahawk was his only chance. Trouble was, the creature knew it too.

Robinson tore the remaining two curtains down, flooding the room with light, but the beast just drew back into the shadowed alcove. One of the long tentacles shot out and tore off half of the render's corpse and swallowed it whole. It spit out the masticated chunk and it ate at the floor, but the tentacles were quick to tear off more portions and heave them in Robinson's direction.

As he dodged the salvos, he reached into his bag and counted the rocks he had left. Four. Not nearly enough. He blinked twice, hoping at the very least he might be able to find some vulnerable spot to blind or stun it so he could run past.

The first rock hit the creature flush, but it only seemed to anger it. As the globs came faster, one of them struck Robinson's boot and he was forced to shed it before it ate through it. His second rock struck one of the creature's massive legs. Although the beast howled, it failed to go down.

Robinson dipped behind a standing column and loaded up his second to last rock. When he started spinning the sling, the creature covered its vital areas and the rock skittered harmlessly away.

The idea suddenly struck Robinson that the beast might have one vulnerable spot after all and he quickly loaded his final rock into the sling. He waited until the creature spit out his next acidic missile and let loose. The shot was perfect, striking the back of the creature's throat, and it roared. Its tentacles flailed wildly, lashing against the walls, tearing down pictures, and hitting the chandelier above.

The chandelier quivered and came further loose from its moorings, but didn't fall. Robinson's gaze fell to the one rock that had skirted out of his sling earlier and was now a dozen paces away on the floor. The creature's paroxysm was subsiding, its focus and rage returning wholly on its target. When it charged, Robinson would have nothing left with which to defend himself. So he tucked his head and ran as fast as he could. The creature's roar filled the room. It stamped the ground with such fury that the walls shook. Tentacles reached into its mouth and pulled out a dozen deadly chunks, firing every one of them off at the same time. Robinson heard the sizzle and hiss as they flew at him. When one struck his shoulder, he fell to his knees and slid. His hand locked onto the rock, dropping it into the pouch in one smooth motion. He only had time for a single revolution, but as he released it, he knew his aim was true.

The rock struck the base of the chandelier with a metal clang and the moorings pulled loose. Six heads and a dozen eyes looked up at once, widening as the giant fixture fell and crushed it with a deafening clatter. Six small mouths and one giant one wailed in unison and then ceased as the tentacles fell one by one and moved no more.

Robinson's shoulder burned and he quickly tore off his jacket. He rushed across the room and grabbed his pack. He opened his water skin and poured the last of the water over his wounds. He collapsed on the ground, unsure how he was still alive.

Eventually he stood and gathered his things before crossing the room and looking over the beast. It was even more hideous up close.

Utterly spent, Robinson looked up at the camera as if to ask "what next." And then he heard a chime. He turned and saw a small light next to the elevator blinking on and off. Somewhere in the bowels of the building, machinery started up and the top of the elevator rose out of the darkness. Robinson stepped inside when it drew even with the floor. Several buttons lined a control panel, but before he could even push one, the elevator started descending.

Chapter Forty-Five
Reunion

The elevator jolted to a stop and the doors parted sluggishly. On the wall opposite Robinson was half of the Seal of the President of the United States. The other half sat in pieces on the ground. An occasional light illuminated the hallway, but to his surprise, it revealed little dust. Even the smell from the elevator shaft hadn't permeated the seal. If this were a tomb, it was the most comfortable one he had ever seen.

As he walked the hall, he perused the framed prints that adorned the walls. All revealed suited men in various poses of public duty. Family or citizens often surrounded them, although one picture revealed a man playing with a dog on the lawn outside. Here and there were photos of a chief looking stern in the face of some crisis. Robinson would never know the history behind any of them.

He came to a set of glass doors, etched with the familiar seal. Inside was a large table with technology in the background, but at some point, part of the ceiling had collapsed and debris lain strewn across the floor. In the far back was a chair and what looked like a suited set of bones canted to one side.

Robinson's footsteps echoed in the hall, competing only with the whir of an air filtration unit that blew from above and the occasional camera that spun to mark his passage.

Robinson passed a kitchen that had been cleaned out long ago. The cabinets were open, some torn off their hinges, and dishes and plates were scattered across the floor.

He came to a door that had been kicked in. Inside were a number of sleeping bays built into the walls. Many of the bays had been torn out and two of them were dark with dried blood.

Farther down the hall was a bathroom complete with showers. Opposite it was a door marked: POWER SUPPLY ROOM: ENTRY PROHIBITED. It bore the symbol that Robinson recognized as meaning nuclear power. It was clear to him now how this place had remained operational after two hundred years.

At the end of the final hallway was a giant, ovoid, steel door. It looked indestructible. Here again was the Presidential seal, but someone had scratched it off. To the right was a control panel; its plating had been pried open and its wiring spilled out like the bowels of the dead.

The camera above the door edged slowly down to him, its eye pulsing from red to dark. He could only think of one thing to say.

"I'm here."

A few seconds later, Robinson heard the sound of clicks and whirs. The door opened and a hiss of cool, purified air escaped.

The inside chamber was modest in size. The only illumination stemmed from a wall of monitors on Robinson's left, half of which no longer worked. The ones that did revealed a few interior and exterior locations. To his right was a table full of lab equipment. A larger monitor sat on the end of the table, but instead of images, it showed streaming lines of text and mathematical calculations.

Robinson stepped in for a closer look.

"It is called a computer," said a husky but feminine voice from behind him. He turned to see her silhouette in the shadows.

"The ancients used them to make calculations and to store data. They have almost limitless capabilities, but they are missing one critical ingredient—humanity. How could they put so much control in the hands of something so incapable of empathy?"

Robinson stepped toward her and the figure raised a hand. "No. Not yet," she said softly.

"Mother?"

He had to ask because he did not recognize her voice.

"You have been through quite an ordeal. When you first arrived all those months ago, I did not think you would live out the week. You were so timid, so frightened. But look at you now. You've become a man."

"Are you her?"

"I was especially pleased when you found Zeus."

"Zeus?" Robinson repeated.

"The Greek father of gods and men, and the protector of cities and of the powerless."

"Oh, Resi. That's what I called him."

"Is he with you still?"

His gaze fell to the floor. "No, he ... No."

"I see."

"Was he yours? Are you the one who sent him to me?"

"Zeus belonged to no one. He was a survivor like you and me. But we cared for each other for a time. That first day you arrived, I knew your need for companionship was greater than mine, so I let him go. He was safer outside anyway."

"Safer from what? The creature in the shaft?"

"That and more."

Robinson took a step toward her, but the figure pulled back again.

"Why won't you let me see you? Are you my mother? Your voice sounds different, but it feels like you."

"You have already been through so much. But if we must."

The figure stepped into the light and Robinson recoiled.

"You're a render!"

It was true. Her body and head were covered with a mass of tumors and boils. She had growths on her hands and on her neck, but she still had his mother's face and her compassionate smile.

"I am infected," she said. "That much is true. But my mind is unchanged, at least for a short while longer."

"I don't understand. If you were bitten, you should have mutated."

"No creature infected me. As you might have deduced, I have been alone inside this room for well over a year now."

"Then how ..." he stammered, but then his gaze fell on the lab equipment, the beakers and tubes, and the data streaming across the screen.

"Oh, Mother."

"I have come close to a cure many times. But with no way to test it ... Well, sometimes one has to make—"

"A leap of faith."

"Yes. But enough sad talk. Tell me about Vardan Saah. I see he's returned."

"He's after something called the FENIX. Do you know what that is?"

"Yes. It is a satellite-based dispersal system from which one can release genetically modified spores into the upper atmosphere. The ancients had hoped that if they could find a cure, they could code it into the machine and with one final swoop, eradicate the disease forever. Unfortunately, they failed to discover the cure in time."

"Why would he want the cure?"

"He doesn't. He wants to destroy it before anyone else can use it."

Robinson groaned. "He has father. Maybe the twins. And ... someone very important to me. If I don't bring him this FENIX by sunset ... you can imagine what he'll do."

She reached under the desk to retrieve a silver briefcase. She opened it and stared inside before handing it to him.

"It doesn't matter now. I no longer have the ability to program it. The irony is that the missing piece was the first thing I stumbled upon in the library under the Crown. I found reports made a decade after the fall of this land, just before the One People were formed. I kept those notes on a small disc, which I hid at home. Had I brought them, things might have ended much differently. Regrettably, Vardan caught on to us too early and I wasn't able to retrieve the disc before I left."

The significance of that moment hit Robinson in an instant. He was holding the salvation of his loved ones in his hands. He had the power to save them. But he had something else too. The disc was inside her locket, which currently rested against this heart. If he handed it over, they might save the world, but to do so would mean condemning everyone he loved to death.

It was the hardest choice he ever had to make.

"Mother?" he said finally. "I have something for you."

When he pulled out the locket and opened it for her, she didn't move.

"Can you make it work?" he asked.

"We'll see. Give me a few turns."

He wandered the halls of the bunker, eating from food supplies that had no shelf life. He tried to nap in the sleeping pod but never came close to closing his eyes.

He thought of Friday and his family. He thought of the One People and his dog. He thought of all the nameless souls out there trying to scratch a living from ashes and mud, trying to rebuild. The sacrifice should have been easy to make, but it wasn't.

He couldn't help but wonder if he was still a coward after all.

Chapter Forty-Six
Departures

His mother eventually called him back. "It's done," she said, falling into her chair.

"Did you activate it?"

"No. I thought I would leave the decision to you."

"Mom—"

"Tell me about the girl."

He took a heavy breath. "Her name is Friday. At least, that's what I call her. Ironically enough, she's the complete and total opposite of you. Hard on the outside, and soft at the center."

"Is it love? True love?" she asked.

"Yes."

"How do you know?" she asked.

"Because I would do anything to keep her from harm. Vareen said that was the measuring stick, but I guess I could have just paid more attention to Father and you."

She seemed to like that. "In my mind, I always had this fear you'd end up with Tessa."

They both laughed.

"For a while, I almost did. But every man needs a Rosalind."

"You read Romeo and Juliet?" she asked, surprised.

"Several times. Bit of a downer ending, but it does resonate in this situation."

Her smile faded. "There are worse things than being star-crossed lovers. As for this," she said as she handed him the silver case, "you are far too young to bear such a burden, but someone must. Knowing the choice is yours gives me comfort."

His lip suddenly trembled. "Mother, is there no hope ...?"

She shook her head. "My time came and went long ago." And then she looked to one of the monitors that revealed the darkening sky outside. "And now comes yours."

He stood resolute, though he felt as if he couldn't draw a breath.

"I could be no prouder of the man you've become," she said finally.

"I am you."

Before Robinson left, his mother showed him how to work the machine. One code would release the spores carrying the render cure. Another would activate the satellites' self-destruct sequence.

Then she handed him one last thing. She gave him back the small disc.

"What's this for?"

"When the time is right, *give it to a friend.*"

Robinson left by a secret door hidden in the garden, the same one Resi had used to find him all those months ago. He knew the cameras were following him, but he never looked back.

The run to the obelisk passed quickly, but the sun was nearly down when he approached the Iron Fist encampment. One of the soldiers called out and Vardan and Jaras appeared, along with Arga'Zul.

"Cutting it close, boy," Vardan said. Then he saw the silver case. "Is that it?"

Robinson nodded and handed it to him. He opened it and looked over the electronics.

"What's the passcode?" he asked.

"Where's Friday?"

Saah nodded to Arga'Zul, who signaled his warriors to fetch her from a cage. She was in terrible shape. Her hands and mouth were bound and she looked pale and weak. But when a savage pushed her, she threw an elbow that broke his nose. Robinson could not hide his smile.

"Now, the code if you please?" Saah said.

"I want my family released too."

"You're in no position to negotiate, *Muckback!*" Jaras spat.

"Actually, I am. If the Regent wants to play despot over the rest of the world, will one man and two children really make a difference?"

Saah considered and shrugged. "I accept your terms. Now the passcode?"

The moment of truth had come. Which way would he decide?

"It's Zeus."

Saah grinned. "God of the sky and thunder. Would that make this his thunderbolt?"

Saah typed in Z-E-U-S and hit enter. The three green lights bloomed and Saah's fingers moved over to the EXECUTE button, where they froze. Then he powered down the unit and looked back to Robinson.

"Now, what's the real passcode?"

Robinson stared at him and then Friday. Jaras sneered.

"Shall I have our large friend make a show of your native?"

Arga'Zul grabbed Friday by the hair and lifted her straight into the air.

"It's ICARUS," Robinson said as his head fell.

Could he live with what he'd just done?

"What's an Ic ...?" Jaras asked.

"Icarus," his father said disapprovingly, "son of Daedalus, the master craftsman. His father made him wings of wax and feathers to escape the labyrinth on Crete, but he ignored his father's instructions and flew too close to the sun. It seemed our predecessors had a gallows sense of humor."

Again, Saah powered the machine up, entered the letters I-C-A-R-U-S and hit ENTER. This time, the three lights went red and the EXECUTE button blinked. Saah looked to his son and smiled. Then he surprisingly turned off the device.

"You're not going to use it?" Robinson asked.

"Everything in its time."

Saah locked eyes with Arga'Zul and nodded. As he and his warriors turned toward their ship, four Iron Fists grabbed and disarmed Robinson.

"Wait! You gave me your word!"

"A Regent beholden to you? Not in this lifetime, *boy*." He laughed as he headed away.

Robinson screamed for Friday. He could see her struggling too, but the Bone Flayers were hauling her quickly toward the boat as their crew readied to launch.

Everything dear to him was being taken away. He couldn't bear to lose her too. So he did the only thing he could think of.

"ARGA'ZUL!" he screamed, his voice so deep and commanding that Arga'Zul and his men couldn't help but turn around.

"Leader of the Bone Flayers, listen to me! You take from me now the woman I love. There is no distance you can sail and no place you can hide that I will not find her. Should any harm befall her, I will kill you and all who carry your blood. This I swear by the sun and the moon."

Arga'Zul paused, not knowing what to make of Robinson, but when his warriors laughed, he followed suit. As they turned again, Robinson spoke once more.

"This I swear by the Aserra."

The laughter stopped immediately. The savages spun. Arga'Zul's eyes grew incensed as he stalked back toward Robinson. The Iron Fists looked to Vardan, who wasn't sure what was happening.

Arga'Zul towered over Robinson and looked in his eyes. He held his gaze without flinching. Then he tore Robinson's sleeve away, revealing the Aserra brand.

The savages readied their weapons as Arga'Zul seized his dagger, but the clatter of Iron Fist weapons being loaded stayed his hand.

"That one is mine," Saah said firmly.

Arga'Zul debated his chances, but common sense got the better of him. He signaled his men to leave before he stalked away.

For a brief moment, Friday and Robinson locked eyes. He saw pride there. He also saw love. Then she was gone.

Saali turned to Robinson in wonder. "You're full of surprises." And then he nodded to Jaras and handed him Robinson's tomahawk.

"I've been waiting for this for a long time."

He raised the tomahawk high and let it fall.

Robinson's world went dark again.

PART THREE

"No man ever steps in the same river twice, for it is not the same river, and he is not the same man."

-Heraclitus

Chapter Forty-Seven
The Return

Robinson awoke shackled and bound with a hood over his head and the most crippling headache imaginable. The fabric of the hood made it difficult to breathe, but the last thing he wanted to do was hyperventilate. So he closed his eyes and thought of the way of the Aserra. His muscles relaxed, his breathing slowed, and soon he felt better.

A low vibration ran through the flyer as the familiar thrum of the engines churned. Two men spoke informally up front. When one of them opened a vent, the crisp ocean air flowed in.

They were heading back to Isle Prime. That's why Jaras had struck him with the edge of the tomahawk and not the blade. Saah wanted him alive. For what purpose? He had his pick of reasons: To capture an escaped killer, the son of his enemy? To use him against any holdouts of his father's old alliances? To draw his brother and sister out? Maybe he simply longed for someone to toy with.

None of these options frightened Robinson. Parading him in front of the Feed would do little more than rile the Isle up. The only real fear he had—one ingrained in every citizen from the day they were born to the day they died—was to walk the Red Road with everyone watching. Was it as terrifying as being eaten by a pack of renders or staved through the head by a group of wanderers? Of course not. It wasn't the pain of the chains or even the plummet to the abyss. It was the shame. It was not knowing if you would hold yourself together or whether the last memory of you would be of some blubbering fit that would be retold for generations.

Since Robinson couldn't gauge how far they'd come, he called out for water in hopes he could get one of the pilots to talk. He received a boot in the back instead.

Turns later, he was awoken as the flyer swooped in and descended for a jolting stop. His body was stiff and cold with sweat, but he offered no complaints when he was dragged to his feet into the chill but familiar night air.

They waited on the tarmac as other flyers arrived and Vardan Saah spoke. Eventually, boots approached and someone pulled the bag from Robinson's head. It was night, but still his eyes shrank from the lanterns nearby.

They were standing on top of the barracks between the Second and Third Spire. New London was gloomy and dark, its walls slick with a heavy mist.

"Welcome home," Jaras said before nodding for the Iron Fists to take him away.

Robinson's destination was the Tower. Two hundred and forty-two steps later, he was escorted into the gaoler's cells. His shackles were removed and he was thrust without ceremony into the main cell. When the door slammed shut behind him and the lock spun, he discovered a cruel irony. This was the very same room he had tried to sneak into nearly a year before so he could see the render.

A group of sleeping men were huddled around the room on beds of straw and stone. There wasn't a single blanket between them. Robinson recognized all of the men. They were men of nobility and influence. Respected Tiers. He looked through their ranks until he found him in the far corner, a shell of the man he used to know.

"Father," he said, touching his arm softly. "Are you awake?"

Leodore rolled over, his eyes wide and glassy. "Robinson?"

He nodded. "Yes. It's me."

Leodore rose shakily and embraced him. His body felt so thin and frail that Robinson worried about crushing him. Other men in the room also stirred.

"Vardan told us you were dead."

"Saah is a liar, a thief, and a coward. But you've always known that."

"Crown's sake, look at you! You're so big and tall! After the fire and our arrest, we never learned where you fled. How did you survive? Why have you come back?"

Robinson gently took his hands. "Sit down and I'll tell you everything."

Over the course of the next turn, he detailed the last ten months of his life, from the coordinates in his mother's locket, to his crash landing on the forbidden continent, and even Friday's abduction. The only thing he left out was his mother's infection. That was a detail no one but him would ever know.

"So she's dead? You're certain?"

Robinson nodded. "But before she died, she succeeded, Father. She developed a cure for the Rendering virus." What he didn't say was that it had been too late to use it on herself.

Still, Leodore's face lit up. "She did it? Oh, Annabess. When you set your mind to something, there was never any holding you back."

Tears came to his eyes, but Robinson did not look away.

"Tell us more about these satellites," Roland Fallow said. "You say Vardan Saah has a device to control them?"

"It's in a silver case. He was carrying it when we landed. If we can somehow wrest control of it from him, I can release the cure."

"Easier said than done, laddie," Gustav Gustafson said. "Especially since we have no clue what he plans to do with it."

"Vardan always had a nose for theatrics," Leodore said. "I would not be surprised if his plan to destroy it coincided with whatever he has in store for us."

"We'll find out soon enough. I heard the Iron Fists tell the Red Guard outside that he would be paying us a visit first thing in the morning."

"Then we should devise a plan. We can charge the guards, overpower them—!"

"Easy, Father. I already have something in mind. But it will take patience."

He looked at Robinson in a new light. "You've changed, son."

"Yes," he grinned. "I'm more like you."

And then Rolland Fallow laughed.

Early the next morning, Vardan Saah arrived as expected. He was freshly showered and groomed, wearing the official robes of the Regent. Behind him, Jaras wore his captain's uniform.

As Saah approached the bars, he saw the uneaten trough of gruel just inside the cage and nudged it with his boot.

"Is it lacking salt?"

Jaras laughed.

"Gloating doesn't become you, Vardan," Leodore said. "It makes that pinched mouth of yours look even more peevish."

Robinson couldn't help himself. He burst out laughing and the other Tiers joined in. Saah flushed before smiling cruelly.

"You, sers, won't be laughing long. Shall I tell you what we have planned for today? Word has already gone out over the Feed that I have thwarted a plot to overthrow the Crown at the highest level, with you, *Tier Crusoe*, being the master architect of this plot. With the aid of your fellow conspirators, your scheme to use a devastating technological weapon from the pre-Rendering Empire to destroy my army of Iron Fists fighting a legion of renders in Reg4 has been quelled."

"A legion that doesn't exist," Leodore said.

"Your ultimate goal: to seize control of the Isle and declare yourself Regent. How do you like the narrative so far?"

"It's insane and so are you. Is this what you really want, Vardan? To become a tyrant?"

"I am no tyrant. I'm a realist. You look at this Isle and see an illusion—a perfectly constructed fairytale born of laws made two centuries ago by people that assumed the remainder of humanity had been wiped off the map. But I've been out there, Leodore. I've seen the truth! That flood that cleansed the world? The waters are breaking back, my friend, and on every shore of every continent, man right now is picking up the pieces left behind and preparing to use them against us. The history books downstairs are full of tales of man killing man, neighbor killing neighbor, brother killing brother, all the way back to the biblical age. Well, I won't sit back and wait for them to come to us again. Not when all we have to defend ourselves with are walls and spears and the Eight. I will take the fight to them to ensure the One People persevere forever."

"Our forefathers chose this path for a reason. Technology nearly destroyed us."

"Then we should take care to learn from our mistakes. The Great Rendering was the result of one country's hubris and yet its effects are still felt throughout the world to this day. I will not leave our fate in someone else's hands."

"Then why destroy the one thing that can rid us of the virus forever?" Robinson asked.

"Isn't it obvious?" Leodore said. "To him, the Rendering is population control."

Saah shrugged. "You have to admit, it's an effective one. And as far as I can see, there's only one wrinkle. One final fly in the ointment."

"Us," Rolland Fallow said.

"Correct, Tier Fallow. Disposing of you earlier would have been messy. We couldn't have a dozen Tiers vanish at once. People would ask questions. The same goes for the Road. Send one fellow down the Red, the citizens overlook it. But march many at once? Pretty soon everyone is watching the door. People can't live in peace if they are living in fear. Which brings us back to the plot. A good plot always has a confessor."

"If you think any of us will stand on a stage and repeat your lies," Roland Fallow said, "you really are crazy."

"Don't be silly, Roland. Every single one of you has wives and children with estates—so much to lose. You're all proud men—I understand that—

but in the end, each of you would sacrifice yourself for the ones you love without pause. Thankfully, it's not any of you I need."

"It's me," Robinson said.

"Forget it," Leodore said. "He'll never do it. I won't allow it. I'm already dead, Vardan. You've said as much. You've given away your leverage."

"Have I?" He grinned.

Robinson realized what that smile meant in an instant.

"Father. He has Tannis and Tallis."

The proof was written on his face.

"I swear, boy," Saah shook his head. "I seriously underestimated you. Had things been different, I would have married you off to Tessa and that intellect and cunning you so obviously possess would have been put to much better use. Still, you'll serve a purpose. The Isle sees you as a young boy yet. When you tearfully corroborate your father's deeds, no one in all the Eight will even think about questioning it."

The silence in the room was deafening.

"Shall we say mid-afternoon? Good. Jaras, have something more appetizing sent up for these good sers. They deserve that much."

Saah and Jaras turned and left. The door slammed shut behind them. The faces in the cell were grim and hard to take in, none more so than Leodore's.

"He's got us," Roland Fallow said.

"Not necessarily," Robinson said.

"He's right, Robinson," his father interjected. "Why kid ourselves? He's thought of everything."

"Father, what would you say Tier Saah's greatest weakness is?"

"I don't know. Vanity, maybe. Arrogance."

"That mustache," Roland Fallow said. "Makes him look like a real poof."

Everyone laughed.

"His greatest weakness is that he thinks too highly of himself. He could have come in here, told us what he wanted, and spared us the speech. But he's proud of his gamesmanship. And that just might give us a chance."

"What are you saying?" Leodore asked.

"If I'm right, Tier Saah still has one move yet to play. One move to tie up all the loose ends and really drive the dagger home. I'm betting that sometime in the next turn, that door will open by the one and only person capable of making certain everything goes according to plan."

"And who would that be?"

"Only his favorite pawn."

Chapter Forty-Eight
Tessa

Two turns later, the door unbolted and Tessa walked in. She was dressed in a yellow cotton dress with long sleeves and a high-collared neck that featured tiny, ruby red studs running down one shoulder and arm. Her hair was pulled back into a ponytail, but it still shone radiantly in the sun that cut through the barred window and filled the room with light. Robinson had almost forgotten how luminescent her skin was and how her eyes glimmered like a field of grass. Even though every man in the room knew the part she'd played in their downfall, the fragrant draw of her perfume still made them all sit up a little straighter.

For Robinson, it brought only memories of longing and pain.

"Good sers," she said with a curtsey before showing a One and Four. "I've brought you an array of meats, breads, and cheeses from the kitchen. Also some wine, should any of you choose to partake."

"Oh, we'll partake, lassie," Roland Fallow said as he and the others collected the delivery from the bottom of the bars. "Of this and anything else you care to offer."

To her credit, Tessa managed to blush but offered no rebuke. Her eyes eventually turned toward Robinson as the others retreated.

"Jaras said you had changed, but I hardly recognize you. Your hair is so long."

"Think I'll start a trend?"

"Lord, I hope not. I have a difficult enough time competing with the women."

They both smiled.

"Is it true you survived in the wild all by yourself?"

"Not entirely. I had some help."

"Ah, yes. The native. Jaras told me about her too."

"Did he also tell you how he and your father sold her to a group of savages? Or how under their authority, Taskmaster Satu was tortured and killed?"

Her mood immediately soured.

"Please. I don't wish to speak of such things."

"Too sordid for your dainty ears? I'm surprised. I was sure a woman so deft in the arts of deception would bask in the successes of all her hard work."

"I knew this was a bad idea," she said and turned to go.

"Wait!" Robinson called and she stopped. "I apologize. That was unfair of me."

"No," she said. "It was perfectly fair. Although I wish you could understand I take no pleasure in any of this."

Oddly, he felt himself wanting to believe her.

"Was it always a ruse?"

"Ruse is too strong a word. What I did, I did out of duty, as any son or daughter of any Tier would do. As a child, I hated you for your recklessness and cavalier frivolity. But as we grew older, I started to recognize that it was your free spirit that drove those things. You had passion and courage, like few in this world do. But marrying you? The thought always terrified me."

"Why?"

"Because I knew whatever path you took in life, you would shine. And I've never been one for the shadows."

"I do believe that's the most honest thing you've ever said to me."

She looked away, embarrassed.

"And now you get to watch me walk the Road."

She pulled close, her face nearly up against the bars.

"You don't have to. When you reach the stage, speak the words my father asks of you. Tell the people what they need to hear and maybe he'll spare your life. He admires you, Robinson. I can see it. You still have much to live for. Maybe after a few years of exile you can return. And then … who knows?"

"And Tannis and Tallis?" Robinson asked.

"They have committed no crimes. With my urging, they might even hold on to their titles."

He stole a glimpse at his father and then agreed. Tessa's relief was immediate.

"Might I ask one thing of you? For old time's sake?"

She nodded.

"I would like to see Slink one last time before I go. You know he was my only friend."

"I'll see what I can do."

Twenty minutes later, the door opened and Slink entered. He was wearing a suit cropped tight at the shoulders and a pair of spectacles on his face. He had grown even bigger, though Robinson wouldn't have thought it possible. This time the Red Guard left the door open, though they glared at him as they stepped away.

"You're doing me no favors asking me here," he said when he reached the bars.

"It's good to see you too."

He looked Robinson up and down. "You've grown some, Nobe. You're nearly as big as me."

"Everywhere but the head."

He chuckled. "I like the outfit too. Very woodland chic. Is that boiled leather?"

"Harder for enemies to grab onto in a fight."

His smile fell. He took in Robinson's scars and couldn't imagine what he'd gone through.

"I hear they let you stay with the Feed," Robinson said. "Do you get to travel?"

"Often. Tier Abett likes my work because he says I can frame a picture well, though personally I think it's because I can hold a camera for turns without griping."

"I'm sure the spectacles help in that regard. And your namesake profession?"

He peered at the Red Guard to see if they were listening.

"I occasionally take in the night air. The old muscles need their exercise too."

"On that subject …" Robinson carefully reached into his belt and pulled out the small disc his mother had given him and set it on the flat of the bar. "You recognize it?"

"It's older, but I've seen one or two."

"My mother gave it to me before she died. I believe it was meant for you."

He didn't take it. He simply stared at it and then shook his head.

"Still trying to get me to follow you on your little adventures. Even if they lead all the way to the ocean floor."

Robinson felt suddenly chagrinned. Then a Red Guard poked his head in the door.

"Wrap it up, Grey. These men have business waiting."

Slink nodded and prepared to go.

"Mayfus?" Robinson called and his friend turned. "I'm sorry."

"For what?"

"All of it. The jokes, the excursions, the trouble. I never appreciated you the way a real friend should."

"That's because we were never really friends. More like brothers. Take care out there, Nobe."

"You too."

And then he turned and walked out the door.

Robinson looked down to see that what he'd left for Slink was gone.

Chapter Forty-Nine
Confessions

The city square teemed with citizens as the prisoners were marshaled out in shackles. Saah had ordered a stage erected under the Feed monitor, which showed shots of the other Townships as their entire populace gathered. Robinson recognized most of the faces in front of him, but he was surprised to see how angry they seemed.

"They're out for blood today," Father said.

"I don't understand why."

"Look in the back."

And then he saw it. Casks of wine and ale were flowing like the Tongue itself. It was barely noon and the crowd was already drunk.

They were greeted with boos and catcalls and a few volleys of trash, but many knew it was a farce. And yet an undercurrent of fear ran throughout the throng as confusion about the societal upheaval had grown out of proportion. Many were looking for answers but none were brave enough to ask the proper questions.

The buzz grew until the Iron Fists appeared and escorted Regent Saah onto the stage where his supporters were gathered. Among them was Jaras, fighting back his giddy delight for the show of blood that was to follow.

At the far end of the stage, Robinson spotted Tessa crying in her mother's arms, lamenting her true love's fall from grace. The crowd ate it up and even Robinson had to admit it was a masterful performance.

Saah held his hands up and the crowd went quiet.

"Citizens of the One People. Today, I stand before you, bringing the worst of tidings. On the dais with me are five men you know well. Tier Shamus Bartell. Tier Siev Cloustern. Tier Roland Fallow. Tier Leodore Crusoe, and his son, Robinson. These men stand accused of a terrible crime—the gravest of crimes—treason. Treason against the One People and violators of the Eight Laws on which our society was founded!"

The crowd grumbled again. Tier Cloustern's wife fainted in the throng.

"These five men have conspired to overthrow the Crown using the influence of their offices. They have travelled beyond the boundaries of our continent in search of weapons and technologies to aid their plotted coup. Tier Crusoe supplied the flyers that transported Tiers Cloustern and Bartell's recruits to establish a base of operations on one of these foreign continents. The food shortage we have all suffered under this past year? It was not due to flooding, as Tier Fallow's reports concluded, but his illegal appropriation for their seditious conspiracy! If any among you doubt the veracity of these charges, look no further than Tier Crusoe's own son. He was declared dead by his father, a victim of a house fire that took three other lives! Only here he stands, miraculously alive, in the clothes of the race he mingled with half a globe away! Do you deny this, ser?"

The crowd roared its disapproval, but the prisoners were meant to say nothing.

"Perhaps the most grievous act," Saah went on once the din had settled, "was in returning to our shores with one of these pre-Rendering weapons. An instrument so vile and so destructive that it can eradicate all of us from a single machine up in the sky!"

At this the crowd turned truly ugly, showering the prisoners with refuse and rocks as a chant of "Expiry" rose through the ranks. To punctuate his point, Saah drew out the silver case and set it on the stage.

"Our forebears knew the dangers of such of technology. They knew the perils of weaponry, religion, and vice. And yet slowly we have allowed these things to snake their way back into our lives under the corrupted system of the Tiers. With their multitude of voices, we have forgotten that only one voice matters: *yours*. And as your Regent, I humbly submit that it is time to do away with the Tiers system and embrace what we were always meant to be. One land speaking with one voice for One People! And I will be that voice for you!"

The crowd exploded in frenzy. On the balconies overlooking the street, many Tiers were growing concerned for their own safety. One was pulled from his loft and trampled in the street.

Saah held up his hand once again.

"But we are not savages. Every accused has a right to defend themselves or to speak their piece. Shamus Bartell, come forward. You stand accused of treason against the One People. How do you plead?"

"I confess, the accusations are true."

Tier Bartell's family wailed as the crowd denounced him.

"For your crimes, you are sentenced to Expiry immediately."

A cheer went up as he was pulled back.

Tier Cloustern was marshaled forward next.

"I ... am guilty of these crimes. I ask for mercy."

"The only mercy you shall have is that your family does not stand with you!"

Roland Fallow was shoved forward next.

"Ser Fallow, do you also confess?"

"I confess ... that you are an asshole, Vardan. And always have been."

An Iron Fist smashed a pommel into his belly. When he recovered, he was thrust in front of the microphone again.

"It's true."

"Then you too are sentenced to walk the Road."

Leodore stepped forward without prompting, his head held high.

"Ser Crusoe. I see you've stepped forward willingly to embrace these charges. Of all the betrayals, yours is the most grievous and the most personal to me. We were friends once. Many years we sat the council together, serving for the benefit of all. I beg you, Leodore, admit to your crimes and free yourself of this burden. If not to return honor to the Crusoe name, then for the good of your own children."

At that moment, several Iron Fists ushered Tannis and Tallis out. Both were crying. It made Robinson's stomach lurch. It was a masterful stroke on Saah's part. He knew Leodore was an impassioned speaker. If anyone could have rallied the crowd it was he. Instead, he simply nodded and stepped back.

"There you have it, citizens. Each man has confessed—"

"What about the boy?" someone yelled.

Robinson looked to see who had spoken. It was a manservant of Tier Soren, one of the boys who had beat Robinson up alongside Jaras. Even this move had been planned.

"The boy acted under orders of his father," Saah said. "He will face the same fate. Now—"

"Let him speak!" a woman yelled. Robinson didn't need to see her to know she was a provocateur as well. "Let him confess!"

The crowd agreed and Saah motioned him forward.

"Robinson Crusoe, citizen of the One People. You stand accused of treason. Do you deny that you willfully left the Isle of your own volition, even though it was in violation of the Eight?"

"No."

"Do you deny that you travelled to another continent?"

"No."

"Do you deny that you recovered ancient technology from that continent and used them to aid your endeavors?"

"I do not."

"Do you deny that while on that continent, you had physical relations with a girl from another race?"

"No."

This one seemed particularly shameful to the crowd. Their jeers continued to grow in pitch. Then Saah held his hand out and Jaras handed him the briefcase, which he opened for the crowd.

"And do you deny that you procured this device, a former weapon of mass destruction, with intent to activate it without full awareness of its consequences?"

"I do not deny it."

"Then confess your part in this treason. In front of this Township, the Eight Regens, *and your brother and sister*! Confess and be done with it!"

In the crowd and on the Feed monitor, Robinson saw citizens gathered in every Township across the Isle, chanting, "Confess!" Their faces were full of anger and resentment, but he knew he wasn't the true target of their rage. They had been subjugated to tyranny for too long and he was the only available outlet.

Robinson looked again for sign of Slink, but he was nowhere to be found. Could he still count on him after all this time? Was he willing to risk his life on a ploy? Equally important, was Robinson willing to risk his siblings' lives on it?

"Confess!" Saah screamed.

Robinson took one glance at his father and saw him nod. He put his lips against the microphone and said, "I confess … nothing."

Chapter Fifty
Icarus

The crowd gasped. Even Saah reacted like he'd been lashed. His head turned as if he were looking for help. Robinson knew he had to speak before Saah recovered.

"*You* are the one guilty of treason, Vardan Saah. *You* were the first to travel to the forbidden continent. *You* raised an army of conscripts to collect weapons and technologies to ensure your reign of tyranny here and abroad. *You* sought that weapon at your feet. *You* framed my parents and these men of their *supposed crimes*. And you're the one who deserves to walk the Road for it."

No one had ever spoken to a Regent like that before. But there was no folding in Vardan Saah. He recovered quickly.

"And have you acquired proof of these crimes?" He said it smugly. He knew Robinson hadn't. So he decided to tell the truth.

"No. But my mother did."

Looking back, he couldn't say for sure why things had unfolded the way they had. The books all told that survival was about the power of will, letting go, and believing in one's self. But no one could survive in a vacuum. Everyone needed help. On the forbidden continent, Robinson had Friday, Resi, and even the Old Man. He was alive because they had earned his trust. And that was how he knew Slink would come through for him. There were few he trusted more.

When all the heads in the crowd snapped up, Robinson didn't even have to turn around. He didn't need to see the footage to know the content and its import.

The first video was Saah inside his office with his conspirators.

"I want electronic devices planted in every Tier home from Regen 1 to Regen 8. Not a single word gets spoken that I don't hear about."

The crowd gasped and Saah's head snapped nervously around.

Then came a second clip of Iron Fists shooting rifles in a field.

"Faster!" Saah ordered. "The renders on the Forbidden Continent are not as soft as our own!"

A third clip had him stepping inside a flyer.

"Are you sure it has the capacity to cross the Atlantica? I don't want to have to transport additional fuel cells unless it's necessary."

"This is a fabrication!" Saah screamed as the crowd turned on him. "These are lies! I've never been off the Isle! I've never—"

The fourth clip showed him stepping out of a flyer at the Air Force base. Three men were pulled out in shackles after him. This time, the crowd was stupefied.

"That's Tier Frostmore! He walked the Red Road!" someone in the crowd shouted. "And Tiers Cork and Ulay were exiled!"

"Look, it's Taskmaster Satu! He was said to have died!"

"Cut the Feed! Someone—! These are technological fabrications!"

But the blood of the crowd was already up. The Red Guard held them back as they surged forward, but it was clear they were in danger of being overrun. Robinson realized that the wall needed one last brick pulled before it completely toppled.

"Vardan Saah is the real perpetrator of treason! He even had the Regent murdered!"

"Lies!" Saah screamed. "Where is your evidence?"

"Here!" a booming voice called. To everyone's surprise, Slink's father pushed through the crowd. He had an Iron Fist by the scruff!

"It was this man's hand that wielded the killing stroke! Tell them!"

"It's true!" the soldier lamented. "Brapo Liesel stole the knife from Tier Crusoe's house. He threatened to kill my family if I didn't help him!"

"This is fabrication!" Saah said and then a final image appeared on the Feed, showing Brapo Liesel handing the blade to the Iron Fist with Saah watching. Robinson quickly turned and saw Slink's father smile. He had helped his son load this final footage from the Crown's secret security cameras.

"Murderer!" the crowd screamed. Then everything turned to chaos.

The Iron Fists rushed forward, their truncheons arcing with killing blows, but the crowd was too many. Robinson heard Tessa scream and turned to see her fighting desperately to hold on to her mother's hand as she was pulled into the mob, her face gouged by women. Jaras was trying to get to his father but quickly realized his sister needed him more. He pulled a hidden pistol from his coat and started firing into the crowd. At last he reached Tessa and dragged her away.

On the stage, Leodore and the other prisoners were freed from their shackles.

"Robinson!" Leodore yelled over the din. "We have to go!"

"The case! We need the case!"

Robinson pointed to the case on the stage. Saah must have heard him, because he lunged for it, his fingers just missing the handle.

"If he sets it off, everything Mother sacrificed will be for nothing!"

"Go!" Leodore yelled.

They fought against the crowd, but on the other side of the stage, Saah dropped to the floor and pulled the case to him. His fingers moved quickly to enter the ICARUS password. Robinson didn't know if he was doing it out of spite or if he really believed destroying the cure would save the Isle from some worse threat, but when he was yanked just short of pushing the EXECUTE button, Robinson knew it was now or never.

He tore through the mob, using every manner of attack Friday had taught him. He was aware he was hitting his own people, but he had no choice. The fate of the world hung in the balance.

Just as he caught sight of the case, a truncheon slammed into his head and he fell to the stage. Behind him, Leodore struggled with an Iron Fist. Robinson crawled forward, blood running down his face, his vision blurred. The silver case was inches away. Robinson's fingers stretched out, about to latch onto it, when Saah made one last leap and hit the EXECUTE button.

He smiled at Robinson's look of horror. And then someone in the crowd gasped.

The riot ceased as all heads turned toward the sky. High in the clouds, a ring of fire grew brilliantly outward. A thunderous boom descended a moment later and people screamed.

Robinson had failed.

He scrambled to his feet and turned to his father. The pain in his eyes was almost unbearable. And then someone said, "Look!"

Back up in the sky, a dozen smaller rockets sped out from the center of the blast like rays of the sun. Contrails marked their path as they sped far apart and then detonated themselves in a nimbus of colored light.

Robinson raised both hands in the air and shouted triumphantly, "MOTHER!"

Only Leodore understood what had happened. But when he wrapped his son in a stifling embrace with tears filling his eyes, people seemed to realize it was a good thing.

At their feet, Saah groaned with defeat. But his troubles were far from over as the crowd grabbed him and hauled him up.

"The Road!" someone shouted. "Make him walk the Red!"

The mob dragged Saah into the street and tore at his clothes before marching him toward the Western Gate. Leodore grabbed hold of Robinson.

"Stop them!" he said. "We need to debrief him!"

"I'll do what I can," his son replied, but knew it would be a tough task. "Get Tannis and Tallis out of here."

Leodore nodded and rushed off. Robinson took off after Saah but couldn't halt the mob for anything. Along the way, he saw Slink calling out from the balcony of a building, but he couldn't escape the sea of bodies.

Saah was barely conscious when someone broke open the Western Gate and dragged him through. But just as the crowd was preparing to toss him to his death, a whoosh of dust and air blew everyone back as a flyer rose up, nearly kissing the edge. A door swung open and Jaras appeared, holding a rifle. Robinson screamed for the crowd to take cover, but it was too late. Jaras opened fire.

The crowd scattered and that's when he saw Tessa standing next to her brother, waving their father in.

"Father!" she screamed. "Jump!"

Saah stumbled forward and leaped, his hand missing Tessa's but catching the runners beneath. Both Jaras and Tessa reached down to help him up, but it was at that exact moment when someone from the crowd launched a rock that sailed through the cabin and struck the pilot in the back of the head.

The flyer bucked and Tessa fell.

Jaras grasped for his sister at the last moment, but the fabric of her dress tore in his hand. He screamed for all his worth, but she was gone.

Saah seemed momentarily numb, but he regrouped quickly enough to signal the pilot to leave. Just as they were pulling away, Jaras looked up and locked eyes with Robinson. The hate in that glance was pure. It was a fury that would carry Jaras for the rest of his life, or until he and Robinson met again.

Before the crowd could reform, the flyer banked away and was gone.

The mob raged throughout the evening, burning homes, shops, and even managing to collapse two of the spires, but by morning, the embers of their rage had cooled and wiser heads prevailed. Still, the damage had been done.

Leodore spent time detailing the events that had transpired, specifically how Tier Saah had sought to destroy the FENIX and the cure it carried, but how in the end, Annabess's final gift had released it into the world instead. Most believed his account. They decided he was the best man to lead the way forward. There were many gifts their forefathers had given them, but to survive, they needed to adapt. They needed change. It would take time.

Early one morning, Slink returned home to find Robinson waiting outside his apartment. Bull had allowed Leodore and the twins to stay there, since Leodore had refused to sleep in the Crown, but Robinson couldn't rest until he'd thanked his friend.

"There's one thing I want to know," Slink said, his face as serious as Robinson had ever seen it.

Robinson raised an eyebrow. "Shoot."

"How many beds *are* in the Tower Keep?"

Robinson cracked up laughing and Slink joined him.

Epilogue
The Promise

He stood at the perimeter of the forest at the edge of the airbase. At first, his intention was to land and set off immediately, but he still had one mission to attend to. He sought out Taskmaster Satu's body, and with Leodore's help, gave him a proper burial.

The two weeks on the Isle had been a bittersweet homecoming. The family had shared stories of their journeys. Robinson had given the twins a good recounting of their mother's goodbye. There had been tears and laughter, but in the end, Robinson had grown restless and everyone had known it was time for him to go.

One benefit of his stay was his new outfitting. A dressmaker who had once served the Crown had crafted him a set of trousers, shirts, and boots of some fabric that he swore was indestructible. Whether they were was beside the point. Either way, Robinson would be the best-dressed warrior on the forbidden continent.

He'd also had a blacksmith craft him two war axes fashioned from something called titanium alloy. They were light and sharp and terrified children whenever they saw him coming. Torches, food, and rope filled out the rest of his modest pack.

"You're sure about this?" Leodore asked, looking out over the forest. "I can have some flyers take you and a legion of Red Guard anywhere you want to go."

"Thank you, but no. This is one task I need to do myself."

"Mayfus is furious that you left without him. He's threatening to bludgeon every pilot he sees until one of them agrees to fly him over."

"Mayfus still thinks I need him to take care of me. I don't. Besides, his newfound celebrity has afforded him a number of female admirers. He deserves to bolster his own reputation for a while."

"Any idea where you'll go?"

"Friday mentioned once that the savages worked their way along the Atlantica in the spring and summer and headed inland by fall, along a route called the Mississippi. I'll start that way and see where it leads me."

Above them, the sun shone brightly. It was time.

"Robinson," Leodore began, about to say the one thing every son longs to hear. But Robinson no longer needed the words. He held his hand out instead.

"I know," his son said.

After they shook, Robinson turned for the forest.

"Come back alive," Leodore called after him. "Preferably with the girl. If my eldest son is to get married or mated or whatever they do here, I think the family should meet her."

"You will," Robinson yelled as his walk turned into a jog.

"How can you be so sure?" Leodore called.

"Easy!" Robinson responded. "I'm a Crusoe!"

As he entered the forest, he was running at full speed. It felt good to have his legs and heart pumping again. He longed to feel the heft of his axes in his hand, but that could wait. His hand was full anyway, holding Friday's acorn.

When he passed too close to a bush, he felt a barb cut into his flesh and a small trickle of blood ran down his arm. He smiled at the pain because he knew he was back where he belonged. He was on the path to her.

And she knew he was coming.

— The End —

DEAR READER

Thanks for reading *Robinson Crusoe 2244*. I really hope you enjoyed it. *Robinson Crusoe 2245 (Book 2)* is already available on Amazon and *Robinson Crusoe 2246 (Book 3)* will be available spring, 2016.

Like most independent authors, I rely on word of mouth for most of my marketing, so please consider leaving a review on Amazon, Goodreads or shouting it from the spires of Facebook and Twitter.

Also, please consider signing up for my spam-free "Newsletter"— an email alert you will <u>only</u> receive when I have a new book out (including *Robinson Crusoe 2246!*). Your email address will remain completely confidential.

Visit http://erikjamesrobinson.com/newletter/ to Sign Up
(Link also available at: http://erikjamesrobinson.com)

Printed in Great Britain
by Amazon